THE SECRET OF
BOW LANE

Center Point
Large Print

Also by Jennifer Ashley and available from
Center Point Large Print:

Death Below Stairs
Scandal Above Stairs
Death in Kew Gardens
Murder in the East End
Death at the Crystal Palace

**This Large Print Book carries the
Seal of Approval of N.A.V.H.**

THE
SECRET
OF
BOW LANE

• *A Below Stairs Mystery* •

Jennifer Ashley

CENTER POINT LARGE PRINT
THORNDIKE, MAINE

To all the readers who love Kat Holloway
and have asked for more.

I

September 1882

"Woman's asking for you, Mrs. Holloway." Elsie, the scullery maid, popped her head into the kitchen one Wednesday morning after breakfast service to make this announcement. "She's waiting up on the street."

"What woman?" I was much distracted, having had to serve a larger than usual breakfast. The family in the Mount Street house had returned unexpectedly early from their summer wanderings, and the lady of the house had presumed they'd slide back into day-to-day life without a hiccup.

Little did they know of my mad scramble to the markets, my despair over the bizarre notes Mrs. Bywater, the mistress, had sent down to me about the new dishes she'd learned of while on holiday. How my assistant, Tess, and I had chopped and boiled and baked and tested recipes until we'd nearly collapsed in the roasting heat of the kitchen. Mrs. Bywater had no understanding of food, and everything she'd suggested had to be rethought and remade until it was edible.

"Don't know, Mrs. Holloway." Elsie tucked her dishcloth into her apron and retreated to her sink.

"She only said she wanted to speak to the cook. It's important, she says."

I glanced out the high windows that gave on to the outside stairs, but I could see nothing beyond the grating and the stone sills that needed to be scraped of summer grime.

Earlier in my life, when I'd first become a cook, I'd have dismissed a woman who didn't leave her name and gone about my business. But these days, as an acquaintance of Daniel McAdam, who had the habit of sending all sorts to me for my help, I felt an obligation to discover what this person needed. Daniel did not always explain clearly what he wished me to do, but perhaps I could learn this from the woman.

"Very well," I said. "Tess, please set that bread in the oven. It will overflow its pan if it sits any longer and be ruined. Give it an egg white wash and sprinkle a bit of those seeds on first. That will be tasty, I think."

Tess, of the freckled face and lively eyes, set to work without arguing or bothering to comment, which told me how much she'd settled since coming to work for me.

Tess separated an egg without mishap and whisked up the white. "If there's another evil person what needs nabbing, you'll let me help, won't you?" she said as her fork clinked against the sides of the bowl. "I'll be staying well out of the way if they're dangerous, of course."

"It is not likely to be anything so dire. Do not overbeat the whites, Tess—you want a thin coating to make the seeds stick, not a meringue."

"Right you are, Mrs. H." Tess hummed happily as she continued to whisk.

I tucked a stray lock of hair into my cap and departed the kitchen for the back door. Anyone arriving at the kitchen instead of the main house was no one I'd need to change my frock for, and I was too busy to even remove my apron.

Cool air wafted to me as I hurried up the stairs, the heat of summer finally broken. My kitchen had often been as hot as my oven these past few months. A sensible person would have found a way to leave London for the summer, but I had a reason to stay, and I did not mean my post as cook in a Mount Street home.

I assumed the woman who stood in a sunny patch next to the house's railings was the lady who wished to speak to me. Her back was to me as she idly watched delivery wagons pass, so all I saw was her serviceable dark brown frock, a straw-colored shawl to keep out the wind, and a hat with one limp ribbon.

"Madam?" I called as I reached the top stair. "I am Mrs. Holloway. What may I help you with?"

She turned and faced me.

My cheerful greeting died as my lips grew numb, my mouth dry. My heart beat in strange little jerks, and I tightened my hand on the railing beside me. If I'd not clutched it, I'd have tumbled back down the steps.

It was her. Charlotte. Mrs. Joseph Bristow.

The woman who'd been married to my husband in the years I believed *I'd* been his wife.

I recognized her because after Joe had died and I'd discovered Charlotte's existence, I'd found out all I could about her. I'd never introduced myself or spoken to her or even made myself known to her. I'd discovered that she lived in Bristol but had come to London to wrap up Joe's affairs. I knew where she'd taken rooms and what she looked like, and realized with dismay that the little boy who followed her closely must be Joe's son. His legitimate son.

I'd learned quite a lot about Charlotte before I convinced myself that I should put her from my mind. She'd returned to Bristol before long, and I'd shifted my focus to my own troubles. I'd been about to bear a child, and I needed to find a way to keep my daughter—*his* daughter—fed.

Charlotte pinned me with eyes that were hard and brown under her dark straw hat. "You know me?"

For a long moment I could not move, could not speak. At last, I managed a nod.

Charlotte studied me in every detail, as I had studied her twelve years ago. She'd been quite pretty then, with sleek dark hair parted in the middle and swept back in wings on either side of her face. Pink cheeked, fresh-faced, slightly plump, pleasant looking.

She'd resembled me a bit, I'd realized, in a superficial manner. Similar hair and eye color, neither of us tall or lean. She'd been in mourning black but had smiled at her son with fondness.

I'd watched her from the other side of a street with my throat closed, not certain why I'd wanted to know anything about her. If I encountered her, what would I say? The sight of the boy, a lad so small and vulnerable, had convinced me to not approach her at all. He was innocent in all Joe's machinations, as innocent as Grace.

The thought of Grace gave me courage. "Do you know *me?*" I countered.

"You call yourself Miss Holloway," she said stiffly.

"*Mrs.* Holloway," I corrected her. "Cooks and housekeepers are *Mrs., regardless.*"

Charlotte eyed me, unimpressed.

The years had not been kind to her, I noted with an unbecoming flicker of satisfaction. Her complexion had grown sallow, her hair now more frizzled than sleek, and she had lines of exhaustion about her red-rimmed eyes. Joe had left me penniless—he'd specified nothing to me in his will, naming only his legitimate wife. He could not have left Charlotte much better off, as the man had never had many coins to rub together.

11

"You were Joe's paramour," Charlotte said. "His bit on the side. I hated you for a long time, but I must put that aside and ask for your help."

She spoke as though each word singed her tongue. The last barely emerged at all.

I regarded her in amazement. "My help? Why on earth should I help you?"

I'd meant to inquire why she'd sought me, of all people, for assistance, but the sentence leapt from me in all bitterness.

"Because you stand to make a few quid from it," Charlotte said.

Her answer made my curiosity flicker, but old anger that should have died years ago flared anew. I'd been quite unhappy living with Joe, but to discover that I'd stayed with him only because of a lie had nearly destroyed me. I'd blamed Joe squarely, but I'd also blamed this woman for stealing the life that ought to have been mine.

"I hardly need your money," I said with all my dignity. "I have a respectable position and want for nothing."

I could have explained that households in Mayfair would offer me the highest wages in order to put my food on their tables, and that I was rarely out a position for long. Also that I could demand a day and a half out a week as a condition of my employment and be granted it without argument.

But I held my tongue. I would not compete

with Charlotte Bristow for accolades. My life had turned out far better than it would have done had Joe lived, I was well aware. I'd gain nothing from crowing about that.

"This might be more than a few quid," she snapped.

I tightened my hand on the railing. "Please explain yourself. I have much to do."

Charlotte scowled. "Give me a minute. I've had to work out what to say, and seeing you sent it all out of my head."

"Do hurry," I said coolly. "My mistress will be expecting me."

My mistress was at the moment deep in conversation with her friends who'd arrived after breakfast, at a very unfashionable hour, to welcome her home to London. Mr. Bywater had fled the female chatter to his office in the City, and Lady Cynthia, Mr. Bywater's niece, had barricaded herself in her chamber. Mrs. Bywater would hardly notice what I did until she wanted her luncheon, but Charlotte did not need to know this.

"Joe might have had a powerful lot of money," Charlotte surprised me by saying. "And someone murdered him for it. We'll find the money when we find the killer, I'll wager."

2

"Murdered him?" I repeated the words in amazement. "For a powerful lot of money? What are you talking about? Joe died at sea. So said the solicitor who came to me after his death." To explain I was not truly Joe's wife and that none of his things belonged to me.

"Joe did die. But not from his ship going down, like they told me, and like they told you."

I made myself release the railing and move closer to her. The rumbling of wheels on cobblestones would ensure we weren't overheard, but I did not want to shout this business on the street.

"How do you know?" I demanded. "Anyone can feed you a rigmarole."

Charlotte was about the same height as me. She stared straight at me, her chin at a stubborn tilt.

"A friend of Joe's has visited me now and then over the years. He's always said something weren't right with Joe's death."

Charlotte spoke the words as though reciting a speech, jaw stiff, hands clenched. She had a haunted look about her, I thought, as though she was unhappy but determined not to reveal any misery to the world.

"What friend?" I asked.

"I'm getting to that. Joe had a man who worked for him, apparently. Fellow doted on Joe, would do anything for him, so this other friend says. After Joe died, the man disappeared, and so did the cash Joe's friend knows Joe had. The solicitors searched for everything Joe had left, but there never was much. I got what they found, as was my right as the widow."

Unlike me, who deserved nothing, the flash in her eyes said.

A bailiff and constable had accompanied the solicitor when he'd come to search my house for any goods Joe might have left behind, intent on carrying off whatever they could to give to Charlotte and her son. That was the day I'd learned about my husband's true wife.

"He never had any money when he was with me," I said.

"No, he went through it fast enough." Charlotte's expression told me she hated to agree with me. "But that was his pocket money. Seems that Joe had much more, stashed away, entrusted to someone, maybe, for the day he quit sailing and retired. This devoted assistant of his stole it—he must have done—and I think he killed Joe while he was at it." Charlotte's bosom, in its drab brown cotton, rose with determination. "If you help me find the money, I'll give you a portion of it."

I digested the story but did not give much credit to it. "I asked you before: Why on earth come to me? Why would you tell me these things and then offer me compensation for my assistance?"

Charlotte's scowl became fierce. "I've heard things, haven't I? On the street, like. I went to Bow Lane and asked about you, and everyone there told me that you were now a snooty cook in a grand house in Mayfair, and that you've helped the police find out a thing or two. I decided you'd be the one person who'd be interested in what happened to Joe's money. Working in a house like this ain't the same as living in it, is it?" Charlotte cast Number 43 Mount Street a disparaging glance.

"You went to Bow Lane?" A chill touched my heart. No one in my old street knew I'd been tricked into a bigamous marriage—they only knew I'd lost my husband and gone to work to support my child.

"That's where the bailiffs said you came from." Charlotte's stare held no remorse. "So that's where I went."

"You had no business doing so." My lips were stiff. "No business coming *here*."

Charlotte cocked her head. "You going to help me, or not? There's plenty in it for ya. Joe, they say, stashed away a good bit before he fell off his perch. Was pushed off, *I* think, by that rat."

So many emotions chased through me that I wondered how I could remain standing at all.

"Your husband never had money in his life," I

said sharply. "Even if he had acquired some, it would have slipped through his fingers or been poured down his throat before long. I want nothing to do with him, or the few coins he might have found by the wayside. And I want nothing to do with *you*."

My jaw so rigid I feared it might break, I turned on my heel and made for the stairs to the kitchen.

"You're a frosty bitch, ain't ya?" Charlotte called to me. "Joe only wanted you on your back. But he came home to *me*."

I refused to listen any longer. I marched down the stairs, pretending dignity, but my heart pounded and bile roiled in my stomach.

Charlotte called me another unflattering name, then stomped away, her boots crunching on loose stones in the street, her footsteps fading into the rumbling of wheels.

I retained the proud lift of my head until I reached the bottom step, out of sight of the road. There, my legs gave way, and I collapsed to the stairs, my arms pressed tightly over my stomach as I gasped desperately for breath.

I have no idea how long I sat on the step, my throat burning, dark spots spinning before my eyes. I was vaguely aware of the noises of the street above, of the cobwebs that should have been swept from the corners of the stairwell, and of the curious cat who sometimes sneaked down the stairs in hopes of scraps, peeking up at me to see if I had brought it a treat.

The cat scrambled away at the sound of a door scraping open, and the next thing I knew, Tess had folded herself onto the step beside me. A second tramp of footsteps sounded, and supple leather boots under finely tailored trousers stopped before me. Not worn by a man, but by Lady Cynthia.

"You all right, Mrs. H.?" Tess asked, her work-worn hands on her knees.

"We saw you descend from the street." Lady Cynthia's light voice floated to me. "And then you vanished. For a dashed long time. Anything we can do?"

When I at last summoned the strength to raise my head, I found both young women peering at me worriedly, Tess with eyes of deep brown, Cynthia's delicate blue.

"It is no matter." My voice, which should have been firm and decided, came out a harsh croak. "I have had a shock, is all. I will be fine in a moment."

"What sort of shock?" Tess's grip on her knees tightened. "Oh no—you haven't given Mr. McAdam the push, have you?"

The question snapped me out of my stupor. "Of course not," I said with more sturdiness. "This has nothing to do with Mr. McAdam."

"Well, that's a mercy." Tess let out a breath of

relief. "He's far too handsome to let slip through your fingers, and that's a fact. Is it something he can help you with? Want me to find James and send for him?"

"No." My answer was abrupt.

"Has Auntie been harping at you?" Cynthia asked. "I don't mind having a word with her. In fact, I enjoy it."

"No." I strove to soften my voice. "It's nothing to do with Mrs. Bywater, or . . . Nothing to do with anything."

I climbed to my feet, my legs trembling so that I had to pause to find my balance. Time had passed, and the stairwell had cooled. If I weren't careful, I'd catch a chill, and then I'd be laid up in bed, my wages docked. Mrs. Bywater refused to pay for a servant who couldn't work—she'd stated this to us bluntly.

Cynthia stepped in front of me. Her suit today was dark gray with brown piping on the lapels, a brown silk scarf filling the space between waistcoat and her throat in lieu of a cravat. The feminine touch of the scarf below her curved face and pale hair rendered the outfit charming.

"You are not well, Mrs. Holloway." She closed a gloved hand around my arm. "Goodness, you are ice-cold. Are you certain you do not wish to summon Mr. McAdam?"

"Or a quack?" Tess was on my other side, cupping my elbow.

"Neither, please." I wanted to shake them off, but truth to tell, I doubted I'd reach the kitchen without their assistance. "This is something I need to think over for myself."

Tess opened her mouth to ask more questions, but Cynthia made a firm shake of her head. Cynthia was curious, I could see, but polite enough not to pry for now.

The two of them helped me over the threshold, past the staring Elsie at her sink, and into the kitchen. Thankfully, none of the other staff were there, not even Charlie, the boy who tended the stove's fire. He must be off on errands for Mr. Davis or Mrs. Redfern.

I fully intended to return to cooking, but when I reached my table, it was all I could do to grasp the back of a chair and lower myself to it. Before me lay vegetable marrows ready for chopping and greens washed and overflowing their bowls.

The warmth of the kitchen penetrated my bones, the familiar scents and colors easing the jarring encounter on the street. Had I really been speaking to Charlotte Bristow, my so-called husband's legal wife? Or had I dreamed it in a trance?

Of course it had happened, my practical mind told me. She had come to me with a bizarre tale, saying Joe came into money before he died, only to have it stolen from him by a murderous thief.

It was preposterous.

And yet . . . Unbidden came the last night I'd spent with Joe. He'd arrived at our lodgings in Bow Lane late in the night, with no explanation as to where he'd been. He had promised we would take our evening meal together before he shipped out early the next morning, but as usual, he'd broken the promise.

I'd realized by that point in my marriage what a hard man Joe was, and that he didn't think it wrong to demonstrate his irritation with me through a slap or even a blow on the back of my head. I should have been happy he was departing for half a year, but I carried a sorrow inside me at his leaving. I'd discovered earlier that week that I was carrying his child, and I'd planned to tell him this over supper.

By the time he'd reached home that night, I was angry at him, the meal I'd worked so hard to prepare cold and ruined. He'd not let me speak, only stopped my mouth with a rough kiss and pulled me with him into our bedchamber.

I'd never found fault with Joe as a lover, and as usual, my anger had dissipated by the time we lay together afterward, his large arms around me. I was sleepy, drifting off in a languor, deciding to keep my news of the child until he said his farewells in the morning.

"You know, my girl?" Joe had whispered into my hair. "One day we'll have so much more than this hovel in this dirty lane. I'll give you gowns of silk with diamonds for your ears and gold for your fingers. You'll be the prettiest lady in London, on *my* arm, and the lads will eat themselves up with envy. Wouldn't you like that? And we'll have a grand house. Where would you like to live, eh? I have my eye on a place in Kent, near the sea. A big house with a garden, and you'll have servants to wait on *you*."

I'd murmured something in acquiescence as I slid into sleep, but I'd paid him no mind. When Joe was in a good mood he'd tell me all sorts of things, claiming he'd take me away from London and give me gowns and jewels that he could never hope to acquire. I never believed him, but I did not curb his pleasant fantasy.

Charlotte's announcement today painted Joe's final boast to me in new colors. What if Joe *had* found a way to make a fortune, or known he would come into money during his voyage? Perhaps he had truly meant to purchase a home in Kent, where I'd live in blissful ignorance of his perfidy.

No, I could not credit Charlotte's tale. Joe had never been the wisest of men—crafty and cunning, yes, but not bright. He might have believed he'd found a way into funds, but that did not mean he truly had done so.

Yet Charlotte claimed that one of his friends—I would have to discover the name of this person— had seen the money and didn't believe Joe had died of an accident at sea.

But if this friend had suspected this all along, why wait so many years to tell Charlotte of his suspicions? Why tell her at all?

Depend upon it, Joe had spun some yarn about this money, and the friend perhaps was spinning another one. I'd waste my time if I looked into it.

Cynthia and Tess continued to watch me in concern, as though fearing I'd swoon or do something else as daft.

"I am well, ladies." I forced myself to my feet, though I had to brace myself on the table to do so. "We must return to work, Tess. These vegetable marrows are not going to chop themselves."

Tess eyed me worriedly but nodded. "Right you are, Mrs. H." She moved to the other side of the table and took up a knife, readying a marrow for slicing.

Cynthia did not obey as quickly. "Something made you pale as a ghost, Mrs. Holloway. Are you certain everything is all right?"

"Indeed, it is." Joe had been dead a dozen years, and the tale Charlotte had told me meant nothing. I was a respected cook with a daughter I loved and friends who cared enough to worry when I faltered.

I sent Cynthia a smile. "Truly it is, Lady Cynthia. I was made to remember something from the past, but it is far in the past and best left there."

So saying, I pulled the bowls of greens to me

and began to shake them out and sort them. I'd make a salad of lettuce, rocket, and parsley seasoned with lemon as a cool dish for luncheon. Mrs. Bywater's friends would enjoy it.

Cynthia watched me quietly for a few moments, then she gave me a nod and left the kitchen.

I busied myself with cooking, switching my focus to it and shutting out the rest of the world, as I liked to do. Soon Tess and I were sending up the luncheon—the crisp salad with cold chicken, fruit chutney, and fresh bread, with an apple tart for the sweet. Instead of resting once that was finished, I ate a quick bite of bread and salad and turned to preparing the next meal.

Cynthia was not without treachery, I was to discover that evening. After Tess and the rest of the staff went to bed, and I had time to sit over my notebook and ponder my recipes, Daniel McAdam came to call.

I admitted him readily, as usual, and poured tea into a cup that I'd prepared for him. Daniel wore his working clothes, the elbows of his frock coat patched, his unruly hair tumbling into his eyes.

"Well now, Kat," he began in his warm voice. "What was this shock you had today? Lady Cynthia says it knocked you flat, which isn't like you. What has happened? Tell me all."

3

I lowered the tea I'd been about to sip, eyeing him in trepidation. I'd served Daniel a chunk of leftover apple tart, and my hand twitched, wanting to snatch the plate from him.

I held my cup to keep myself from any gesture of rudeness. Daniel scooped up a large mouthful of tart as he waited for me to explain.

"Lady Cynthia had no business telling you such tales," I said in vexation. "In any case, when did you see Lady Cynthia today? Did she rush to Kensington with the news? Or Southampton Street? Or wherever else you may be dwelling these days?"

Daniel lived a peripatetic life, and I never knew where I could find him. I had to rely on his son, James, who sometimes hung about Mount Street waiting to run errands, to take messages to him.

"I did not see her," Daniel answered around a mouthful of apple and pastry. "She and Thanos were working on his paper at the Polytechnic, and Thanos told me after she left him."

Lady Cynthia had begun an unofficial position as Elgin Thanos's assistant at the new Polytechnic in Cavendish Square, he being a brilliant mathematician who could never find pens or paper or ink or whatever book he was looking for on any given day. Cynthia helped keep his office tidy and wrote things down for him. She'd begun this task at the end of spring and had resumed it now that she'd returned to London from her summer in the country with her parents.

"She had no business telling Mr. Thanos either," I said indignantly. "It is a private matter."

"I am certain it is, or you'd not have nearly fainted."

"I was in no danger of fainting," I declared. Though I'd sat myself down rather abruptly after my interview with Charlotte and hadn't been able to move, I saw no reason to tell him this. "Please forget about it."

"That I cannot do." Daniel put the last bite of tart into his mouth—the pastry had disappeared quickly. "This is wonderful, Kat. You have outdone yourself."

"So you say about every dish I give you." I slid the empty plate aside. "I believe you pay me such compliments so that I will continue feeding you."

"Not at all. I've never tasted an apple tart so fine. You didn't drown the apples in sugar or cinnamon, but there was just enough of both to keep them from being too tart. The crust—neither too hard nor too soft. The perfect casing for your delicious filling."

I softened to the fact that he understood how thoughtfully I'd prepared the dish, but I was not wrong that he flattered me on purpose.

"Thank you." I was not too proud to accept a compliment.

Daniel leaned across the table to speak quietly, though we were quite alone. "Has it anything to do with Grace? Is she well?"

"Grace is perfectly fine," I answered without a qualm. "No worry there."

"Good." Daniel sat back in relief. "I feared something dire, but when you opened the door to me tonight, I could see that you were not as distressed as all that. But I thought I would inquire. You are able to hide your feelings well."

"Am I?" I asked in surprise. "I thought I wore my feelings on my sleeve."

"Not at all." Daniel's smile was wry. "Believe me."

Was that a criticism? Or was he teasing me? I was not always certain with Daniel.

I rose abruptly to carry the plate and fork to the sink. I'd wash it myself and put it away so Elsie wouldn't question in the morning, though she might simply believe I'd eaten the last of the tart myself.

When I turned back to the kitchen, Daniel stood directly in front of me.

I smelled the damp wool of his coat and the smoke from outdoors that clung to it. I'd not seen much of him over the summer, as he'd been working not only on his delivery jobs but on the secret assignments the man at Scotland Yard liked to send him on. The most dangerous tasks seemed to be left to Daniel.

However, we'd been able to meet on a number of my days out, Daniel and I taking Grace to walk in Regent's Park, or to the zoological gardens there. James would often join us, Grace and he laughing together like mates. Once, Daniel had taken us to dine at a restaurant near Charing Cross Station, and it had thrilled Grace to be invited to do something so grown-up.

I'd reveled in these outings, all of us cheery and friendly. I'd dared to pretend we were a real family.

In these past months, Daniel hadn't pressed me to assist him in his cases, and he'd been more forthcoming to me about what his guv'nor asked him to do, as much as he was able. I worried about him, but I appreciated his honesty.

As Daniel put his hands on my arms, I knew he'd ask me to be just as honest with him.

Before I could speak, he leaned to me and kissed me. A warm kiss, lingering. Our kisses had become more like this lately, with a taste of passion. I hugged these moments to myself, but they also frightened me. The last time I'd given way to passion, I'd ruined my life.

Daniel eased from the kiss, leaving my lips tingling, but he did not release me.

"You know I will help you with anything," he said in a low voice. "I owe you that."

"It is a perfectly ridiculous circumstance." My voice shook. "One I wish to forget rather than pursue."

"Sometimes facing it is the best way. Lay the ghost rather than run from it. You can run from ghosts for far too long."

A haunted light flickered in his eyes. I was not privy to all of Daniel's history, but I knew he had lost people close to him, and that he'd had to fight for his life even when he'd been a wee lad.

He'd just stated that he owed me, but it struck me then that I owed him. He'd stood by me many a time, had once saved me from prison and possible hanging.

I let out a long breath. "Very well. But it is a preposterous tale, you will soon agree."

I told him all of it. We ended up at the table again, me pouring more tea for both of us. Daniel sipped, but I held myself rigidly, hands on the table, as I relayed what Charlotte had told me, and then, steeling myself, what Joe had said to me the night he'd departed.

I'd never had the chance to give Joe the news that I was quickening with Grace. I'd awakened in the morning to find him gone, and I'd not seen him alive again.

By the time I finished my narrative, Daniel had covered my cold hands with his large, warm ones.

"I am so sorry." His eyes held true compassion.

My heart squeezed, but I kept my tone brisk. "As I say, it is ridiculous. Joe must have been duped, or he duped others. He could spin a story."

"Apparently." Daniel withdrew his clasp. "Joe Bristow. This is the first time you've told me his name."

He'd asked me before, but I'd refused to answer. "I never liked to speak it. I only did tonight because it would be difficult to tell the story otherwise."

"Mmm." Daniel sipped his tea, but I could see him tucking away the information I'd given him. He'd be finding out all about Joe for himself. "The story might not be as absurd as you think, you know. Sailors meet all sorts of people, all over the world. Joe might have fallen in with someone who pulled him into a lucrative scheme."

"You are not suggesting I look into this, surely? The man visiting Charlotte might be telling her a tale, perhaps attempting to pry money from her."

"True. But it must have been a compelling enough story for her to seek your help."

"I suppose." A flame of anger had burned inside me since I'd seen Charlotte this morning, as much as I'd tried to suppress it.

Why not go after Joe's treasure? some part of me whispered. *The bailiffs took everything from you. Why should you not have something back?*

"I would have no idea where to start," I said, half to myself.

Daniel laid his hands on mine again, the comfort of his touch too beguiling. "You begin at the beginning," he said. "Where it all started for you, and for him. Bow Lane."

My mum always told me that true Cockneys were only those born within hearing range of Bow Bells—the bells of the Church of St. Mary-le-Bow in Cheapside. I don't know if she spun me a yarn, as she always had a twinkle in her eye when she said it, but I knew others who claimed the same.

The next morning, Thursday, my day out, I walked up Bow Lane from Cannon Street, toward the rear of the church, from which the bells were ringing the hour. I'd been born in the narrow Bow Lane, in the bells' very shadow, which meant, said my mother, that I was Cockney to the bone.

Daniel had not accompanied me. This first step, he'd said, I must make on my own. I expect he wanted to give me time to settle my nerves without him watching every emotion that crossed my face.

Likewise, I had not brought Grace. She lived not far away, in a comfortable house near St. Paul's with my friend Joanna Millburn and her husband. I'd been mates with Joanna since we were tykes playing in the middle of this lane, she being the kindest and most trustworthy woman I'd ever known.

I rarely came this way, though Grace lived so

near. It was bittersweet, this homecoming, like the chocolate I melted over the top of a walnut torte.

It was sweet because of the memories of life with my mother here, in the house at the corner of Bow Lane and Watling Street. We'd shared a flat there above the tobacconists, a tiny place, but snug for the two of us.

I halted when I reached the corner and peered down Watling Street to the familiar dome of St. Paul's in the distance, remembering the days I'd raced downstairs and outside into the bracing wind. I'd been younger than Grace then.

It was bitter because it was here I'd lost my mother, my prop and friend, and found emptiness in her place.

The greengrocers who had a shop opposite our old flat was still there. The man who'd run it in my day had passed on, but his daughter bustled about inside, arranging vegetables for women who hurried in with baskets to buy their daily provisions.

She caught sight of me as she emerged to set a box of carrots outside her door, eyes widening. "It's Kat Holloway, ain't it? Oh, I mean Bristow. I forgot."

Nettie Sheppard, who was a bit older than I was, had never liked me, claiming I put on far too many airs for the daughter of a charwoman. *Her* father, of course, owned his own business. What were the likes of us to her family?

"It is indeed," I said cordially. "Fine-looking carrots."

Nettie preened as though she'd grown them herself. "I always make certain to stock the best."

They were not the best, in my professional opinion, but I decided to be polite. They were small specimens, too puny to be sold to chefs or cooks in fine houses. Housewives on Bow Lane, however, would not complain.

"What brings you here?" Nettie asked. She looked me up and down as though trying to find fault with something, shrugging when she could not. I wore my best frock and carefully kept hat as I always did on my days out with Grace. The day was a bit warm for the woolen fabric, and the dress's cut was out of date, but it was clean and crisp, as I made certain to take good care of it.

"Happened to be passing," I said.

"That's right, your little girl boards around here. Such a pity she can't live with you, but likely she's getting good training for going into service."

Nettie instinctively knew how to cut. My greatest regret was that Grace and I had to live apart while I made enough money to keep us both. Nettie could not know that, as I rarely spoke to her, but her words stung nonetheless.

Also, I was determined that Grace would never go into service. I did not much want her to become a shopgirl, having to face unsavory patrons, but far better that than being a maid to a master who had no compunction about pawing at his servants.

I hadn't come here to argue with Nettie Sheppard, so I only sent her a vague nod and pretended to be absorbed in her wares.

"Woman was asking about you the other day." Nettie leaned to me, but her reedy voice did not lower. She smelled of licorice, and her frock under her long pinafore was a drab purple. "Didn't like the look of her."

"Oh?" I pretended surprise, as I assumed she meant Charlotte. "What woman?"

"Weren't from around here. Asking did I know you, where I could find you. I didn't tell her much. I know you're cook in a house in Kennington or some such, but I wasn't certain which street."

"Mayfair," I corrected her. "Not Kennington." They were entirely different places, Kennington, in fact, lying south of the Thames.

Nettie's mouth puckered. "As I say, I didn't remember. When you're down in a kitchen, don't much matter where the house is, does it?"

It made every bit of difference, but I did not pursue the matter. "I suppose she was someone I met on my travels," I said, as though I had done the grand tour. I'd been as far afield as Devonshire, and that was about all.

"Sour, she was," Nettie said darkly. "If you met her on travels, I'm glad I've stayed home."

"Indeed. There isn't a much better place than England."

Nettie had nothing to add to this, so I took my leave. I felt Nettie watching me walk away, but when I turned back, she dove inside her shop, chattering in her shrill way to a customer there.

I did not like how my stomach knotted at Nettie's jabs—I thought I had grown out of my annoyance with her taunts. But at least Nettie hadn't told Charlotte much about me. I felt slightly better to know that even a woman who didn't remember me fondly had been loyal to me against an outsider.

A short stroll northward on Bow Lane, continuing toward the church, brought me to the rooms I'd lived in with Joe.

4

The bittersweet taste on my tongue shifted toward acrid as I gazed up at the house I'd shared with my husband.

I could find no fault with the abode on the outside. Plain brick rose four stories from the ground floor, which held a tiny haberdashery shop. The building immediately next door sported a pub, which was shut at this early hour.

The rooms we'd let had been stuffy in the summer and cold in the winter, but they'd kept out the rain and wind. I'd furnished our two rooms the best I could on the money Joe occasionally gave me, combined with the few treasures that had belonged to my mother.

The windows two floors above the haberdashery had been ours. Mostly what I remembered about the flat was how much I'd wept in it.

I squared my shoulders. I was not that frightened young woman any longer, the one who'd fallen in love too readily and had been hurt too deeply. I was much more sensible now, happy with my growing daughter, able to earn my own keep, and content with the dear friends I'd acquired.

"Good morning, Mr. Miller," I sang as I entered the shop.

Mr. Miller was an elderly, stooped man who'd been elderly and stooped as long as I could remember. He sold buttons and thread, ribbons and lace, as well as remnants of fabric he obtained from the more prosperous drapers in Cheapside and Cornhill.

"It's young Miss Holloway," Mr. Miller said in his thin voice. Unlike Nettie, he didn't correct himself and call me *Mrs. Bristow,* for which I was grateful. Mr. Miller had always seen me as little Miss Holloway.

"It is indeed." I beamed at him.

Mr. Miller had always been kind to me, slipping me tiny buttons and scraps of cloth he never could have sold, pressing his finger to his lips as he glanced at my mother. Mum would never have let me accept his charity, but thinking it through now, she must have known. How else could she explain the bits of cloth and lace I'd sewed together for my one doll?

"What can I do for you this morning?" Mr. Miller leaned on his counter, his pale, bony hands protruding from black serge sleeves. "You've hardly come for my paltry things. You're a famous cook now, in a grand home in Mayfair. I always knew you'd flourish."

His praise warmed me. "I'm only a domestic, Mr. Miller. Not the lady of the house."

Mr. Miller waved that aside. "Why would you want to be? Frail things, those ladies, too thin to lift a finger. It's better to be robust, like my Agnes."

"How is Mrs. Miller?" I inquired. She was, indeed, a stout lady, but strong. I'd always admired her.

"Quite fit. Races around after our grandchildren in blissful content. How is your dear daughter?"

"Also fit," I answered proudly. "And so clever. She can do arithmetic marvelously quickly, and read volumes, and her spelling is excellent."

"Ah, she will go far, then. Her mother is a fine example."

I contrasted the cozy feeling of his kindness to Nettie's needling. Mr. Miller had worked in this shop under the flat Joe and I shared, and knew what a disastrous marriage I'd made. He'd also been one of the very few who'd known that I was increasing with Grace, though it had become obvious when I'd waddled through the shop.

I clasped my hands in my close-fitting gloves, drawing in a breath. "I have come to ask you a few things, Mr. Miller. About Joe. My husband."

I winced as I said the word *husband,* but I stuck to it. I'd never told anyone here the truth of my marriage, and I prayed they'd never find out.

Mr. Miller's white brows rose. "Why do you want to talk about him? You know, my dear, that while his death was a tragedy, I've always considered it an escape for you." He looked slightly ashamed of himself as he stated this—

our training to not speak ill of the dead was well ground into us.

"I agree with you." My fingers tightened. "I came to realize Joe was not a good man, as you no doubt discerned for yourself. But I am trying to find out a bit more about him."

He stared at me blankly. "Are you? You were married to the man, you know."

I flushed. "Yes, but a woman sees one side of a husband, while his cronies and acquaintances see another."

"That is true," Mr. Miller conceded. "I am certain that what Agnes says of me and what my friends say of me are entirely different." He chuckled. "Might I ask the obvious question, young Miss Holloway? Why now? He's more than ten years gone, isn't he?"

"Twelve."

I'd not formed a thorough plan when I'd decided to revisit Bow Lane today. For some reason I'd thought it would be more changed, and perhaps I'd hoped that. Easier for me to expunge the past if the past itself had already vanished.

"Grace is of an age where she ought to know more about her father," I extemporized. "For good or for ill."

Mr. Miller regarded me shrewdly. "Has it anything to do with the woman who marched in here inquiring about you a few days ago?"

Mr. Miller had never been a lackwit. He'd

managed to live well on the proceeds of this tiny shop and the rooms he let upstairs—he had a house with his wife in a court off Lombard Street. They didn't dwell in this narrow building.

"Perhaps," I said, my face warming. "She said a few things that made me think I did not know Mr. Bristow as well as I ought."

"A nicely evasive answer." Mr. Miller nodded approvingly. "None of my business, you mean. But I am fond of you, young Miss Holloway, and would not like to see you hurt by anything that man did. What would you like to know?"

I wasn't certain. I wanted to pretend this investigation had nothing to do with me, that I was inquiring with my usual curiosity about a problem brought to me by someone else. But my hands were clammy under my gloves, my mouth dry.

"Did he have friends come by whenever I was out?" I asked quickly. "Speak to anyone? Perhaps from the pub next door?"

"I wouldn't know what went on in the pub." Mr. Miller folded his arms on the counter and leaned comfortably on them. "I never darken its door. And Mr. Bristow went out more than you did."

I nodded. "I am grasping at straws, I admit. Rather humiliating to say I know nothing about the cronies of my own husband."

"My wife has many friends I barely see," Mr. Miller said. "Probably best. Stay out of the way of the womenfolk." He chortled. "I do recall, now that you bring it to mind, that Mr. Bristow did have a visitor a few times, not long before he went on his last voyage. The man didn't come into the shop, and Mr. Bristow didn't invite him upstairs. I see much out my windows, though the panes are always dusty."

He gestured to the small, grimy windows that gave on to the street.

"What did this man look like?"

"Well, it was years ago now." Mr. Miller raised a thin finger to rub one ear. "I remember he walked a bit funny, swaying from side to side. Not from drink, just the way he moved. I recall it made me think he was a sailor."

"A sailor?" I jumped. The man Charlotte had called Joe's assistant? Or the friend who'd gone to see Charlotte about the money?

"As I say, I can't be certain. And maybe I thought him a sailor because Mr. Bristow was and all." Mr. Miller gazed at me apologetically, as if he wished to help but believed he was no help at all.

"Do you remember anything else about this person?"

"He and Mr. Bristow did squabble. About what, I could not hear. But I could see they were arguing. One time when they met, the second fellow threw up his arms and stormed away. I didn't see him after that."

Part of me was disappointed that Mr. Miller couldn't tell me the man's name, where he lived, and where I could find him now, but I knew I could not expect much after so long a time. That Mr. Miller remembered the man at all was a blessing.

"I do wish I could help you more, my dear." Mr. Miller no doubt saw the dashed hope on my face. "If you don't mind me putting my oar in, I think it's best you let sleeping dogs lie, as it were. Not much can be gained from digging up the past, especially when it was a painful one."

He gently straightened a skein of lace on his counter. I wondered if he believed Charlotte had been Joe's mistress, and that I was trying to discover if this had been the case.

Mr. Miller was so kind that I almost broke down and confessed the entire tale of the money to him, but I stopped myself. Even if I remained evasive about who Charlotte truly was, the story would sound as absurd as I'd thought it yesterday.

Also, I feared what effect the mention of a lost fortune might have on Mr. Miller. People became a little peculiar when they believed a great lot of money was loose in the wind. Though Mr. Miller did make a living here, a fortune was much different from eking out an existence.

The thought crossed my mind in that moment that the only person who didn't seem to care much for money was Daniel. He never expressed the worry over funds that so many did, though his patched and mended clothes spoke of a man careful with his coin.

Then again, he rented a small house in Kensington, more rooms in Southampton Street near Covent Garden, and who knew where else. Not to mention the tailored suits he wore when playing his part as a gentleman or man-about-town. Did his boss, Mr. Monaghan, keep him well paid?

The speculation flitted through my head as I pondered what to tell Mr. Miller. "Thank you," I said. "If you remember anything else, will you send word to me? You can leave it at Mrs. Millburn's. You recall my friend Joanna?"

"Indeed. A lovely girl. Married well."

"She did." I was proud of Joanna for making a good life for herself. "She has four children now, all of them fine lads and lasses."

"And looks after your girl." Mr. Miller gave the counter a decided tap. "Never hold a friendship like that lightly, my dear. It can so easily be taken away."

A shadow crossed his face, as though he spoke from experience. I reached over and patted his arm.

"You are a good man, Mr. Miller. Please give your wife my best wishes."

His sorrow faded. "I will do that, Miss Holloway. Or do you prefer to be called Mrs. Bristow?"

"Mrs. Holloway," I said. "I have returned to my own name, for my profession."

Mr. Miller gave me an approving nod. "For the best, I think, my dear Miss Holloway. Thank you for looking me up again. You've brightened an old man's day."

I left the shop after I'd purchased a skein of ribbon for Grace, not liking to pop in here and take up Mr. Miller's time without giving him something in return.

I returned to the street not much enlightened. A sailor—who might not have been a sailor—visiting Joe before he died might be significant, or mean nothing at all. Joe could rarely speak long to anyone without quarreling with them. The man could have been someone Joe owed money to. The assistant, Charlotte claimed, had been devoted to Joe, and a man throwing up his hands and storming off did not sound like one devoted. A bloke who was owed money was a more likely prospect.

I studied the public house next door, still shut. Joe had frequented this pub nearly every day when he'd been in London. A sailor between voyages did not have much to do, so he'd warmed a seat there most days.

I remembered that in the last months, he'd also taken to frequenting a gin parlor in the next lane. I walked back to Watling Street and around the corner to Bread Street. In the Middle Ages, I'd been told, this was the only street in the area where bakers were allowed to sell bread—they had to have a shop here if they wished to peddle their loaves. These days Bread Street still had a few bakeries, but most had become little shops that sold everyday wares or, as in the place I headed toward, gin houses.

The gin parlor was already open, though it was only shortly after ten in the morning. I saw, to my disapproval, that more than a few people, men and women both, already lounged inside in a stupor.

As I debated whether to enter and ask the proprietor a few questions about Joe, two men approached, intent on the house. I stepped aside, as though I was gathering my bearings to continue my shopping, but the two men halted suddenly in front of me.

"It's her," one said. Not a friendly greeting.

"I beg your pardon?" I answered coldly. "I do not believe we are acquainted."

The man's larger mate glowered down at me. "You're Joe's wife."

"Was," I said quickly. "His widow now."

"Don't we know it?" the first man said. "A good man like Joe gone all this time, and his high-and-mighty wife is still plaguing the earth."

His friend moved to one side of me, hemming me in. Bread Street was plenty crowded with women shopping for the day, workmen on ladders repairing gutters of a house not far along, and men and women heading purposefully through to other streets. I decided I could cry for help if my assailants became too persistent, and so I faced them with my head high. I'd wanted to know who Joe's friends had been, and here was an opportunity to find out.

"You knew Joe well, did you?" I asked.

The first one's brows drew down. Both men were large, as Joe had been, with hard faces, big hands in thick gloves, and hobnailed boots on giant feet. They weren't brothers—they looked quite dissimilar. One had greasy tow-colored hair sticking out from under his hat, and the other had darker skin and black-brown hair. The towheaded man was thinner than the other, but they were both tall and threatening.

"Why wouldn't we have?" the light-haired man said. "We was his mates. You was his Trouble, didn't he always say so?"

Trouble and strife—wife. Much of the Cockney slang about wives was disparaging.

"Then you would know about a man who worked for him," I said without acknowledging the slight.

"Worked for 'im?" the second man demanded. "Joe didn't have no one working for him."

"Perhaps aboard ship he did. He must have mentioned this person who aided him."

"Listen to her," the first man said to the second.

"She sounds like a right hoity-toity. Think she's forgotten where she comes from."

I met the man's gaze without flinching. "There is nothing wrong with speaking well. It helps you get on in the world."

"No wonder Joe ran away to sea." The first man's face cracked a smile, but it wasn't a warm one. "I wager he was tired of having this bitch yammering at him to better himself."

That was the second time I'd been called such a name in two days, and I was tiring of it. "What did Joe tell you about the men on his ships?" I persisted. "Or who he met on the voyages?"

I knew I risked much being so direct, but I also knew these men would give me no information otherwise.

Both closed in on me, and my heartbeat quickened, a trickle of fear touching my spine.

"Why are you asking these questions?" the second man demanded. "Just like the other one?"

By "the other one," I assumed he meant Charlotte, who'd apparently stirred up plenty of suspicion in this locale. She was expecting me to find things out, but she'd not smoothed the way for me.

I dropped the neutral accent I'd worked hard to master and resumed my native tongue. "Joe was me husband, weren't he? Why shouldn't I know who he met and who were his mates? Maybe there's something in it for 'em."

The change in tone eased some of their belligerence and caught their curiosity. "What somefink?" the first man answered.

"That's for me to know, innit?" I countered.

I'd baffled them, which was to my advantage, but the second man leaned to me. "We could beat it out of her."

I backed away, but the wall of the gin house was behind me. "One more step, and I'll scream, won't I?"

The second man gave me a nasty grin. "Start screaming then, love."

He came for me. I'd sucked in a breath to give him a scream that would batter his ears, when a strong hand pulled me aside, and a man in warm-scented brown wool interposed himself between me and the two men.

"Now then, gentlemen." Daniel bathed them in a wide smile. "Why don't we discuss this over a glass in this fine house? If I were you, I'd let me stand you a drink, because if you try to lay a finger on her, I will certainly break all of them."

5

How Daniel managed to talk the two ruffians into leaving me be while we adjourned to the gin house to converse about Joe, I am still not certain, but he managed it. Before I knew it, we were seated around a table, a tired barmaid depositing glasses of clear gin before us.

I not only disapproved of gin, I loathed the taste of it. I'd rather drink vitriol. But I realized that lecturing about the sins of strong drink would not be wise in this place, nor would refusing to drink a drop. I wet my mouth with the gin—my lips immediately became numb—then idly turned the glass on the table while the other three men talked.

Once lubricated with gin, the two men lost their belligerence and became loquacious. Not only had they known Joe, they'd admired him.

"Always good for a laugh, was Joe," the tow-haired man, whose name was Cedric, told Daniel. Neither of them would speak directly to me, but they'd already learned respect for Daniel.

"Always," the second man, Ned, chimed in. He mostly confirmed what Cedric said, I noted, without adding new information of his own.

Daniel agreed that a man good for a laugh was a fine thing.

"Joe weren't from around here," Cedric went on. "Didn't get on with people hereabouts because he came from Stepney. Not from inside the walls, was he?"

"Snobs everywhere, eh?" Daniel said congenially. "But he married a Bow Bells lass."

Cedric glanced at me, almost as though he'd forgotten my presence. "Many couldn't accept him, no matter what. Except me and Ned. We were mates."

"Did he have mates in Stepney?" Daniel asked. "Or was he glad to see the back of the place?"

Stepney, as well as its neighbor, Bethnal Green, was a slum. Whitechapel and Shadwell were a slight step above, but those stuck in the slums were a sad lot. My fear had been ending up there or in a workhouse, Grace taken from me, hence my determination to be the best cook in London.

"Naw, he had a lot of mates," Cedric said. "Men he went to sea with. They lived around Shadwell and down into the docklands. Knew everyone, did Joe."

They raised their glasses to him, while I sat mutely and listened.

The two men spoke of a man I barely recognized. A man who stood drinks for his friends, had ambitions of wealth that he thought going to sea would bring. Not through hard work, but by meeting the right people who would boost him up. Joe had planned to buy a plantation in the Lesser

Antilles, Cedric claimed—Barbados or Antigua. He'd amass a fortune raising sugar and return to England to buy himself a fancy country house, lording it over those who'd trodden on him before.

His words echoed what Joe had said as he'd lain next to me that last night, promising me fancy frocks and a manor house by the sea.

But it was ridiculous. Any coin Joe earned from his voyages he promptly drank or spent on worthless items. Whenever I asked for more money for the household expenses, he told me I needed to make do with less.

"How did he plan to buy a plantation?" Daniel asked in amazed admiration. His words slurred a bit, but I could see that he was far from drunk. "Takes a clever chap to do that."

Cedric puffed himself up, pleased he was privy to the information. "Oh, he knew how to bring together coins when he wanted."

"And then there was his grand plan," Ned put in.

Cedric glanced quickly at him as though he was unhappy Ned had let such a thing slip. "We don't know about that."

"Grand plan?" Daniel noisily slurped at his gin. When Cedric and Ned likewise lifted their glasses to drain them, Daniel surreptitiously spilled most of his drink on the floor.

Ned flushed as he lowered his glass, as though regretting his words.

"Like I said, we don't know much about it," Cedric answered.

Daniel signaled to the barmaid with his empty glass. "The poor man is dead and gone," he told Cedric. "What harm can it do to know what his plans were? I want to hear more about this plantation and his country estate. It doesn't hurt to dream."

Cedric lifted his broad shoulders in a shrug. "I wish I did know all about it. I wouldn't mind coming into funds meself, though I'd stay right here in England instead of running around to the far corners of the earth. I was a sailor for a while, but only on barges that went out to the end of the Thames and back. Soon as a swell hit on the other side of Southend, I was down on the deck, spewing me guts out. I can't think what it would be like sailing clean across an ocean."

"I'm a landsman myself." Daniel nodded at him. "Safer to keep my feet on dry earth."

"Or muddy muck, like in England." Cedric chortled. "Not everyone can be a sailor."

"Not like Joe," Daniel said with much respect in his voice. "I can imagine him puttering around an estate in the Cotswolds, all in tweed, like a good country squire. Seeing to the sheep and buying his lady plenty of gold plate to eat off of."

Ned snorted a laugh, but Cedric said, "Kent. Not the Cotswolds."

Daniel's brows rose. "He'd picked out a site?"

"Aye, down Folkestone way. He had a house in mind, one standing on a cliff overlooking the sea, with a long green leading up to the front of it. Can't recall its name."

"Seagate," Ned said. "I always thought it sounded so beautiful."

To witness these two ruffians, who'd not an hour ago tried to accost me, going dreamy eyed about a house my wretch of a husband had convinced this pair he would purchase, was unreal. They'd believed every word he'd told them.

But it matched what he'd said to me, that he'd wanted a house in Kent, where we could watch the sunrise over the sea.

Joe could be persuasive, the scoundrel. He'd duped these men as much as he'd duped me.

It wasn't long before the gin worked its spell. When Cedric and Ned slumped into each other and against the wall behind them, Daniel slipped a crown to the sallow-cheeked barmaid and led me out of the shop.

"Joe could spin a yarn," I said as we left Bread Street for Cheapside and walked east toward the lane where the Millburns lived.

Daniel tucked my arm through his. "Do you think he was lying?"

I'd come to know Daniel well enough to understand he'd already made up his own mind but wanted my opinion.

"I'd say yes, but for two things." I tapped my forefinger to his arm. "Charlotte believed the story enough to come to me, the woman who, in her mind, stole her husband. The second is that his choice of a house near Folkestone is very specific, and he mentioned Kent to me as well. Had this house gone up for sale? Had he inquired as to the price?"

"Worth looking into."

I sidestepped an errand boy who barreled along the road with no regard for anyone in his way. "Please do not tell me you have connections in Folkestone who will deliver you every bit of information on this house called Seagate."

"I don't know anyone in Folkestone," Daniel said, eyes glinting with amusement. "But I can make inquiries through those who do. Or pretend to be a gentleman searching for a suitable house in the area." The slur had left his words, Daniel as sober as he'd been before we'd entered the gin shop.

"Well, I shall leave that to you." I had no time to be traipsing to Kent, as pleasant as that journey might be. "You certainly had those two men confessing all to you. Butter wouldn't melt in your mouth, as they say."

"I've always wondered where that adage came from. It has never made sense to me. Anyway, the gin melted in their mouths and made them talk. The fact that I paid for the gin likely helped.

When they recover from the aftermath of so many glasses, they might forget all about us and anything we discussed."

I hoped so. "Joe obviously didn't trust those two enough to bring them in on the details of his plans."

"It would help if we could find someone he did trust, such as this servant or assistant or whoever he was that Charlotte mentioned." Daniel pulled me closer to him as the traffic became thick. He didn't speak again until we stepped into the narrow and much quieter lane that led to the Millburns' home. "I will look into that too. I do know people in Stepney."

"Be careful if you go into the East End." My blood chilled thinking of him there. Daniel had made an enemy of a man who ruled the East End's underworld, and I had no doubt this man would be happy of an opportunity to snare Daniel.

"I will take great care." Daniel squeezed my hand on his arm. "Here we are, and I see Grace watching for you. Where shall we go today?"

My heart lightened as I beheld my daughter waving at us from behind the thin lace curtains at the front room window. I untangled myself from Daniel and waved back.

"Do you not have work to do?" I asked Daniel, as it became clear he would accompany me inside.

"Nothing that can't allow me to spend the day with two lovely ladies."

Before I could answer, he had stepped up to the door, which my friend Joanna herself opened. Then Grace was there, and my arms were around her, and nothing else mattered.

We took Grace to Primrose Hill, north of Regent's Park, a very pleasant space with a view of London to the south and Hampstead to the north.

I stood on the green and surveyed the vista of the metropolis, its brick chimneys leaking smoke into the air despite the fineness of the day. Food still had to be cooked, factories to function, and trains to run, no matter the weather. Coal fires were the necessity and the bane of everyday life. But here, on this hill, fresh air dissipated the smoke, and I could breathe.

"We ought to have our cottage here, Mum." Grace held my hand loosely as we gazed at the view. I panted a bit from the walk up the rise. Daniel wandered the lower slope of the hill, looking for I knew not what. "When you have your tea shop, and we live in a cottage," Grace finished. "It's nice here."

"A fine idea." It was likely we'd only be able to afford tiny rooms over the shop at first, but I liked to hear Grace's confidence that we'd have our cottage one day.

I was as much a dreamer as Joe had been, I mused. He with his country estate on the coast of Kent, I with my tea shop and cozy cottage with Grace. We all wanted pie in the sky.

"Found it!" Daniel called to us, waving his arms.

Grace slipped from my grasp and skipped down the hill to him, her knee-length skirts bouncing. She'd be wearing longer skirts in no time, as my beautiful girl was becoming a lovely young woman.

Suppressing the pang in my heart, I followed Grace to where Daniel waited next to a tall oak.

"What have you found, Uncle Daniel?" Grace chirped. Daniel had been calling himself that to her, and Grace had decided it was a good enough moniker for him. Grace knew that Daniel and I were closer than brother and sister, but she good-naturedly went along with the name.

"Shakespeare's Tree." Daniel patted the thick bole beside him.

"Shakespeare's?" Grace gazed at it, wide-eyed. "It must be very old. Did he sit under it while he wrote *Julius Caesar*?"

I felt a surge of pride that a daughter of mine knew about Shakespeare and his works. Joanna was making certain Grace learned of the grand traditions of English drama.

Daniel's eyes twinkled. "Shakespeare never knew this tree. It was planted, oh, nearly twenty years ago now, to mark his birthday." He pointed to a plaque of faded lettering that proclaimed the tree had been set here by the actor Samuel Phelps, and funded by the Workingmen's Shakespeare Committee.

We admired the tree for a time, its shade welcome in the September sunshine. Trees lasted, I told myself. This one would watch over the park and the metropolis after the three of us were long gone. A sobering thought.

To shake myself out of these maudlin musings, I said brightly, "I believe it's time for tea. With plenty of cake."

By tacit agreement, Daniel and I never discussed Grace's father on our outings. I had not told Grace much about Joe, only that he'd been lost at sea. She'd not asked many questions, though I imagined that would change as she grew older.

I hugged Grace good-bye in the front parlor of the Millburns' home and took my leave, my eyes misting as they always did when the day was over.

"I will see you Monday," I promised her.

Grace kissed my cheek. "A happy day it will be."

She liked to reassure me, the darling girl.

I patted my stomach as Daniel and I strolled back toward Cheapside. "I did eat rather a lot of cake in that tearoom. You ought to have stopped me."

Daniel slipped his arm through mine. "You were enjoying yourself."

"I was rather." I had liked watching Grace's eyes light up as Daniel continuously ordered different sorts of cake at the tea shop we'd found at the edge of the park.

"Are you too stuffed for some proper supper?" Daniel asked me.

"It is nowhere near time for supper." It was five o'clock, and twilight had not yet gathered. "Although I should be home preparing it for the Bywaters."

"Your day out is not quite over yet," Daniel said. "Enough time left for us to take in a meal. There is a restaurant in Kensington I believe you will like—sauces prepared in a way you'd approve. If we take a train from Cannon Street, we'll be there in no time."

"Why this sudden rush to eat? If you are hungry, I'm certain I can find leftovers in the larder, as long as Tess hasn't softened and given them all to the footmen."

Daniel removed his cap, scrubbed his hands through his thick hair, and clapped the hat on again. "Can't a chap take his young lady to dine without her pestering him with questions?"

"Oh." I halted and peered at him in confusion. Daniel had escorted me to dinner twice this past summer, but Grace had accompanied us both times.

Daniel regarded me with exasperation. Beyond us, the traffic in Cheapside had, if anything, thickened. The train would be the best way for me to return to Mayfair, as much as I disliked riding underground.

"Is your objection supping too early, or supping with me?" Daniel demanded. He'd released my arm and now faced me, shielding us from the gazes of the passersby in the busy street.

"Why would my objection be supping with *you?*" I asked in amazement.

His exasperation increased. "You confound me, Kat. If it is not having consumed too many cakes nor eating with me, then what *is* your objection?"

"Well, I . . ." I spluttered while I tried to make sense of my thoughts. I could tell Daniel many things, such as that my frock was dusty from climbing the hill, that it was a long way to Kensington even on the train and then I'd have to journey back to Mayfair, or that I wasn't certain any restaurant's sauces would meet with my approval.

The answer that emerged surprised even myself. "Because I am not your young lady."

6

Daniel went very still, the animation vanishing from his voice. "I see."

His tone was flat, uninflected. I'd observed Daniel press his emotions into a tight, cold ball before, but never when he was alone with me.

"Forgive me," I said quickly. "That sounded dreadful. Not what I meant at all."

"Then what did you mean?" The quietness of the question alarmed me.

"That we are hardly sweethearts," I babbled. "We are friends, in the best sense of the word. You do not have to take me to restaurants as though I were a gentlewoman and you my beau."

As the light in his eyes turned hard as crystal, I realized with a jolt that this was exactly what he thought of us. A young woman and her beau, a gent and his lady.

His invitation this evening had not been so he could give me a treat as a friend, but because he wanted to escort me, on his arm, as though he courted me.

"Daniel . . ."

Daniel took a step back. He removed his hat again, smoothed his hair more tidily, and replaced the cap. "Apparently, I have presumed too much."

"No, I don't think you have. I so enjoy my outings with you, and I look forward all day to you arriving for a late cup of tea . . ."

Daniel's stolid face and unmoving stance made me trail off to silence. He stood like a pillar at the edge of the lane, the people rushing past of no interest to him.

"I thought it obvious what I feel for you, Kat," Daniel said after a time. "You call us friends, but I want so much more than that."

My heart beat faster. When I'd first met Daniel, he'd smiled at me as though I was the most beautiful woman in the room—and in Mrs. Pauling's kitchen on that day, I suppose I had been. He'd flattered me with his attention, and for the first time in years, I'd felt a flicker of interest in a handsome man.

If Daniel had made the declaration he had just now before I'd known he was more than a simple man-of-all-work, I'd have warmed with pleasure. But I did know him, chameleon Daniel, who did dangerous jobs for Scotland Yard, though he claimed he was not part of the police. He could not tell me everything about his past, himself, and his obligation to the cold Mr. Monaghan, which I quite understood. Sometimes what they did involved the fate of the nation.

Also, if I had not made an utter fool of myself over a man in the past, resulting in me raising my illegitimate child on my own, I'd be much more welcoming to Daniel at this moment. But I'd made a huge mistake once before, and I'd vowed that Grace would never suffer for my mistakes again.

But, I argued with myself, did I not know the real Daniel? He of the kind heart who looked after his own by-blow of a son and had plenty of time for my daughter, and for friends like Mr. Thanos. Elgin Thanos, a brilliant gentleman, couldn't speak highly enough of Daniel.

As I swallowed, unsure how to respond in my confusion, Daniel grew even more grim.

"I suppose I've become so used to being cryptic that I have been too much so with you," he said. "Another thing I can be angry at Monaghan about."

"I understand that you have to be cryptic. And secretive. You told me."

"But, damn it all, that is not who I am." Daniel's calm cracked. "It is a job I do. One I'm forced to do, when I'd give anything to simply be by your side. To take you away from drudging in the kitchen of that ungrateful woman and have you putter about in your own, doing whatever you wish, while I take care of you. That is what I want."

My mouth went dry, my tongue heavy. "What exactly are you saying, Daniel?"

"I think you know what I am saying." Daniel straightened his cap with a decided tug. "And I believe I know what your answer would be, so I will not ask the question. Good day, Kat."

He turned and walked away from me. I remained on the spot, rooted by numb feet that refused to move. I should run after him, beg him not to go, tell him I would answer however he liked. I needed Daniel in my life. Needed him more than I wished to admit.

Frozen in place, my body flooded with both heat and an icy coldness. I saw Daniel raise a hand, heard the sharp whistle through his teeth as he signaled a hansom cab. I assumed he'd board it, but he shouted something to the driver and pointed my way. The cabbie nodded, caught the coin Daniel tossed him, and headed for me, as Daniel crossed Cheapside and faded into the teeming crowd.

Even in his anger at me, in his belief that I was rejecting him, Daniel was making certain I reached home without harm.

I boarded the cab with shaking limbs, closed the flap door, and thumped into the seat as the cab jerked forward. I now should fall into a fit of weeping, but my eyes remained dry and aching. All the way home, no tears would come.

I moved woodenly through my duties that night, reassuring Tess, who inquired if I was all right, that I was merely tired from my long day out. She frowned at me, but fortunately did not pursue the matter.

Mrs. Bywater wanted another of her unusual meals—grouse sausages, oysters in milk, sole-stuffed giblets in a curried soup, and a complex soufflé with out-of-season fruit and jelly—and Tess and I had to do our best to make it all into something edible.

I wanted to rail and curse, but I held myself tightly, knowing if I did not, I'd become a shrieking harridan. Tess, Mr. Davis, and the maids and footmen assisting me had done nothing to earn my wrath, so I clamped my lips closed and said nothing at all.

Focusing on cooking helped me push troubling thoughts of Daniel aside, but as supper was sent up, and the staff partook of their own meals and drifted off to bed, I could no longer stave them off. I was left alone to sharpen my knives, make notes on my meals, and ponder what had happened this afternoon.

The quietness was unnerving. I knew Daniel would not come tonight, and the knot in my chest began to ache, far more than I thought it could.

I did hear a thump of boots on the back stairs, but I knew it was not Daniel's tread. Soon Lady Cynthia, clad in a man's suit, stood silhouetted in the kitchen doorway. She paused, the gas sconce in the hall behind her outlining her slim figure, then she headed for my table, her bootheels loud on the flagstones.

"It is ghastly dark in here," she announced as I politely rose.

I'd extinguished the lamps except for one lone candle on my work table and the sconce in the hall to guide me to the stairs when I was finished.

Cynthia turned up the gas on the sconce near the dresser, lighting it with a long match struck competently on the brick wall. The white-blue light rendered her pale cheeks and hair still more wan. I preferred candlelight, with its more flattering glow.

Cynthia turned to me, studying me as I studied her. She'd been out, that was certain, but she must have returned before Mr. Davis ordered all the main doors locked. Otherwise she'd have had to tap on the door that led to the outside stairs and wait for me to admit her.

Her cashmere suit held the scent of cigar smoke. Cynthia herself did not often imbibe in smoking, but her friend Bobby did. Perhaps she and Bobby had surreptitiously entered a gentleman's club or gaming parlor, as they daringly liked to do. I also scented whiskey, but Cynthia did not seem to be inebriated.

"Gambling den?" I asked her when she did not speak. "Or a risqué club you and Lady Roberta enjoy gaining admission to?"

"Neither. A private party hosted by Miss Townsend for those of like minds. Thanos was there."

Likely why Cynthia had not allowed herself to become intoxicated. She valued Mr. Thanos's good opinion.

"What did he think of it?" I imagined Mr. Thanos blinking at everyone through his spectacles—if he bothered to put them on—in his intrigued way.

"He was fascinated. I am rather more interested in why you look as though you were run down by a police wagon."

I touched my face. I hadn't realized my low spirits had manifested themselves on my countenance.

"I had a rather long day," I began.

"Poppycock. You were burbling with vigor this morning, and you usually return home from your days out most refreshed. Is anything the matter? Is Grace ill?" she finished worriedly.

Cynthia was the only member of the household, upstairs or down, who knew of Grace's existence.

"No, no. She is in excellent health."

"Thank the Lord for that. Do sit down, Mrs. H. I'm not the sort who expects the staff to stand at attention, when they're not bowing and scraping and all that rot."

"So many do." I resumed my seat, taking up my pencil as though ready to continue writing in my notebook.

Cynthia peered at the book as she seated herself on a stool and stretched out her legs. "You're only making little squiggles. A new sort of cipher?"

"Don't be silly." I closed the book I'd not been able to write legibly in and laid down my pencil. "As I say, I am tired."

"I don't believe you. Something happened. Is it to do with the woman who visited you? What did Daniel say about that?"

At Daniel's name, my face tightened. I tried to suppress my sudden emotion, but Cynthia, with the benefit of the brighter gaslight, noticed and leapt on it.

"What the devil happened, Mrs. H.? Tell me immediately, or I'll be imagining all sorts."

I hardly wanted to confess all to Cynthia— my mother had always taught me not to push my troubles onto others. Unfortunately, my unhappiness came tumbling out.

"I am afraid Daniel has given me the push."

I heard the tears in my voice, but even now, with a sympathetic friend, I could not cry. My throat remained tight and dry.

Cynthia's eyes widened. "Never. Of course he did not. Did you quarrel? You must have misunderstood him."

Some of my dignity returned. "I understood him perfectly well. He intimated that he wanted to ask me for marriage, but he knew I'd refuse, and so he stormed off. Well, retreated rapidly down the street once he'd seen me into a hansom. He did not visit me tonight, and I'm not certain he will again."

Cynthia's mouth hung open. "He said he wanted to marry you? Damnation."

"He did not say that exactly," I corrected her. "He hinted. And said that I should have known his feelings. But how could I?"

Cynthia leaned across the table and eyed me severely. "Good Lord, anyone who ever saw McAdam could realize his feelings for you. The man is head over heels. And I've seen the way *you* look at him." She jabbed a long finger at me. "Your sentiments for him are quite warm. The pair of you rub along better than most of my married friends—tenfold better, I'd say. Why on earth would he decide you'd refuse him?"

"Because how *can* I marry?" I burst out. "I have a daughter to look after, a job to do, a living to earn. Daniel's life is not his own—he is obligated to a man who works for the police. It is all convoluted, and I do not understand it. Daniel pays for his own son to board elsewhere so he will not encounter the dangers Daniel might bring home."

"Perhaps, but—"

"Shall I put Grace into this danger?" I went on, ignoring her interruption. "How am I to move my daughter in with Daniel when I would never know what peril he'd be plunged into next? What peril he'd plunge *us* into? And how would it be for me, expecting the day when a constable or Inspector McGregor told me that Daniel had been offed by some villain? And anyway, neither of us has much coin that I can see, so I might be obliged to remain in service, no matter what. Marriage is not simply a moonlit night and a grand passion, my dear Cynthia. It is a great undertaking with no assurance that any happiness will come of it."

I ran out of breath, finding myself holding on to the table as I swayed on my chair. Cynthia had closed her mouth, but her gaze was fixed on me, her cheeks flushed.

I realized that I had addressed her by her first name, without any honorific, as I had no business to do. She let it pass without comment.

"Not all men are like your first husband," she said when it was clear I had finished. "Some are thoroughly decent chaps, like McAdam and Thanos."

"A thoroughly decent chap who cannot even tell me if Daniel McAdam is his real name."

"Ah, names." Cynthia waved that aside. "My father, as you know, stole the title of Lord Clifford—at first anyway. I'm called Lady Cynthia Shires and not plain Miss Shires because of my father's duplicity. Bobby prefers that moniker to Lady Roberta—I can hardly blame her. You told me you resumed your maiden name after your husband died. So what do names matter? It is the person behind the name who is important."

"Your father, while quite charming, is a

confidence trickster," I reminded her. I'd become acquainted with the eloquent Lord Clifford when he'd come to stay in this house last spring. I'd grown to like the man, but I was well aware that he dabbled in deceit.

"While that is true, I am not, nor is Bobby, nor you. And McAdam uses deceit to catch criminals, which is not the same thing as using it for personal gain, as dear old Papa does. I am trying to point out that I trust McAdam far more than I do most people, including my own relations. Perhaps you should as well."

She was scolding me. I balled my fists on the table. "I do trust him. Mostly. But when you have been thoroughly deceived, it is difficult. If he were as transparent as Mr. Thanos, perhaps I would not be so hesitant."

Cynthia's tiny smile told me much. "Yes, one knows exactly who Thanos is, and that he is kind to everyone."

I forbore to mention that while Cynthia was surprised I hadn't guessed Daniel's intentions toward me, she was oblivious to Mr. Thanos's about her. However, this was not the moment to point out such things.

"Mr. Thanos is a dear," I said warmly. "I believe you are saying, Lady Cynthia, that I ought to accept Daniel's proposal—not that he made any such thing—regardless of my ignorance of his past deeds and his true name."

"His present deeds tell me he is a man of integrity," Cynthia said. "He catches very bad men and has them banged up. You ought to know. You've done plenty to help him—and he you."

I fell silent, realizing the futility of arguing with her. I cared for Daniel, more than I wanted to admit. The fact that he might never darken the door of my kitchen again formed a hollow in my chest.

I knew Daniel could erase his presence from my life as easily as he'd inserted it, if he wished. The sight of him striding away from me through the press of carts in Cheapside had sent a shudder of finality through me.

Cynthia's warm hand on my wrist brought me out of this bleak place. "All is not lost, Mrs. H. Would you like me to have a word with him?"

My eyes widened. "Dear heavens, no. It is good of you, Lady Cynthia, but no. This is a private matter between Daniel and me."

She squeezed my arm. "I dislike seeing you look so forlorn. But do not worry—he'll come around. He's damned fond of you."

"But we return to the same problem. I do enjoy his company." My face heated as I recalled the rather passionate kiss we'd shared in this very kitchen the previous night. "I wish things could stay as they are. No difficult decisions to be made."

Cynthia gave my wrist a final pat and released

me. "I do not believe that will be enough for McAdam. Or you either, I daresay. Here's an idea—instead of waiting for Daniel to confess all to you, why not use your clever brain to find out about him? Make Daniel McAdam the focus of your investigation."

I shook my head. While I longed to know everything about Daniel, I shied from the knowledge at the same time. What if I didn't like what I discovered?

"I would rather Daniel told me plainly, when he is ready," I said, trying to speak with conviction.

"What rot. If you'd known what sort of blackguard your first husband was, you'd never have married him. In my circles, the parents of the young lady make it a point to know everything about the gentleman who has the audacity to propose to their daughter. It is difficult for any man without an impeccable pedigree and his exact history known from the time he was in the cradle to find himself a wife among my benighted friends."

Her obvious disgust stemmed from the parade of eligible gentlemen her aunt had pushed in front of her, the young men carefully screened before being given an invitation to dine. Cynthia so far had loathed every one of them.

I held up a hand, which shook a little. "You are an aristocrat. Even if your father finagled his way into the title, he still was an heir with the correct bloodline. Daniel and I are creatures from the working classes. At least I am," I finished. I hadn't the faintest idea where Daniel had been born or to whom.

Cynthia's grin chased away her melancholy. "Are you supposing McAdam is a long-lost heir, perhaps to a duke, or even better, royalty?" She guffawed. "That is the stuff of pantos. Though it would be such fun if he were, wouldn't it?"

"Not for me," I said. If Daniel did turn out to be some sort of prince in disguise, he'd never be able to take a cook born in Bow Lane to wife.

"I still say you should discover all you can," Cynthia said, breaking the nonsense of my thoughts. "You have several excellent resources at your disposal already."

"Do I?"

"Yes. Thanos for one. He and McAdam were at Cambridge together. Thanos has known him for years. I'm certain he can allay your worries."

"Mr. Thanos is a kindhearted gentleman, as we have mentioned," I said. "He will give me the rosiest picture of Mr. McAdam, both to please me and to remain loyal to his friend."

"True." Cynthia nodded. "But Thanos is also as honest as he is kind. If he thought there was something dark you needed to know about McAdam, he would tell you. So would McAdam's son."

James. "I am not certain I should interrogate

James for information about his own father," I said quickly. "I don't want to distress him."

"Not an interrogation. You simply want to know more about the man. I'm certain James would eagerly supply what he knew. He's fond of you, Mrs. H."

James had a sunny nature, his brown eyes free from the shadows I sometimes spied in Daniel's. "I am quite fond of him in return, but I worry that he too would paint Daniel in the rosiest colors."

"Possibly, but the other resource I have in mind would not."

I had a feeling I knew of whom she spoke, but I dutifully asked, "What other resource?"

"Mr. Fielding, of course." Cynthia's eyes sparkled. "He will not varnish his thoughts about McAdam, no matter that he's a vicar and all. If anything, Mr. Fielding might exaggerate the other way."

"I have no doubt that Mr. Fielding will be quite anxious to tell me all sorts of foul things about Mr. McAdam." I pulled my notebook to me and opened it again. "Mr. Fielding considers Mr. McAdam his rival in all things. Never mind they call themselves brothers."

"Then why do they?" Cynthia asked in curiosity. "If they are rivals and not blood brothers, why do they refer to each other as such?"

I paused in the act of reaching for my pencil. "I really do not know."

"That tells me they have a shared bond they do not want to break, no matter how much they protest to the contrary." Cynthia lounged back in the chair, crossing her well-made boots.

I lifted my pencil. "Daniel intimated his intentions, realized I did not return his wishes, and has departed. Now I must get on. I have much to do and to think about."

Cynthia remained seated, though I began to scribble in the notebook. She had been right to observe that my writing tonight was crabbed and illegible.

"Do not give up, Mrs. H.," she said gently. "You and McAdam are meant to be. Like Beatrice and Benedick."

I blinked at her. "Who are they?"

"From *Much Ado About Nothing.* Shakespeare. Sorry, just saw the thing at home in Hertfordshire, performed by some strolling players, who were ghastly. But highly amusing."

Shakespeare had come up twice today. No doubt my daughter would know all about the play and its characters.

Cynthia hadn't finished. "Beatrice and Benedick had much to work through before they declared their undying love at the end of act five. But they suited well, as do you and McAdam. Perhaps you are only in act four, when everything seems lost."

"This conversation has become quite silly," I

said briskly. "I do need to finish my notes and retire."

"That is the Mrs. H. I am used to finding in this kitchen." Cynthia laced her hands under her knot of fair hair. "I actually came down here for another reason, before I saw you so unhappy. I wanted to ask about the problem you shot out of here this morning to solve. The one I sent McAdam to winkle out of you in the first place."

7

So relieved was I that Cynthia turned her attention from the question of Daniel and me, that I explained all to her.

Perhaps she had not believed I could shock her twice in one night, but when I described how Charlotte had claimed that my husband had been murdered and robbed of a fortune, her mouth dropped open again.

"A house in Kent, eh?" Cynthia sprang to her feet with her natural energy and began to pace the kitchen. "That would be easy enough to discover—whether he picked a name from the air to wind up his mates or if he actually spoke to someone about purchasing it."

"After he'd doubled his fortune in Antigua or Barbados," I clarified. "Inquiring there would be somewhat more difficult."

"Not necessarily." Cynthia ended her circuit at the dresser full of crockery and swung around to march past the table once more. "Miss Townsend and Bobby know half of those who built up fortunes in the Antilles. Between the three of us, we should be able to find out if a sailor had been flush enough with cash twelve years ago to try to buy a plantation. The gossip on the islands is apparently rife." She chuckled. "Mummy knows all these people too, but she won't speak to any whose family hasn't been listed in Debrett's for the past hundred years."

She continued to laugh, amused by the foibles of her mother.

I could see by the softness in Cynthia's face that her stay in Hertfordshire this summer had done her good. Her bitter anger at her parents had faded, I hoped fueled by a new understanding. Cynthia was their only surviving child—I had seen their love for her when they'd stayed in this house, though emotions on all parts had been somewhat strained.

"I suppose it could do no harm to ask," I ventured.

"Also, we can find out if this house called Seagate exists. If it does, it supports the idea that your husband had come into funds, or believed he would. It is one thing to say, *Oh, I'd love to purchase a country house and live the life of a squire.* Another to say, *I am going to buy that house, for this price, on this date.*"

I agreed with her. "The question remains—did he actually find this money? From where? Did he come by it honestly? Knowing Joe, I doubt it. And what happened to it?"

"All good questions." Cynthia ceased her pacing and flung herself onto the stool. "And did this assistant bloke the Charlotte woman speaks about really kill him and steal the money?"

"We must hunt him up," I said. "Daniel would be very handy for such a task . . ." I trailed off and swallowed, forgetting that Daniel might wash his hands of the whole affair.

"I'm sure he'll help," Cynthia said quickly.

I decided not to reopen the topic. "Another person to question would be this man who came to Charlotte and told her the tale. Who is *he?*" I sighed. "I will have to speak to Charlotte again, I'm afraid."

Cynthia wrinkled her nose. "I can see where that would be difficult. But never you mind. I will go with you. I'll make sure she's civil to you, at least."

I would be foolish to proudly resist Cynthia's offer of help, and so I gave her a nod.

"That would be most welcome," I said. "Thank you. I would be glad of your assistance."

The next morning, I returned to the kitchen, apron clean and pressed, schooling my face so my moroseness over Daniel would not reveal itself.

I'd had a bad night, waking whenever my tired body made me drift off, first drowsing in the happy memory of Daniel, Grace, and me at the top of Primrose Hill. Then I'd remember Daniel's parting, and my stomach would knot.

I'd often worried for his safety, fearing losing such a friend, but I hadn't realized until now exactly how much of an ache his absence would cause me. Telling myself to put my feelings aside was doing me no good.

I would have to wait to continue my investigation into Joe's death and his supposed fortune, though Cynthia would be able to inform her friends and start asking about the plantation and estates in Kent. I wasn't certain the information would help other than to confirm the story Cedric and Ned had told Daniel, but I would still welcome their assistance.

For now, I was a cook, and cook I must.

Mr. Davis banged into the kitchen after breakfast service, just as I was finishing my own breakfast and carrying my plate into the scullery for Elsie to wash.

"She has sent you the menu for the afternoon meal." Mr. Davis's coattails fluttered as he slammed a paper to my table. "She's having guests again," he said with an air of disgust. "She ought to know that the menu should be delivered through the *housekeeper,* not *me.* Ignorance."

Mr. Davis, who had been a butler in the best houses for years, was quite the snob. A lady who didn't understand the hierarchy of servants was in no way worthy of his respect.

"Never mind, Mr. Davis," I said placatingly. "Perhaps Mrs. Redfern is busy."

"She is—organizing the drawing room for the mistress's gathering of fussy, middle-class women. Lady Clifford, for all her shortcomings, at least has elegance and taste."

"Indeed, Lady Cynthia's mother is quite fashionable. But since you've seen the menu, you at least know what wines to bring out."

"Ugh." Mr. Davis stabbed a finger to the neatly written lines on the page. "What sort of wine is served with *this?*"

I examined the paper in some disquiet. I'd hoped Mrs. Bywater's phase for extremely odd foods she thought fashionable would fade, but that appeared not to be the case.

"I possibly could cook these," I said. "After a long trip to the market and possibly a journey to France. Tess and I will have to make do with what we have."

Tess chuckled at my joke, but honestly, Mrs. Bywater was becoming unreasonable. Her husband much preferred simple dishes, and usually she gave in to his wishes. But for some reason, upon her return to London this autumn, she'd decided to abandon simplicity for pretension.

The paper was blazoned with the title:

Luncheon for Twelve. The Meeting of the Ladies' Society for Training Girls of Good Character to Enter Service.

My mother had always had a horror of such organizations. *They take a sensible girl and fill her head with ideas that she is good for nothing but fetching and carrying for others,* Mum had snapped. *The more compliant and biddable she is, the more they praise her. When you are in service, my Kat, you must always know your own mind. Being courteous to your mistress is not the same thing as being downtrodden by her. Better walk away from a post than let the master or mistress strip you of your pride and your faith in yourself.*

I could hear her voice plain as day, which reminded me how much I missed her.

I firmed my resolve and skimmed through the paper. I'd change every one of these blasted recipes into a good, wholesome dish—I secretly doubted Mrs. Bywater would be able to tell the difference anyway.

Tess and I gathered our supplies and went to work. The fricassee of eels in chowder became a straightforward fish soup. The curried duck served with a paste of skate and potatoes became slices of duck breast with a smooth curry sauce. The calf's brains mashed and served in a pastry case became vol-au-vent stuffed with minced beef.

Thankfully, the puddings Mrs. Bywater asked for were apricot tarts with fruit jelly. I ignored her instructions for a saffron soufflé with candied oranges, which was ridiculously complicated, not to mention expensive, and instead made a sweet cream soufflé drizzled with orange water.

Simple was always best, in my opinion.

Mrs. Bywater believed a convoluted recipe with a long name made it sophisticated and aristocratic. I ought to tell her about the duchess I'd worked for, who'd been satisfied with cold chicken pie and a cup of tea for her midday meal.

Cooking kept me occupied, however, especially when I had to answer Tess's questions or calm her amazed remarks on Mrs. Bywater's choices. When the last of the dishes went up, I turned my hand to cobbling together leftovers for the staff's luncheon.

When that was finished and those who'd come downstairs were happily eating in the servants' hall, I feared that my mind, released, would wander back to my sorrows and worries.

But it was not to be. Mrs. Redfern entered the kitchen and told me that the mistress had requested me to go upstairs and take my bow.

"Did she?" I demanded in irritation. My apron was stained, my hair straggling, my hands cracked and dry. I had no inclination to hurry upstairs and bob curtsies, pretending to be humble, while Mrs. Bywater and her guests critiqued what I knew had been a magnificent meal.

"Never worry," Mrs. Redfern said, trying to sound kind. "They are quite happy with the food, from what I overheard."

While this observation was encouraging, it was quite trying to have to change my apron, straighten my hair, wash my hands yet again, and appear as though I'd prepared the entire feast without so much as perspiring.

I left the kitchen and climbed the back stairs, noting how weary I was. After my sleepless night and much work today, I wondered if I could nip to my chamber for a quick nap.

Mr. Davis sent me a sympathetic glance when I appeared in the dining room's doorway. He stood stiffly by the sideboard, where he kept an eye on the footmen who circled the table to serve the food. The footmen were just finishing handing around the soufflé, which sat plumply on plates as it should, the orange sauce perfectly ladled out under Mr. Davis's watchful gaze.

I halted, curtsied, and waited to be noticed.

"Ah, there is Cook," Mrs. Bywater said. She knew I preferred to be called by my name, but either she did not remember at this moment, or she did not care. "The ladies wish to thank you for your excellent meal." She beamed at the company. "Our cook is clever at putting together the recipes I give her."

Not only was I not to have a name, but I was given no credit for making certain her meal wasn't ghastly. I hid my annoyance and curtsied once more.

Thankfully, Lady Cynthia sat in the middle of the pack of ladies on the right side of the table, dressed today in a tea gown of mauve silk. To my surprise, Miss Townsend, her friend and a genteel young woman, reposed next to her. I hadn't thought Miss Townsend interested in Mrs. Bywater's societies.

Miss Townsend's dark brown eyes flicked to mine as she sent me a small smile. I pretended not to notice her and kept my eyes averted as a good domestic ought.

"You are familiar to me," a lady opposite Cynthia said as she peered at me. She had iron gray hair pulled into a large bun, an unlined face, and eyes of steely blue. "I am certain you must have been cook to one of my friends. Were you with Lady Atkins?"

I curtsied to her, my legs already tired from all the bobbing up and down. "No, ma'am."

"Hmm. Lady Wilkinson? No? The Countess of Garrowby?" She frowned as I negated name after name. "It must have been *someone*. You ran off, I remember, to get married. And had a child, I believe."

8

My heart constricted so hard I feared it would stop. The identity of the person this lady was groping for was Lady Aston-Were, who lived in Grosvenor Square. She'd had two cooks—I'd been the under-cook, as I'd not had much experience at that time, only having finished my training before I'd been hired in her large house.

My mother had died while I'd been in that post. I'd met Joe on my afternoon out, when I'd been wandering the Embankment grieving my mother, where she and I used to watch the boats on the river. On leave between voyages, Joe had been traversing London to see the sights. He'd lent a sympathetic shoulder, and things had progressed rapidly from there.

I'd told few that I was leaving my post to marry, but of course I'd had to explain to the other cook in the house. While Mrs. Dyson, that cook, had not approved, she'd understood and wished me well. Somehow the story must have leaked from that house to this woman now sitting at Mrs. Bywater's table. I doubt Lady Aston-Were had much cared where I'd gone—she'd likely made an offhand remark to the effect that her under-cook, newly hired, had run off to marry, so tiresome of her.

I swallowed and made my stiff legs curtsy once more. "I beg your pardon, ma'am," I said. "I've never been married."

Cynthia's brows rose slightly at this declaration, but it was perfectly true. My marriage hadn't been legal.

"Are you certain?" the woman persisted. "Lady Cynthia told me your name was Mrs. Holloway. I would swear it was a Holloway I'm thinking of."

It was not my place to argue with her or correct her, or point out that there must be many women with the name of Holloway kicking about London. I could only brace myself while Mrs. Bywater peered at me narrowly.

"And there was a child," the woman rattled on. "Quite a disgrace, I thought when I heard of it."

"Hardly a disgrace," Miss Townsend interposed smoothly. "If this cook you are thinking of was married."

The woman's brow puckered. "I heard there was something wrong about it. Perhaps they had to wed in haste. You understand what I mean." She sent Miss Townsend a knowing look.

"Well, it wasn't *our* Mrs. Holloway," Lady Cynthia said stoutly. "Must have been some other cook. My own sister hired her, and Mrs. Holloway has impeccable references."

If Mrs. Bywater checked those references, she'd find Lady Aston-Were listed as a past employer. If this lady today managed to remember the name she searched her faulty memory for, Mrs. Bywater might ask the Aston-Were household why I had left it. My entire future hung on that thread.

"No, indeed," Miss Townsend put in. "Mrs. Holloway is a single lady. *Mrs.* is a badge of respect for her position. Besides, if she'd married, her name would no longer be Holloway, would it?"

The lady's expression cleared. "Ah, of course. I hadn't thought of that, Miss Townsend. How silly of me."

She made a deferential nod to Miss Townsend. Miss Townsend came from a very wealthy and prominent titled family, and I saw that this woman was awed by her. Mrs. Bywater, who adored aristocrats, also beamed Miss Townsend a smile.

At this moment, I too loved Miss Townsend, and with her, Lady Cynthia, my heart overflowing with gratitude. One never understands who one's true friends are until one is in a tight situation.

Mrs. Bywater dismissed me. I smothered a sigh of relief, gave the room yet another curtsy, and fled.

I reentered my kitchen gratefully. As elegant as the upstairs rooms were, I felt much more at home with the brick walls and stone floors of the kitchen, my table laden with provisions, and the dressers and shelves stocked with crockery and a fine array of pans. Lady Rankin—Cynthia's sister, who had originally hired me—had not stinted in fitting out the room.

"Did they give you a vail?" Tess asked eagerly upon my return.

So agitated had I been that I hadn't noticed how none of the ladies had offered me a sixpence or half crown in appreciation for my cooking.

"Not even a farthing today," I answered.

Tess glowered. "Mean of them."

"Do not disparage the mistress's guests, Tess. It is not for us to decide who she should or should not invite to the house." The admonishment was automatic—I had been more interested in escaping scrutiny than worrying about gaining a tip.

I had not liked that the woman had come so close to guessing my secrets. If Mrs. Bywater investigated further and found out the truth of my past, I could be out on the street. Only the fact that she admired Miss Townsend had made her dismiss the matter.

Mr. Davis arrived on the heels of Tess's declaration. He did not join my scolding, only shook his head. "Bloody women," he muttered.

"Not your place either, Mr. Davis," I said good-humoredly.

"Twittering shrews, and you know it." Mr. Davis removed his coat and scooped some of the duck and vol-au-vents I'd saved for his lunch onto a plate. "They insisted on me serving a lemon-infused sherry with all courses, no matter I'd decanted a perfect red and had a crisp white to finish. A waste of decent wine."

"I always tell ya, Mr. Davis, I'd drink it up." Tess grinned at him. In truth, Tess drank very little wine and no spirits, but she could not resist teasing Mr. Davis.

"Never," Mr. Davis growled. "I'll serve it to the master. He at least appreciates the wine. Damned cheek of that old biddy to make out you're a tart with a by-blow. What the devil did she mean by that? Trying to get you the sack?"

Tess's eyes widened. She opened her mouth, but I shook my head as Mr. Davis bent to mound my food on his plate.

"I suppose she thought nothing by it," I said. "Simply spoke on impulse. Some people enjoy intimating that they know more about a person than anyone else."

I hoped that was all it had been. A silly woman wanting her friends to listen to her with interest.

Mr. Davis muttered more uncharitable words about Mrs. Bywater's guests before he stomped across the passage to the servants' hall to eat his luncheon.

Tess stepped swiftly to me. "Did she truly say you were a tart with a by-blow?" she whispered. "Cheeky bitch."

"Please do not use such language, Tess. Yes, she

91

did." I rested my hand on the table for support. "But Lady Cynthia and Miss Townsend managed to convince her she was mistaken."

"Cor. Thank the Lord for that." Tess backed away but studied me worriedly. "Why don't you go out for a walk or some such? Take in some fresh air, if ya can find any in London. You look knackered."

"I am quite tired, yes." I put my hand to my forehead to find it slick with sweat.

"Off you go, then. You have a brief constitutional, and I'll start preparing the victuals for supper." She shooed me away then began to collect the bowls of greens and beans I'd selected from the larder.

A walk did sound nice. A change of scenery might allow me to collect my thoughts. I could nip to Hyde Park or simply walk up and down the streets for a time. I also knew that Tess was eager to show me that she could be responsible for preparing all the ingredients to my standards.

I removed my clean apron and my cap, which was now limp, donned my coat over my gray work dress, and left Tess to it. She waved cheerily at me, which would have been more reassuring if she hadn't been holding my best knife.

Cool air touched me as I emerged from the cellar to the street. A few clouds blotted out the sun, enough to make the temperature comfortable, while most of the sky remained blue. We'd have cold and rain soon enough, so I determined to enjoy the fineness while I could.

Unfortunately, the turmoil in my head negated the diversion of the good weather. So too did the presence of Charlotte Bristow, who swooped down Mount Street from the east end of the road, as though she'd been waiting to pounce on me.

"Well?" she asked. "You going to help me, or not?"

I took Charlotte's arm and turned her firmly around, walking rapidly with her in the direction of Berkeley Square. I hardly wanted Mrs. Bywater to catch sight of her from the windows.

"Yes, I have decided to help," I told her. "Joe might have stumbled across some scheme to make money, though after all this time, whatever he acquired—if anything—is likely long gone."

"Don't think it is," Charlotte said. "It's just a matter of getting our hands on it."

"That would be welcome." I could not stop myself admitting this. "However, it was a long time ago, and it will be difficult to retrace his steps." I halted us at the corner of Charles Street, deciding we were sufficiently far enough from the house. "It would help me to speak to this man who gave you the information in the first place. What is his name?"

She jerked from me. "What you want to talk to him for? Just find out what Joe were up to, that's all."

Gracious, what on earth had Joe seen in this woman? She had once been pretty, and I supposed that was it. Many a man never looked beyond a comely face or well-shaped figure.

I held on to my patience. "If this person was a friend of Joe's, he might know things we do not. I'd like to understand why he is so suspicious of Joe's death and why he believes the story about the money."

Charlotte scowled. "Don't know if I can find him again."

"Nonsense. You say he has visited you from time to time in the past years. I hardly care if he has become your lover, if that is what you are worried about. What is his name?"

Charlotte flushed, and I knew my guess had hit home. A man visiting his friend's widow frequently might simply be worried about her for his friend's sake, or, more probably, he'd formed a relationship with her.

"Don't know if I want you to see him." Charlotte stuck out her chin, which made her face tight. "You stole my last man off me, didn't ye?"

I made an impatient noise. "I am hardly of an age or inclination to have interest in any man. I assure you, I wish to speak to him only for information."

I heard the lie from my lips, the second time I'd evaded the truth today. I was interested in *one* man, I could have told her, and I doubted any other could pull me from him.

"If ye speak to him, I'm next to you the whole time," Charlotte said. "Agreed?"

"Of course," I answered impatiently. "Where can I find you, if I need to send word to you?"

She did not want to tell me, I could see, but she spat out, "Boardinghouse at Half Moon Court. Off Aldersgate Street."

"I know the area. Inform me when you have arranged the meeting. And soon."

"All right, all right. Don't fuss." Charlotte eyed me belligerently, and I gave her a cool stare in return.

Without a good-bye, she whirled and strode hurriedly away toward Berkeley Square as if to shake off the touch of me.

I sighed as I watched her go. She and I ought to have forged a bond over the bad way Joe had treated us both. But I knew she would never forgive me.

When I turned back toward the Mount Street house, my walk spoiled, I encountered Lady Cynthia and Miss Townsend, arm in arm, strolling toward me.

"Splendid afternoon," Cynthia said as they neared. "And a splendid meal, Mrs. H. Take no notice of what my aunt's harridan friends say to you. They form charitable organizations but can't abide to actually be charitable to anyone."

"You are not a girl who needs to be molded into the ideal servant by their committee, and so they feel they can be rude to you," Miss Townsend added.

I understood they were trying to soothe me, and I was grateful.

"I will be well," I said when they'd finished. "It was a shock, is all. I was rather surprised to see you there, Miss Townsend. Though, I am very happy I did."

Cynthia huffed a laugh. "Auntie asked me to attend and bring a friend to fill out the ranks. Evidently, she is having trouble recruiting ladies to her cause. As I knew Bobby would rather die than accept such an invitation, I begged Judith."

"I am always happy to help a beneficent society." Miss Townsend's shapely nose wrinkled. "Perhaps I can keep them from quashing the girls into spiritless automatons."

"I think the servant girls of London are safe from them so far," Cynthia said. "The organization doesn't do much more than have tea parties with Auntie and slurp down Mrs. H.'s finest foods."

I sent Cynthia a smile. "You and Miss Townsend are very good to me. I thank you."

"I say you give Auntie the push and run off to a better place," Cynthia said.

"An easy thing to suggest, but difficult to achieve, unfortunately," I answered. "Good places are hard to come by, and I am content with your aunt's kitchen, barring the few mishaps."

"You are a saint, Mrs. H."

"Not at all. Now, I must get on. Good afternoon, ladies."

Cynthia stepped squarely in front of me. Her gown caught the shifting light and brought out the blue in her eyes.

"We confess, we came to seek you. Fresh air was only the excuse. I saw you beetling off down the road and suggested a walk to Judith."

I waited politely, though I did not wish to discuss things at the moment, on the street where others could hear us.

"Miss Townsend has agreed to help," Cynthia continued. "She knows everyone in the county of Kent and plenty of directors of shipping companies, and perhaps can help you uncover details of your husband's demise."

"Cynthia exaggerates, of course." Miss Townsend spoke smoothly. "She told me of your problem, and I would be happy to assist. That is, if you will let me. I will not pry if you do not want that."

I wished they would cease being so generous. I'd melt into a puddle soon if they continued to gaze at me as though I were a poor soul who needed a hand up from the mire.

"I would be silly to proudly tell you I could discover all these things on my own, when I know I cannot," I made myself say. "I would be most grateful. And obliged. I do not know how I could repay you."

"I've done nothing yet," Miss Townsend said with good cheer. "And a lemon cake similar to the one you bestowed on Bobby and me last spring wouldn't go amiss. We devoured it in one sitting. We shared it with my butler, and I believe he fell in love with you."

Miss Townsend's butler was a faded, elderly man who never expressed much emotion. I took her exaggerated words to mean he found the cake tasty.

"You will have as many cakes as you like," I promised. "I must say, I am rather baffled about how to begin my search. How does one discover what happened to a ship twelve years ago? And one man on it—or not on it? And whom he met, and anything else that happened to him? My husband was never forthcoming about much in his life."

"Shipping company records," Miss Townsend said promptly. "They can tell us exactly what happened to the ship and all the crew—including what it was carrying and on what route. Also, we can scour newspapers, which will let us know what was happening in London or the Antilles near the time of his departure. There is nothing to say where Mr.—?"

She paused. I'd never actually told her that

Holloway was my maiden name, but either Cynthia had imparted this information or shrewd Miss Townsend guessed.

"Bristow," I said. "Joseph."

"Bristow." Miss Townsend absorbed the name without a pause. "There is nothing to say where he planned to acquire this money, or whether he'd already been saving it for years."

"I doubt that." I spread my hands, letting the soft breeze touch my work-worn skin. "Joe was always tetchy about money, growling how he never had enough of it. Until that last night."

I relayed to her how Joe had hinted that he'd be flush by the time he returned home, and added that this had been the last time I'd seen him. That had been in April, in the year 1870.

Miss Townsend's eyes gentled as I finished explaining, as though she understood the hardship I'd faced. "I have access to archives that I can peruse. Tedious work that you have no time to do. Cynthia and I need activities to fill our empty days."

"Ha," Cynthia said. "*I* apparently have nothing to do but sit under a tree until a husband falls into my lap, but you have your painting, Judith. Bobby and I can pore over old records and newspaper stories."

"Nonsense, I will find it a diverting task."

"You are now assisting Mr. Thanos," I reminded Cynthia.

"Yes, and jolly good fun it is." Cynthia beamed. "Sifting through dusty pages is exactly what Thanos is best at. We'll recruit him, too."

My limbs were definitely loosening in gratitude. What I'd done to deserve such devoted friends, I did not know. They had no obligation to me, and yet they were eager to help.

"If you bring documents and newspapers to me, I can scour them as well," I said, trying to remain businesslike. "I spend my evenings making notes and reading—I will read these things instead."

"Of course." Miss Townsend gave me an understanding nod. I wanted assistance, not charity, and she comprehended that.

"Then it is agreed," Cynthia said. "Judith, Bobby, Thanos, and I will round up all the records we can, and the five of us will go through them. I'm sure that between us, we'll scare up all there is to know about what happened to your husband. Ladies are thorough and scrutinizing creatures, far more than gents give us credit for. Ah, and Thanos is, of course, as well."

She stuck out her hand as though wanting to seal the bargain, but it would look very odd for me, a servant, to be seen shaking hands with Lady Cynthia. I took a slight step back, and Miss Townsend hid her laughter before sliding her hand into the crook of Cynthia's arm, tugging back the offered hand. "Come along, Cyn. Let us go speak to Mr. Thanos instead of embarrassing Mrs. Holloway."

"Rot," Cynthia said, but she allowed Miss Townsend to tow her away. "Good afternoon, Mrs. Holloway," she called over her shoulder. "Don't mind my odd ways."

Her laughter floated back to me on the fine September air.

By the time I returned from my truncated walk, Tess had prepared the mise en place for tonight's dishes, with carrots washed and chopped, herbs minced or torn, onions diced. The only food I'd instructed her not to cut before we began to cook were the potatoes, as they would brown if sliced up too soon. Some cooks dropped them into cold water to keep, but I liked them fresh and starchy in the boiling pot or frying pan.

Tess had done very well and flushed with pleasure under my praise. "You'll make a fine cook yet, my girl."

"It's nothing special, I'm sure," Tess said with humility. "Just a few carrots and onions."

"It is very special. When you are a cook, and your mistress compliments you, you must say *thank you,* and take it as your due."

Tess dropped a very proper curtsy. "Thank you, ma'am." She peeped at me slyly. "How about if me husband is pleased with me cooking? What do I do then?"

She joked, but I felt a qualm. "Are you running off to marry Caleb already, Tess?"

Her flush deepened, but she shook her head until her curls danced under her loosened cap. "Not me. I told you, I'm not one for the chop. Besides, he hasn't asked me."

I turned to the stove to inspect the broth reducing on the back burner. "He might, you know. You certainly walk out with him enough."

"We get on, like." Tess joined me at the stove, straightening her cap and pinning it back into place. "But Caleb knows he can't afford a wife. Not on his constable's pay."

"Did he tell you that?"

"He did. Like he's apologizing for not proposing, but I told him I didn't mind. I like things as they are."

As I did with Daniel. Why did we all have to rush into marriage the moment we were attracted to another human being? The courtship state was the most pleasing, I thought. Before the problems of paying the rent and the grocer's bill reared their heads.

On the other hand, if two people got on well, and helped each other through times of crisis, was that not worth striving for?

I did not know any longer.

"Caleb is a nice young man." I felt I should give Tess some advice, but none sprang to mind at the moment. "I'm sure all will turn out for the best."

It was a weak thing to say, and Tess knew it. She chuckled at me, and then we turned our conversation to cooking.

I did sleep much better that night, worn out from work and my restlessness of the previous evening, aided by relief that my friends would help discover whether Charlotte's tale was true.

Charlotte hadn't exactly promised to let me meet this mysterious man of hers, but she must see the sense in it. I could ask him any questions she hadn't thought to and judge for myself whether his information could be trusted.

Going through old newspapers would be a tedious chore, but I looked forward to it. I preferred practical work to wild speculation.

Thankfully, Mrs. Bywater had not summoned me to ask about her guest's scrutiny of me in the dining room. I was no longer that young cook for Lady Aston-Were, who'd given notice to marry the handsome bearded fellow who'd swept her off her feet.

Perhaps I'd taken to Daniel because he was clean-shaven.

All these things helped me drift off, though I unfortunately dreamed too much of Daniel.

As I prepared breakfast and then luncheon—alone today, as Saturday was Tess's day out—I thought over Cynthia's advice for me to speak to Mr. Thanos, James, and Mr. Fielding about

Daniel. I wanted very much to speak with them, but did I have any business subjecting them to my prying?

Before I could make up my mind about this, I was surprised and alarmed by Mrs. Bywater marching down to the kitchen.

Mr. Davis swept in before she did, snapping me a warning, then he escaped into his butler's pantry just before the click of Mrs. Bywater's heels sounded on the slate floor of the passageway.

My worry that Mrs. Bywater had come to question me about her friend's speculations yesterday evaporated when I saw she'd brought a different guest with her.

This one was a vicar. He had dark hair slicked back with pomade, a trim dark beard, a handsome face, and a winsome smile.

"My dear Mrs. Holloway," Mr. Fielding gushed. "I was fortunate enough to partake of one of your marvelous luncheons today, and I begged my hostess to allow me to descend and thank you for your wonderful meal."

9

Mr. Fielding, a fatuous smile on his face, came forward and caught my hand, which was rather floury—I'd started to roll out pastry. I felt a coin pressed into my palm.

I stepped back, closing my fist, and gave him a brief curtsy. "That is very good of you, sir."

"It is not the first time I have been so fortunate." Mr. Fielding pressed his hand to his heart. "I am pleased to be thus blessed again. Your mistress is a bountiful hostess."

Mr. Fielding was laying it on a bit thick, but Mrs. Bywater, behind him, appeared vastly pleased. She believed Mr. Fielding to be nothing but the effusive, slightly dim East End vicar he pretended to be. Mr. Fielding truly was a vicar—he had taken a degree from Oxford, had been given a living in his parish, and was now an assistant bishop for the Shadwell and Whitechapel areas—but he was also Daniel's "brother" and a talented swindler.

"I never mind doing my part for the downtrodden," Mrs. Bywater crooned. "Mrs. Holloway is an excellent cook, I do agree. She follows my instructions beautifully."

Mrs. Bywater could not see Mr. Fielding's face as he beamed at me, and so he dared to roll his eyes and send me a cocky wink.

When he turned to Mrs. Bywater, his expression was once more a careful blank. "Mrs. Holloway is quite charitable in her own way. She has given me what she can for my orphan fund and contributed to the upkeep of my church."

Mrs. Bywater almost simpered. "Mrs. Holloway is a kindly woman. I have always said so."

She had not, and I had not exactly donated to Mr. Fielding's causes. What I'd done was give him solid advice about caring for the children he'd rescued from a horrible life, and my investigations had helped remove the previous suffragan bishop so Mr. Fielding could be appointed in his place.

"Perhaps there is somewhere we can sit and chat with Mrs. Holloway?" Mr. Fielding put on exactly the expression of a man with little funds who saw the opportunity to pry more donations out of a willing herd.

"Of course," Mrs. Bywater answered readily. "The housekeeper's parlor will be perfect. Mrs. Redfern is very busy with her duties."

"Excellent." Mr. Fielding rubbed his hands together. "And I would be happy to lead us in prayer, thanking the Lord for the largesse of cook and mistress."

"Ah." Mrs. Bywater's enthusiasm became strained. "I unfortunately have much to do—I run many charities myself, as you know. But you may sit with Mrs. Holloway and discuss things and say as many prayers as you like. This way, Mr. Fielding."

Mrs. Bywater bustled from the kitchen and along the passage to the housekeeper's parlor. Mr. Fielding sent me another wink before he followed her. Resigned, I dusted off my hands and went after them.

"Enjoy your visit, vicar," Mrs. Bywater cooed before she hastened toward the back stairs and up.

Mr. Fielding ushered me into the parlor and closed the door behind us. I faced him in the middle of the small but comfortable room and held out the silver crown piece he'd handed me.

"Thank you, Mr. Fielding. I am not in need of a charitable donation myself."

Mr. Fielding dropped his vacuous expression and lifted his hands. "Oh, keep it, Mrs. H. You deserve it for putting up with her. And the food she served me was damned good."

My pride was stung, but common sense told me he was right. I did work hard, and other guests occasionally sent extra cash my way. I would put it into my savings.

I dropped the coin into my pocket, murmured my thanks, and indicated the chairs. Mr. Fielding waited until I'd perched on the end of the worn wing chair before he took the Belter chair next to it.

"The most agreeable chamber in this house,"

he declared. "The rooms upstairs are far too formal for my taste. I'm constantly worrying I'll track in a piece of mud or leave a wet footmark. Your Mrs. Redfern has a glare that could stop a train, and your butler can make one feel like a recalcitrant schoolboy."

"Part of their jobs is to ensure the house remains spotless," I said in their defense. Secretly, I agreed with him about the upstairs. I constantly worried I'd put a greasy hand on a table or handrail and earn a disappointed look from Mrs. Redfern.

"And they carry out their duties well," Mr. Fielding conceded. "You wouldn't have any whiskey hiding here, would you? Everyone brings out the Amontillado for the vicar, and I can't abide the stuff."

"Mrs. Redfern does not approve of spirits, but I can hunt up a glass of wine. What do you prefer?"

Mr. Fielding's disparaging air fled. "A choice? How novel. Does your old butler have a Bordeaux he will part with?"

I rose and made for the door. "Mr. Davis is not old, and I will inquire."

I found Mr. Davis holed up in his butler's pantry, taking stock of the silver and choosing pieces for the table tonight.

Mr. Davis had been kindly disposed to me of late, believing Mrs. Bywater abused me with her strange menus and dismissal of my talent. He agreed to the wine for Mr. Fielding, but only after I told him I'd use the Bordeaux later in a dish— he'd never uncork an entire bottle simply to offer Mr. Fielding a glass.

He decanted the wine for me, and I carried the decanter and goblet to the parlor.

"You'll have none?" Mr. Fielding asked me as I poured for him and slid the stopper back into place.

"I have much work still to do. An inebriated cook might reach for the saltcellar instead of the sugar."

Mr. Fielding chuckled. "Fair point, though I know you'd never make that mistake, my friend." He sipped the wine, his face softening in pleasure. "I will never mock your Mr. Davis again. A fine vintage."

I set the decanter on Mrs. Redfern's writing table and returned to my chair. "I did not know you were a connoisseur of wines, Mr. Fielding."

"I'm a connoisseur of many things." He took another sip, making a noise of satisfaction. "At the moment, of this marvelous Bordeaux. I've had a fine day so far in your house."

"Why did you wish to see me?" I eyed him severely. "That rigmarole in the kitchen was to finagle a private conversation with me. Lead us in prayer, indeed."

"That was to rid ourselves of the tiresome

Mrs. Bywater. Ladies rhapsodize about the beneficence of the clergy and how much they themselves support the church, but as soon as you mention prayer, they hurriedly find something else to do. Easy to espouse Christian teachings without actually having to participate in them."

"You say these things glibly." I pointed at the white collar that encircled his neck. "I am surprised you can wear that without bursting into flames."

"My dear Mrs. Holloway, it is a dog collar, not a magic talisman. I doubt the Almighty cares whether I wear a collar at the pulpit or dance about in my unmentionables. It is about what we are inside, not outside, that matters to Him." His grin flashed at my skepticism. "I am in truth eternally grateful to the Lord and believe He rescued me from a life of squalid horror. I took the divinity degree because I knew it would lead to me being fed and housed for the rest of my life, if I played things well, but I have learned much about faith along the way. Real faith, I mean, not the ravings of lunatics."

My brows had risen during this speech. "I am pleased to hear it, Mr. Fielding. But again, I wonder why you have come. Do you wish my help? Perhaps with your children?"

"Ah, the children. Some of whom are no longer children, but nearly grown, the wretches. No, we have come to an agreement—they refrain from terrorizing me and my housekeeper, and I refrain from trying to reform them. I will have to arrange employment for them, something enjoyable, or they will return to their former deplorable practice. And why not? It put food in their bellies."

"Perhaps I can help with that. Not everyone takes to being in service, but I can inquire—"

Mr. Fielding raised the wineglass and made a shushing noise. "If you will cease interrupting, my good lady, I will tell you why I've come. I have heard that you wish to know all about Daniel McAdam, and that I am the soul who can impart this wisdom."

I started. "You heard?"

"Indeed. Lady Cynthia sent me a note. I do not blame you at all for giving Daniel the boot, but I decided to present myself to you and answer your every question."

I had no idea what to say. I hadn't realized Lady Cynthia would leap to recruiting Mr. Fielding so quickly. I wagered she'd sent a similar note to Mr. Thanos, and possibly even James if she knew how to find him.

"I have no business prying into Daniel's affairs behind his back," I said stiffly.

"Of course you have business." Mr. Fielding scoffed. "He is wooing you, and you do not want to make a blunder."

"Wooing?" I curled my fingers around the soft

arms of the wing chair. "You make us sound like silly lovers in a melodrama."

"I was thinking a comic opera, but there you are." Mr. Fielding took a sip of wine and peered at the glass. "This truly is bloody good stuff. Your butler knows a thing or two."

"Yes, he does." Mr. Davis had impeccable taste, hence the reason Lord Rankin had hired him in the first place. "May we stick to the subject?"

"Your pardon, dear lady. I am easily distracted by the finer things in life—we poor vicars have so few of them. Yes, you should know all about Daniel. A question, Mrs. Holloway. Does he know many things about you?"

I went silent while Mr. Fielding watched me with his shrewd gaze. Daniel had learned far more about me than I had ever told him. He'd once relayed my past to me, knowing all about my false husband, my daughter, my struggles. It had unnerved me how much he'd discovered.

Mr. Fielding's perceptive shot made my irritation rise, both at him and at Daniel.

"He does," I said tightly. "Very well, Mr. Fielding, you have made your point. Tell me about Daniel's sordid past."

Mr. Fielding became somber. "I am afraid it *is* sordid." He set the glass of Bordeaux gently on the table beside him. "Daniel may be the model of propriety now, but in his youth, he was unrepentant. He smashed his way into buildings, stole whatever he could find, and thumped those who tried to step in his way. Admittedly, those he thumped were villains themselves, but he was a demon of a fighter. Rarely did anyone get the better of Daniel."

I recalled the few times since I'd known Daniel when he'd fought fist to fist and come out unscathed. The only time he hadn't was a day when he'd wanted to keep his disguise as a tramp and let several young aristocratic gents work him over.

"He set fire to a warehouse once." Mr. Fielding began to lift his glass to drink but at my appalled expression set it down quickly again. "It was empty and no one was inside. He made certain. He was sent to do it by the villain he currently worked for, who'd been hired by the warehouse's owner—insurance racket, you understand. The warehouse's owner was caught, and the owner grassed on the villain, who would have grassed on Daniel, but Daniel had the sense to flee to Ireland for a time."

I listened in growing disquiet. "I'm certain all this is exaggerated. Daniel told me he'd wanted to become a constable. How could he have made the attempt if he'd been a known criminal? The metropolitan police turned him down, but he'd not have been able to walk through the door of one of their stations without being arrested, if you are right about the things he's done."

Mr. Fielding opened his hand. "By the time our

Danny decided to reform and become a peeler himself—he'd know all about how to catch villains, wouldn't he?—he'd changed his name. Scotland Yard does not have anything on Daniel McAdam, but they have a very thick sheaf of papers on Daniel Carter."

My eyes went wide. "Carter?"

"Yes, the name of the man who adopted us as tykes. I have remained Errol Fielding all my life, but Daniel learned that it is good to keep his name fluid."

Daniel had been very fond of Mr. Carter, who, as I understood, had been a criminal himself. The leader of a gang of villains, Daniel had told me. He'd looked after Daniel and Mr. Fielding well, and both had been very grateful to him. Unfortunately, Mr. Carter had been killed by the leader of another criminal gang, and Daniel and Errol had been left to fend for themselves as lads of only ten years old or so.

"Daniel was very upset at Mr. Carter's death," I said slowly.

"As was I, dear lady. He was a decent chap. Is it your theory that Daniel became a miscreant for grief of Carter?"

"He could very well have done."

Mr. Fielding favored me with a smile. "You will look for the best in him, of course. But Daniel had been a bad 'un before that. He simply carried on once Carter was gone."

"While you were angelic," I remarked.

Mr. Fielding laughed. "I adore you, Mrs. Holloway. You have a way of making a man speak the truth. No, I was every bit as bad as Daniel, but in a more selective way. He loved the smashing, the fighting, the running. I liked to keep my clothes clean and whole, and my limbs unbroken."

"Therefore you became a confidence trickster. You can wear fine suits for that." I motioned to his fashionably cut black tailored ensemble, far finer garments than a vicar of a poor parish should wear.

"Exactly." Mr. Fielding's eyes twinkled. "Not for me the rough coats of a deliveryman. The baron who adopted me after Carter died burned the clothes he'd found me in, and I wore well-made things from then on. He was a horrible person, a bastard of the first water, but he did have excellent taste. At least, his valet and tailor did. I learned how to make friends with good tailors. So did Daniel, but only when he started going about in his infernal disguises."

"Why did he?" I asked abruptly. "Begin the disguises, I mean? Why did he decide to be a City gent or an upper-class twit?"

"That, my friend, I cannot tell you. I do not know if after he began working for the police he realized he could investigate better if he could blend into the middle- and upper-class worlds, or if he'd decided long before that in such guises he could more easily rob them. As I indicated when I first met you, Mrs. Holloway, I hadn't seen Daniel for about a decade before I ran him to ground again. I heard of him now and then, and knew he'd turned informer for the police, but that is all. For what he's become since then, you will have to ask him."

"He easily takes on the manners and speech of other classes," I said. "As do you. I'd never have known you grew up on the streets if you hadn't explained about your past."

"Ah, but I had my gentleman's ways beaten into me by good Baron Symington and his brutal tutors. No foundling was going to embarrass *him*. Daniel, on the other hand, has always been a good mimic. He could have gone on the stage and had the world at his feet."

"He does not like to draw attention to himself," I said with sudden insight. "He prefers the guises, so he can look like any number of people in whatever group he chooses to infiltrate."

"Interesting choice of words." Mr. Fielding drained his goblet, gave a satisfied sigh, and clicked the glass to the table. "I decided on a profession and worked very hard to obtain it. Daniel infiltrates."

I sent him a sharp look. "You cannot pretend you are a superior creature because you charmed your way into a respectable post. You were a swindler, and still are. I saw how easily you helped the Earl of Clifford with his ruse last spring. You slid seamlessly into the role."

"For a good cause, dear lady, for a good cause." Mr. Fielding ruined his beatific expression by chuckling. "And you are a very perceptive woman. You frighten me sometimes. Though I can't blame Daniel for being enchanted with you."

His exaggeration amused me. "You are a mountebank, Mr. Fielding. As flattering as you are, I cannot believe the compliments you toss out."

"And now you've broken my heart." Mr. Fielding heaved a sigh. "Have I fed you enough about Daniel today? Or do you want to know more?"

"Is there more? You have not said much about what he was like when you lived with Mr. Carter."

Mr. Fielding shrugged. "Daniel was a friendly enough chap when we were lads, though not soft. Definitely not soft. He held his own quite well. We were rivals, but I like to think, friends. We'd defend each other from outsiders stoutly enough no matter how much we fought between ourselves. You might be right that Carter's death sent Daniel a bit mad."

"And you have no idea why he decided to reform?" I asked.

"None whatsoever." Mr. Fielding shook his head. "I'd be interested to learn that myself."

"I suppose it will remain Daniel's secret, unless he decides to tell us," I said, resigned.

"Well, he should certainly tell *you,* in any case."

I agreed with him. I wanted very much to know what had made Daniel into the man he was now, the cheerful fellow who aided others and had sold his life to assisting the odd Mr. Monaghan.

I also knew that while Mr. Fielding had been quite forthcoming to me today, I should take what he said with a large grain of salt. He'd openly stated that he'd been rivals with Daniel, and I could sense that he still was.

"I thank you for your candor, Mr. Fielding," I told him.

"Pleased to help, dear lady. I would like to see old Daniel happy, but not at your expense. Please do thank Mr. Davis for the excellent wine. He has earned my respect, and I will cease poking fun at his hairpiece."

Mr. Davis's hairpiece did slip from time to time, and I'd sensed he'd do anything to not reveal the bald patch beneath it.

Mr. Fielding waited for me to rise—he'd not stand before I did—but I was not finished. "Before you depart, I would like to ask you another question," I said. "You are acquainted with illicit means of obtaining money, are you not?"

Mr. Fielding leaned to me with every display of interest. "Yes, but that is all in the past, I assure you. Are you asking me to help *you* with these illicit means? How delightful."

"No, indeed." I frowned at him. "I would like to discover how might a sailor—an ordinary man who worked no harder than his fellows and could never hold on to his pay—come into a great deal of cash."

10

Mr. Fielding's bearing changed. He sat up and spoke to me sternly. "Why do you want to know that?"

I hadn't intended to bring Mr. Fielding into my story. I was certain Cynthia had said nothing of it in her letter to him—her purpose was to pair me with Daniel, and I doubted she'd betray the secrets of my past to Mr. Fielding. She was well aware of his easy duplicity.

However, I found myself explaining to him all Charlotte had revealed to me, which, as I thought it through, was little. I did not explain exactly what Charlotte had been to my husband—I let Mr. Fielding make up his own mind. The flicker in his eyes told me he speculated on her relationship to him, but he said nothing as I spoke.

When I finished, Mr. Fielding sat back in his chair, hands on his knees, and studied me as though he'd met me for the first time today. The clock ticked steadily behind us, and a particularly heavy cart rumbled by outside the high window.

After an extensive pause, Mr. Fielding let out a long breath. "A very interesting account. Very interesting, indeed."

"I have no idea if any of it is true. I have yet

to speak to the man who gave Charlotte this information. He may not be reliable."

Mr. Fielding huffed a laugh. "Your composure is admirable, my dear. A woman comes out of the past to impart that your dastardly and unlamented husband might have scraped together a fortune, but no one has set eyes on it. And then his old pals tell you he'd planned to buy a plantation—and a house in Kent after that. To finish, your husband *might* have been murdered for this fortune, and simply reported to have perished on his ship. And here you sit with your hands folded, quietly asking for my advice."

"I have already had several sleepless nights because of it," I said without moving. "I believe I am now beyond the shock of it, and wish to turn to practical matters."

Mr. Fielding peered at me as though he did not quite believe me. But what good would it do if I clutched my hair and swooned every ten minutes? I'd accomplish nothing if I carried on so.

"Practical matters," he repeated.

"Yes, such as how a sailor could gain so much money he believed he could obtain a plantation."

"I'm flattered you believe I can help you." Mr. Fielding tapped his fingertips together. "Ask a reprobate how another reprobate could procure a fortune, is that the idea?"

"I have no wish to offend you," I said quickly.

121

"If you do not know, I will try to find out another way."

"I am not offended in the least. Very wise to ask an old trickster about plots and schemes. Now, let me see." Mr. Fielding touched his left forefinger. "First, a man can be frugal and save the money, of course."

"Joe was not, and did not."

"I gathered that, but I am running through possibilities." He touched his second finger. "A scoundrel could take it from the ship's cargo. Tricky, as manifests are jealously guarded—investors like their cargoes to reach their destinations unscathed. However, Mr. Bristow could have pinched a valuable piece here, a valuable piece there, over the years, until he'd amassed a hoard."

I thought that over. "Again, Joe was not good about savings. If he ever stole something valuable from a ship, he'd sell it immediately and spend the take. I doubt he'd have the discipline to squirrel things away."

"Very well, then let us assume he found the whole thing in one lump. That could mean smuggled goods he stumbled upon and decided to keep." Another finger tapped. "Or Bristow was entrusted with these smuggled goods and then he swindled the smugglers. A very dangerous proceeding, I will add. Charlotte's man claims Bristow was killed, so it is a good possibility he took a grave risk."

"Which is something Joe might have done. He believed he could get away with anything."

"That is obvious, from the way he behaved toward you." The affable vicar vanished and the hard lad from the streets now occupied his place. "I am sorry this Joe Bristow is dead. I'd like to wring his neck for being evil to you."

"It was a long time ago," I said. I did not like to talk about it.

"Time does not erase his deeds. I am so very sorry you had to experience them."

Mr. Fielding spoke sincerely, and I was grateful. I shrugged. "I was the silly girl who married him."

"No." The word was sharp. "Another man's brutality and lies are not your fault. *He* was entirely at fault. Your trust is a beautiful gift, Mrs. Holloway . . . Kat. You do not give it lightly. The fact that Bristow took this gift and mangled it makes him a contemptible bastard who deserves no one's pity. I hope he rots in hell."

His adamance touched me. Usually, I did not approve of such violent words, but today I would forgive them.

"Your kindness is much appreciated, Mr. Fielding," I said warmly.

Mr. Fielding acknowledged this with a nod. "If my fool of a brother would see that you were worth fighting for . . ." He drew a breath. "Never mind. I could go on about Daniel's shortcomings all afternoon. But let us return to where your knave of a husband might have found this money, if he did. You deserve all of it, my dear."

"It is a phantom fortune at the moment, remember. Now, we have him saving it—unlikely. Stealing it from the ship's legitimate cargo. Finding smuggled goods and stealing them, or stealing goods from smugglers who entrusted him with them."

"I notice neither of us mentioning him earning an honest crust." Mr. Fielding shot me a grin, the hardness on his face easing.

"I gave up on that idea long ago. Let us think—how else could he have found this money?"

"He might have inherited it," Mr. Fielding conceded. "Or perhaps thought he would. Who were his relations?"

"Joe never spoke about his family. I assume they are long gone."

"Or estranged. Not every family is a happy one." A bitterness entered Mr. Fielding's voice. "I've seen in my own parish how fathers push aside sons, how sons turn their backs on mothers. In Shadwell, unfortunately, more people are fixed on surviving than sticking by their families."

"It was similar in Bow Lane. When the belly needs to be fed, sentiment can go out the window. But not always," I finished, softening. "My mother and I were very close, bless her."

"You were lucky," Mr. Fielding said.

"Remember that. Returning to Bristow, even if he shunned all his relations—or they shunned him—sometimes an eccentric uncle or aunt or a sentimental cousin decides to reward a ne'er-do-well with a fortune. Where was he from?"

"Stepney. His mates said he had trouble fitting in, in my part of London, because of it."

"Yes, the men who couldn't praise him enough." Mr. Fielding's chuckle was disparaging. "Likely time has painted Bristow in a rosier color, or he promised them money, too."

"You are very cynical," I observed.

"Blame my sad, lonely life. I can poke around Stepney, which is not far from my haunt, and see what I turn up."

"Daniel said he would—" I broke off.

Would Daniel still help? Or had he washed his hands of me? I imagined Mr. Monaghan would soon have Daniel off on a dangerous assignment, in any case, if he hadn't done so already.

"Hmm." Mr. Fielding slid on his gloves, the supple leather fitting him like a second skin. "I wager I'll find out more than my brother can. Daniel will go in, friendly-like, and stand men pints, which is all very well, but a suffragan bishop will be able to access parish records and chat with parsons who will know who is who and what is what in every street."

"I would be forever grateful." I had been saying the word quite a lot recently.

"I will expect a reward, I warn you." Mr. Fielding settled his gloves. "A lavish meal, cooked specially for me. And my urchins. They'll charge out of the woodwork when they smell food."

"I would be happy to." I rose, sending him a smile. It would be a delight to bang about Mr. Fielding's kitchen for those poor souls, as long as his housekeeper didn't mind.

"What will you do?" Mr. Fielding took up his coat, which was light for the sunny weather, and shrugged it on. "While I am beating about Stepney and thinking of more ways a common sailor could stumble upon a fortune?"

"Peruse newspapers." I turned Mr. Fielding around, straightened the collar of his coat, and brushed down the back of it. "Miss Townsend had the idea to go over records and stories from a dozen years ago, and Lady Cynthia has agreed to help. We will look for unusual happenings involving large sums of money, or involving Joe's ship. Besides it capsizing, I mean."

"How tedious." Mr. Fielding scrunched up his face. "Might turn up something, yes, but it sounds dreary."

I eyed him narrowly. "When you took your degree, I imagine you had to read all sorts of old books, did you not? And write papers, and things of that nature? I hear that is what students do at university."

"Ha. I did indeed, and this is why I know it's dreary. I got around much of it by hunting up elderly tutors and lubricating them enough to spill out their knowledge. What is the difference if they read the books or I did? They were founts of information."

"Unfair, Mr. Fielding."

"Not really. They did make me interested in some of the old writings. Augustine, for instance. He was a wild and unruly lad before his conversion—I rather took to him. And Thomas Aquinas and his forward-thinking ideas—for his day. Though I had to read those fellows in the best translations I could find. My Latin is atrocious."

Again I wondered how he'd managed to take his degree. I'd worked in a house where the son had been attending university, and from what he'd complained of when he was home, I assumed almost everything was taught in Latin or Greek.

On the other hand, Mr. Fielding was charming. He'd charmed his way into university, I was certain, and he must have charmed his way to finishing.

"Thank you for all your help," I told him, sounding a bit stiff, but I feared if I did not hold myself so, I'd turn into a blubbering fool.

Mr. Fielding seemed to understand. "Not at all, Mrs. Holloway. We are friends, I hope. I never mind giving a friend a leg up."

I warmed. Mr. Fielding was a charlatan, yes, but he had been a great help in the past and not for his own gain.

I stuck out my hand. "Good day, Mr. Fielding."

He took it and bowed over it, and then impudently kissed the backs of my fingers. "And you, Mrs. Holloway. I will go forth and tear up Stepney, and report when we meet again."

"Cheek," I said, snatching my hand away. "Hurry along, before Mrs. Bywater returns and recruits you for her committees."

I hid a laugh at the dismay on Mr. Fielding's face. He made for the door, opening it a crack and peeking through before he slid out. He raised a hand to me, and then he was gone.

I let out my breath and sat down again. Conversation with Mr. Fielding, and the revelations he'd given me about Daniel, had wearied me. I needed a very strong cup of tea.

Thankfully, supper that night was a simple one, as Mr. Bywater dined alone. His wife had gone out with her friends to the theater, and Cynthia had done the same—likely to a different theater—with her own friends.

I enjoyed making the plain beef au jus with roasted potatoes and a bowl of greens, with crisp bread finishing off the meal. I warmed leftover apple tart and sent that up as well.

Mr. Davis was much more cheerful when he

descended. "Mr. Bywater enjoyed the rest of the Bordeaux, claiming it an excellent pairing with your beef. Which it was." He sighed contentedly. "Happy is the day when I can wait on someone who truly appreciates our efforts."

"Happy indeed, Mr. Davis," I agreed.

Mr. Davis went off to feast on the remains in the servants' hall, where the rest of the staff was already enjoying it. Tess had just returned from her day out, speaking for a few minutes with Elsie, before Elsie abandoned her sink and joined the others for supper.

Tess charged in from the scullery as soon as the kitchen was empty of all but me, tore off her coat, and glared at me.

"Elsie tells me Mr. Fielding came to visit you today," Tess announced. "That is, she said, *That nice-looking vicar and Mrs. H. were closeted in Mrs. Redfern's parlor ever so long*." Tess folded her arms. "There are things afoot, ain't there? And you haven't told me a thing about them."

II

"Do lower your voice, Tess." I glanced through the open kitchen door across to the servants' hall, but the staff was eating and conversing, Mr. Davis pontificating on some point. As far as I could tell, they'd heard nothing from the kitchen.

Tess did not move. "I don't mean to pry into your business, Mrs. H., but I don't like that you have adventures without me."

I turned from her and began straightening my work table. "Why do you suppose I'm having adventures?"

"Because you'd not have been chatting with Mr. Fielding for so long. Elsie thinks he's courting you, but I know that's daft."

"Please tell Elsie he is doing nothing of the sort," I said in some disquiet. I beckoned to Tess and spoke in a low voice as I scraped the remains of the greens into a slop bowl. "I have not had a chance to speak to you, which is the only reason I haven't taken you into my confidence. As a matter of fact, I would like to ask for your help."

Tess's transformation from belligerence to eager interest was comical. "Anything. I'm your girl. You know I am."

"I do not have time to outline the entire problem to you at the moment, but I would like you to ask

Constable Greene for a favor. But only if he is discreet and does not get himself into trouble."

"I'll make sure," Tess said confidently. "What ya want him to do?"

"To find out—if he can—whether there were cases about a dozen years ago that were never solved. Shipments coming into the docklands that went missing, for instance. Or ships being robbed. That sort of thing."

Tess's eyes widened. "Is this one of Mr. McAdam's cases? Are you after bad villains?"

"No, no," I said quickly. "It's something I am looking into for myself. And I'm not certain if there are bad villains involved, or simply men trying to quietly abscond with cargo. Or coins. Or valuables. Or something. The trouble is, I'm not certain exactly what I'm looking for."

"No matter. Caleb can keep his eyes open for ya. His sergeant would probably praise him for sorting through dusty boxes of old cases."

"He must tell no one, however," I said. "Not Inspector McGregor, not his sergeant. If Constable Greene does not think he can do this without his superiors questioning him, then I'd rather he did not. He does not need to get the sack because of me."

"I'll explain. Caleb is actually quite bright if he's shoved in the right direction, and he likes helping you. Besides, if you can catch someone who stole things a long time ago, wouldn't that be a good thing? Caleb might get a promotion."

"I am not certain there is anyone to catch. Or any goods or money to be found," I had to admit. "I am simply trying to be thorough."

"Asking Caleb to do a bit of extra police work won't hurt him. He likes it, and as I say, even if he is discovered, he'll probably be praised for his earnestness."

"Perhaps." I thought of Inspector McGregor's formidable frowns and did not share her optimism. "Do tell him to take care. If he discovers nothing, then there is nothing to discover."

Tess's eyes danced, indicating she didn't agree. "I'll tell him." She flung her arms around me in an impulsive hug. "Thank you for not shutting me out. Now, I need some of your delicious victuals."

She spun away and dashed across the passageway, calling to Elsie that she had better have left a helping for her.

Tess's lightness of stride and her ready smiles as she joined the other servants told me she'd spent all afternoon with Caleb. I knew that as much as Tess protested that Caleb was not ready to marry, I would soon lose her. I wanted to be happy for her sake, but my heart was a touch heavier as I returned to clearing my table.

Sunday was uneventful, except for when Mr. Bywater put his foot down at breakfast, telling his wife she could ask for no more exotic dishes at his table. Mr. Davis reported this gleefully.

"The mistress tried to argue, but Mr. Bywater was having none of it." Mr. Davis chortled as he entered the servants' hall and helped himself to sausage and potatoes. "Said he didn't want to have to guess what was on his plate. Your excellent beef last night persuaded him, I think."

"Let us hope so, Mr. Davis." I finished off my own helping of bangers and mash, secretly pleased that my plain but good meal had done the trick.

"Mrs. Bywater sat in chagrin, and Lady Cynthia banged her glass with her spoon and shouted, *Hear! Hear!*"

I hid a smile, imagining Cynthia doing so.

"A triumph for you, Mrs. Holloway."

"A relief, I will say, Mr. Davis."

I carried my empty plates to the kitchen and left the staff to fill their bellies and gossip.

I heard nothing more from Lady Cynthia, who, after attending chapel with her parents, departed to spend the rest of the day with her friends. My morning and afternoon were taken up with preparing meals, happily without the aid of Mrs. Bywater's bizarre menus.

I tried, in vain, to stave off thoughts of Daniel. We'd had our quarrel on Thursday. Three nights he'd not come by to speak to me, and it felt like three years.

Cynthia had implied she thought me a fool for rejecting him, but the man had thrown his intimations at me out of the blue.

Well, possibly not out of the blue. We'd known each other for nearly three years now, and we had been growing closer over the last months. We'd shared plenty of kisses and warm moments, though Daniel had never strayed into impropriety.

Why did I regret that he hadn't? I should rejoice that he made it easy for me to have a care for my reputation.

My head said these words, but my heart ached. I craved the familiar sight of his thick wool coat, the smoothness of his hair, the scent of soap and coal smoke that clung to him, the warmth of his breath on my cheek.

Blast the man. I missed him so.

For luncheon, Tess and I sent up mutton with a sauce of meat juices flavored with capers and scallions, a light partridge soup, and a charlotte. I was pleased with the charlotte, despite the fact that its name reminded me of my husband's wife. We lined a round cake mold with ladyfingers—I had made the biscuit-like cakes yesterday—then filled the center with whipped cream that had been flavored with liqueur and sugar.

"Make sure to brush all the edges with the egg white, or the ladyfingers won't adhere to one another in the mold," I instructed Tess.

"And there'd be cream everywhere." Tess

grinned as she dutifully painted the edges of each ladyfinger with egg white.

I noted there were one or two fewer ladyfingers on the plate than when I'd put it down, but I'd deliberately set out a few extra. We did get hungry while working.

Tess put the finished crust into the oven for a few minutes to set the egg, then we filled the interior with the cream. A few spoonfuls of cream found their way into our mouths, but then, we did have to make certain it was flavored correctly.

The luncheon was a success, according to Mr. Davis. Mr. Bywater had praised it thoroughly, and Mrs. Bywater seemed surprised by how much she liked it. I told Mr. Davis to make certain Tess gained the credit for the charlotte, and then we moved on to the next meal. There is not much time for accolades in cooking.

Lady Cynthia planned to spend that night with her friends, and I did not see her at all that day. I spoke with no one but Tess and the other servants, including young Charlie, whom I was teaching to read. He did not much care for it, but I told him that a young man who knew how to read would go further in life than one who did not.

"I'll be a footman, Mrs. Holloway," he complained. "I won't need any book learning for that. Mr. Davis will teach me all I need to know."

"One never knows one's future," I told him sternly. "The ability to read might land you a post as a clerk or some such thing. You'll earn more money and not have to do so much labor."

Charlie clearly did not believe me, but I was firm, and we soldiered through the reader I'd bought for him at a secondhand bookshop.

Monday dawned, and with it came the fine anticipation of spending the afternoon with Grace. I had pushed aside the problem of my husband and his fate, and planned to ask Cynthia, when I returned this evening, if she and her friends had made any progress with their inquiries. I did not want to interrupt my time with my daughter with such questions.

When I gained the street, however, ready to find an omnibus to take me to the City, Charlotte Bristow stepped from the railings of the next house along Mount Street and clutched my arm.

"If you want to meet Mr. Tuck, you'd best come with me now."

"Who is Mr. Tuck?" I asked impatiently, but I realized who she must mean before she answered.

"My friend. Joe's friend. The man you asked to see." She glared at me as we hurried along the pavement.

I pulled from her grasp. "I have no time today. Tomorrow, perhaps."

"No. Today. He's off to Reading tomorrow. If you're so keen to talk to him, come with me. If not . . ."

She shrugged and quickened her stride toward

Charles Street. I fumed as I hurried to catch up to her. My days with Grace were precious to me, but I knew I needed to speak to this Mr. Tuck.

We went north on Charles Street and around Grosvenor Square, the park behind its gates beckoning. We traversed Duke Street beyond the square to Oxford Street, Charlotte keeping a rapid pace. She turned east on Oxford Street, the thoroughfare busy with carriages and delivery carts, maids and kitchen assistants darting among the traffic, baskets swinging.

Charlotte took me a good way along Oxford Street, my feet in my best shoes beginning to ache. The area became less salubrious as we traveled. When I was about to demand why we didn't hail a hansom or step onto an omnibus, she turned south toward Soho. Charlotte's steps slowed as we reached Soho Square, the music halls and gin shops already doing a rowdy business.

We rounded the square to a lane called Sutton Street, and here Charlotte led me into a tavern. The place was full even this early in the afternoon, with plenty of workingmen pausing to down a pint. Some of these men I could tell did not work at all, but sat here and drank away their time, hunkered in corners with heads down over mugs.

Ladies could not enter the taproom, and we hurried past it and along a small, cool passageway to the snug, where a very obvious lady of easy virtue was entertaining two men at a corner table.

Charlotte sent the woman a sneer of disgust, and we seated ourselves in the inglenook in the opposite corner.

"Where is Mr. Tuck?" I asked her. "I hope he is not one of that lady's paramours."

"He ain't here yet." Charlotte turned the sneer to me. "He'll be along."

I signaled to the barmaid who had stuck her nose in to see who her new customers were. She did not appear pleased that I wanted to order something, but sashayed ill-naturedly to us.

"Yeah?" she asked.

I did not wish to drink even ale before I set off to see Grace, so I asked for a pot of tea. The barmaid stared at me as though I'd run mad, but when I did not back down, she nodded.

"A half for me," Charlotte said defiantly. "And bring a full pint of bitter for me man. He's on his way."

"I hope he will not be long," I said as the barmaid disappeared. "I have an appointment."

"You'll be able to run off and enjoy yourself soon enough." Charlotte scowled. "Who are you tarted up for?"

I hardly believed my long-sleeved brown frock buttoned to my chin constituted being tarted up, but I ignored the question. I did not know if

Charlotte knew about my daughter, and I did not intend to tell her.

I wondered if her son was well, and who was looking after the poor chap while she trotted about London trying to discover if Joe had hidden any money. He'd been a small lad when I'd seen him twelve years ago, and he'd be a youth now, only a few years older than Grace.

The maid brought the tea, which was bitter but tolerable. Charlotte slurped her half-pint of lager and pulled the pint for Mr. Tuck closer to her as though guarding it.

We sat without speaking for perhaps a quarter of an hour. I sipped tea. The lady in the corner chose her fellow and they left together. The second man, smiling, sauntered out after them. He sent a hopeful glance our way, which withered as soon as he saw the reproving stares from the two of us. He hurried out.

The silence was awkward, but I did not break it. Charlotte too seemed in no hurry to begin a conversation with me. The widows of Joe Bristow were not friends. I noted the haunted look in her eyes once again, and I wondered, perhaps too charitably, if she was missing her son.

I was on my second cup of tea, the pot rapidly cooling, when a tall, angular man with a thin beard and wearing a drab brown suit entered the snug. He had a battered homburg hat, the dent in its crown rather more pronounced than I wagered it had been when new.

The man moved to the table where Charlotte had sprung up with gladness on her face. She was almost pretty again when she looked at this man, with his narrow face, sunken eyes, and scraggly beard.

"Are you Mr. Tuck?" I asked, as Charlotte clung to his arm and pulled him to sit. She made no introductions.

"I am." His voice was deep and strong, in contrast to his gaunt appearance.

He seated himself without shaking my hand or inquiring how I was. I ignored his rudeness and sipped tea as Charlotte pushed the pint toward him. Mr. Tuck drank deeply and wiped his mouth, the tension leaving his face.

"You were Joe's friend," I prompted, as Mr. Tuck seemed in no hurry to begin.

"I was. He was a good man, Joe."

This was the second time I'd met a person who claimed Joe had been good and true. Perhaps he'd been more congenial with the men in his life than with the women.

"Miss Holloway don't believe ya," Charlotte said.

I did not correct her with the *Mrs*. Mr. Tuck did not need to know all about me.

"You must admit, your story is far-fetched," I said.

To my surprise, Mr. Tuck nodded in understanding. He'd removed his hat and set it on the empty place beside him, revealing that he had thick red-blond hair threaded with gray. He ran a long-fingered hand through this mop.

"I imagine it would seem so," he said. "But I've always been troubled by Joe's death. He was careful, was Joe, when he was at sea. His ship, the *Devonshire*, did indeed capsize, off the coast of Antigua, but I've discovered that Joe was not on it."

12

Charlotte had hinted this to me at our first meeting, but I regarded Mr. Tuck sharply. "How can that be? The solicitor and policeman who hunted me up at his demise assured me that the *Devonshire* had sunk with Joe trapped on board."

Mr. Tuck answered me calmly. "He stepped off in Antigua and did not step back on."

I clutched my teacup to keep my fingers from trembling. "Then why was he reported to be on the ship?"

"Because the ship's roster listed him. Possibly, no one missed him right away and didn't put his absence in any report. The ship went down not half a day out of port. A sudden storm, a large swell . . ."

I didn't like to think of it, whether Joe had been aboard or not. "Then how did he die?" I felt a qualm that nearly made me sick. "Or did he?"

Mr. Tuck laid a hand on the table, almost as if he'd been reaching out to calm me. "He did indeed. He turned up in the London Dockyards, in fact. The coroner's report, which I have read many times now, described him thoroughly, even if the police didn't know his name. Five feet, eleven inches tall, brown hair, beard, brown eyes, tattoo of a seahorse on his left upper arm, missing small finger on his right hand."

That was Joe all right. He'd told me a shark had bitten off his finger on one of his voyages, but I imagined he'd lost it in a fight. The tattoo he'd obtained not long after we'd wed. It would be too much of a coincidence for another man to be walking this earth with a missing right finger and the same tattoo on his left arm.

I breathed out in relief. Though sad to find myself relieved that a man was dead, having Joe in my already difficult life had only made it more trying.

Charlotte blinked away tears. "Poor old Joe." Mr. Tuck squeezed her hand.

"How did you know he was killed?" I demanded of Mr. Tuck. "If Joe wasn't named in the document? How did you know to look for the report? And why did the coroner let you read it?"

Mr. Tuck shuffled his feet. "Reports of crimes in the dockyards come across my desk—or across my employer's desk—all the time. We track theft there, and hear about everything that goes on. Bristow had sent word to me to expect him in London—which surprised me very much. He did not turn up for the appointment, and then I saw this description of a man, unknown, turning up dead. I read it and knew it was Joe. I was shocked."

"But you did not inform the police who he was?" Or tell me about it, I did not add.

Mr. Tuck flushed, and Charlotte touched his arm. "He told me," she said. "But why muck things up? Everyone already thought Joe dead, a hero going down on a ship. They didn't need to know."

The police might have a different opinion, but I did understand her thinking. Why face the distress of a police questioning when Joe was already dead and at rest? I had some sympathy for her on this point—the police could be unnerving and quite rude to women of the working classes. If they'd decided she had a hand in his death, they'd be even harsher.

"When did the report say he died?" I asked.

"Not long after the ship went down," Mr. Tuck answered. "The *Devonshire* sank on the tenth of August, 1870, and Joe's death was listed as August twentieth the same year."

I wondered how long Joe had been in London before his death. He'd not turned up in Bow Lane, proudly proclaiming that deserting his ship had saved his life. By the time he had truly died, I'd already moved out and to a boardinghouse. He wouldn't have found me in Bow Lane even if he'd come there.

"He must have taken another ship, then," I said. "One sailing from Antigua before the *Devonshire* did. I'm sure a crossing takes more than ten days."

"My thinking, too," Mr. Tuck said. He spoke

well, not exactly with a cultured accent but without the cant of London or a thick accent of any other region of England.

"What did the coroner list as the cause of death?" I asked.

"Misadventure," Mr. Tuck answered. "A heavy blow to the head, which could be accounted for by the thick pole he'd been found against. Blood on the pole. The police did not investigate further."

Charlotte made a sound of distress. Mr. Tuck caressed her hand before he gently released her.

I kept my tone matter-of-fact. "But you don't believe it was an accident?"

"Why should Joe fall against a pole, in the middle of the dockyards?" Mr. Tuck asked. "He was careful, as I say. If you are about to claim he could have been drunk, he never went drunk to the docks. Too dangerous."

"It seems you knew him quite well, then."

Mr. Tuck regarded me with light blue eyes nearly the same shade as Lady Cynthia's. "I did."

"He never mentioned you," I said.

"He never mentioned *you*." Mr. Tuck's demeanor became less friendly. "I suppose he was ashamed he had taken a mistress." His lips tightened as though he believed I should show some amount of contrition.

I needed to clear things up immediately. "As far as I understood, I was married to Joe," I said crisply. "I had no idea of Charlotte's existence until the solicitor told me Joe was dead. I certainly am no seductress who lured him into sin—I married him in good faith, in a parish church with a record and all. This is the sort of man your dear friend was."

Mr. Tuck flinched, but I am not certain he believed me. It did not matter, I told myself. I was here to discover whether Joe had come into money. That was all.

Charlotte's expression was stony. "Don't try to claim my marriage to him was a lie. I know it weren't."

"It was not," I acknowledged. "I looked into it when I inquired about his will. I could not credit it when the bailiffs came and ransacked my rooms, but I did find the record of your marriage at Somerset House, along with his will. Joe did marry you first."

I disliked to say the words, but I espoused that the truth should always be accepted. Joe had been a bad person, no matter what Charlotte and Mr. Tuck believed. He'd married me knowing it was wrong. I could flatter myself that Joe had been so enamored of me that he persuaded himself to take a second wife, but I knew that he simply had decided to see if he could get away with it.

"He did," Charlotte said. "Don't you forget it."

I flattened my lips. "If you wish my help, please leave off the admonishments until we are finished. Now, Mr. Tuck, you must tell me why on earth you believe Joe had come into a fortune before he was killed. You relayed to Charlotte that he had a servant or assistant or some such, and you claim this servant murdered him and stole the money."

"I do suspect that," Mr. Tuck said. "I did not at first, but the more I've come to learn about this man called Thomas Smith, the more I am convinced he is a villain."

"Smith?" I asked skeptically.

"Apparently, that is his true name," Mr. Tuck said.

"Where is this Mr. Smith?" I inquired.

Mr. Tuck shifted uncomfortably. "I'm not certain."

"Presumably, he is still alive?"

"I'm not certain of that either."

I wrapped my hands around my cold teacup. "What you are telling me, Mr. Tuck, is that you believe a man called Smith attacked Joe—an able-bodied and strong sailor—killed him, stole whatever money Joe had managed to assemble, and fled to who knows where? Never to be seen again?"

"Yes." Mr. Tuck's disapprobation changed to resignation. "I do agree it sounds dubious, but I can find no other explanation. Joe had money. He showed me some—coins of gold. Beautiful they were. Promised to share with me after he'd bought things with the rest. And then he was dead."

"Bought things like a plantation in Antigua?"

Mr. Tuck started. "Plantation?"

"I have reason to believe that he used most of the money to buy land, although I have not verified that yet. Charlotte has employed me to discover things, and this is what I have discovered."

Mr. Tuck sat back, grudgingly impressed. "I see."

"Why have you waited all this time?" I asked him. "Joe died a dozen years ago. Why wait to tell Charlotte all this and decide to track down the money now?"

Charlotte answered while Mr. Tuck regarded me uneasily. "Oh, he told me. Long ago. But I wasn't certain I wanted to tell *you*."

Meaning they'd exhausted other avenues of discovering what had happened, and Charlotte had decided to seek me out in desperation. "If Mr. Smith stole the money, he might have spent it already," I pointed out.

"Unlikely," Mr. Tuck said. "Even if he spent ten guineas a day, he'd have much left over. It was a fortune—this I know."

This he believed, at least. But I carried on as though Mr. Tuck was right about the amount.

"What do you do, Mr. Tuck?" I asked him abruptly. "Why do reports of dockland crimes appear on your desk?"

Mr. Tuck's fair face reddened, freckles standing out in dark specks. "Insurance clerk. I work in an office that insures cargo."

"And how did you know Joe?"

His flush deepened. "He came to me to insure this money. He needed to get it safely to Antigua."

I sent him a severe look. "When the money went missing, did your insurance agency pay out? Charlotte ought to have obtained some compensation for it, is that not true?"

"There was no payment." Mr. Tuck swallowed. "I took Joe's premium, but my company refused to grant the policy. Too risky, they said. Didn't like the amount he wanted to insure, didn't believe Joe came by the money honestly."

I agreed the insurers had been astute. "You took Joe's premium? Why didn't you give it back when your company wouldn't comply?"

"Because he was already gone." Mr. Tuck balled his fists on the table. "When I knew he was dead, I returned the premium money to Charlotte. I hunted her up to give it to her." He paused to send her a fond glance that was unmistakable. "I am very glad that I did."

Mr. Tuck had little to add to his story, but he had clarified many things. Charlotte could have told me all this herself, I supposed, but her anger at me hadn't let her converse with me with much lucidity.

Once I knew all Mr. Tuck had to say, I declared the interview over. I had to meet Grace, and I was already an hour late.

I thanked Mr. Tuck and shook hands with him properly, and thanked Charlotte for allowing me to speak to him. Charlotte remained surly but said good-bye without too much rancor.

Though I was in a hurry, I waited for them to leave first. They walked down the passageway together, hands nearly touching, and out into the afternoon.

I followed more slowly, pausing to gaze into the taproom at a man in the corner who still hunkered over his pint. His seat was against the wall that separated the taproom from the snug, a large crack in the plaster not quite hidden by his right shoulder.

I held my gaze on him, then turned and walked out, keeping my steps slow.

I had not passed three doors on the street when he fell into step beside me, his hunched shoulders now straight.

"Well," I said to Daniel. "I assume you heard all?"

13

Daniel did not appear one bit ashamed that he'd both followed me to the tavern and found a place to eavesdrop. I'd thought I'd noticed a shabby-looking man with a cap hiding his face dogging us from Oxford Street onward.

"I did," he said.

"Well, that is a mercy, so I will not have to repeat it to you. Have you been keeping an eye out for me leaving Mount Street all weekend?"

"Not exactly." Daniel's rumbling voice tempted me to soften to him and perhaps kiss him right here in Soho Square, but I held myself firm.

"You mean you had James watching," I concluded. "He did well. I never saw him."

"That will please him." Daniel flashed a smile, threatening my resolve once more. "Yes, I followed you today. I had no intention of letting you meet a stranger in a pub in Soho with only Charlotte Bristow at your side. She could have led you into the worst sort of trap."

"I did think of that," I said indignantly.

"What did you plan to do if she took you to a place where men waited to do you over?"

"Not followed her inside, of course. I have passed that pub many a time in my life. It is not the most respectable place, but nor is it a den of thieves and murderers."

"What does a den of thieves and murderers look like?" Daniel asked, eyes wide with feigned fascination.

"Cheek. You've seen them in the rookeries, as have I. This is not that sort of pub. No gang leader conducting the worst kind of business from the back room."

Daniel took my arm to steer me away from three men who came pouring, drunk, from a gin house. I did not object as I had no wish for the men to career into me.

"What did you think of Mr. Tuck's story?" I asked when the men had staggered past us.

"He believed every word of it." Daniel paused. "I wonder how many cargoes he has 'insured,' not bothering to tell his customers that the company did not actually underwrite them."

"Pocketing the fees himself, you mean?"

"Possibly. Or possibly he truly meant to return Bristow's money and was not able to find him before his ship to Antigua had sailed."

"Mr. Tuck does not carry himself like a thief," I mused. "But perhaps he has convinced himself he has done nothing wrong."

"Embezzlement is often committed by lofty gentlemen," Daniel said as we made our way back to Oxford Street, a slightly safer road, though pickpockets ranged everywhere. "Those you would never suspect of doing anyone harm. That is why it is so shocking when the truth comes out."

He spoke with authority, and I wondered how many lofty embezzlers he'd caught.

We turned east—Oxford Street would become High Holborn, which would eventually take me south toward St. Paul's and Cheapside.

I did not know if Daniel meant to escort me all the way to the Millburns', or accompany Grace and me on whatever outing we decided upon, or if he'd drift away when he finished with our conversation. I also did not know which of these choices I hoped for.

"Mr. Tuck is another who believes Joe's motives were honorable." I had to raise my voice to be heard over the rumble of wheels and the sharp clop of horses' hooves on the road. "I'd had no idea Joe Bristow was such a saint."

Daniel sent me a sideways glance. "If you will pardon my saying so, you believed he was a good man at one point in your life."

"That is so." My face heated. "But I soon discovered that he was not the considerate man he made himself out to be, and this was long before I knew about Charlotte."

"You were with him two years?"

"Nearly, but not quite that." I sighed. "I was so young, Daniel. A girl can be very easily led at eighteen."

His fingers tightened on my arm. "I was not the best judge of character myself at that age. Including my own."

I recalled a few of the things Mr. Fielding had told me about Daniel. I had difficulty reconciling this solid man I trusted with the wild malefactor Mr. Fielding had painted for me.

"We have both grown wiser, I hope," I said.

Daniel grinned. "Ah, Kat, do not portray us as two elderly people just yet. We are still in the prime of life."

I tried not to melt at his smile. "I meant that we have put the rashness of our past behind us. At least I believe so."

Daniel's brows drew together as his amusement fled. "You believe so? Are you questioning my rashness?"

"Why? Have you done something rash?"

Daniel chewed his lower lip, gazing along the road to the slight rise of the Holborn Viaduct that would take us over streets below us.

"I have upset my greatest friend," he said in a low voice. "With my impatience and my temper. I want to apologize to you for behaving like a boor the last time we met."

My breath came faster, and not simply because the wind had begun to push at us. "I made you unhappy."

"It was not your fault at all, my dear Kat. I was presumptuous and wanted too much."

I did not like to hear him say that. Did he regret his implication that he wished to marry me? Had he given up the idea? I did not like the pang that caused in my heart.

"I was abrupt and dismissive," I said. "Please say we can be friends again." I pulled him closer. "I have missed you."

The last words came out softly, and I thought he did not hear them, but he lowered his head to mine. "I've missed you too, Kat. Dreadfully."

We walked along in silence a few moments while a sort of relief coursed through me. I'd feared I'd never see Daniel again, never see him send me that sly glance with his smile, never hear his laughter, never feel the warmth of his hand in mine.

What was between us had changed, I knew. We'd gone from flirtation and enjoying each other's company to something deeper, something unexplored, something we both hesitated to name.

Someday I would have to come to terms with that more complex idea, but I would not have to face it at this moment, not while descending the Holborn Viaduct to Newgate Street.

I disliked taking this route to Cheapside, because I had to pass Newgate Prison and remember the very bad hours I'd spent there. I'd been rescued from this horror by the man at my side. I owed him my life, and I could never forget that.

Daniel's voice drew me from my uneasy musings. "Since I last saw you, I have been wandering the East End, looking to learn more about Mr. Bristow. I could not find out much. He went to sea for the same reason many in the slums do—it is a way out of the backstreets and offers steady pay. Dangerous work, but appealing to those who have nothing."

I wondered if Daniel had ever been tempted to run away to sea. "Did he return to Stepney after he became a sailor? Before he met me, I mean. When we married, he wanted to move into my neighborhood instead of taking me back to his."

"Probably so you wouldn't meet anyone who might mention he had another wife in Bristol," Daniel said, scowling. "I still want to hit him for that."

"Apparently, someone else already did," I reminded him.

"Yes, in the London Docks. You said he usually sailed from Gravesend, farther down the river. What was he doing in the dockyards, then?"

The London Docks were a series of enclosed wharves near the Tower, just east of the St. Katharine Docks, where ships could unload directly into warehouses. Larger and newer docks had been built down the river—the West India Docks and others on the Isle of Dogs, the many wharves south of the Thames in Rotherhithe, and the Royal Victoria and Royal Albert Docks in Woolwich.

I knew about all these because on the rare occasions when Joe had talked about his job, he'd told me of the extensive networks of docklands along the Thames. So many ships came from all over the world to disgorge goods into London.

"Was he meeting someone?" I asked. "He was supposed to meet Mr. Tuck, but didn't turn up. Did he have his money on him, and was robbed? Or was he on his way to retrieve it?"

"Learning of his movements the last days of his life would be helpful," Daniel said. "As would finding this chap called Smith. If Smith took the money, where is it now? I agree with you that in twelve years, he's likely spent all of it, but we ought to make certain."

I did indeed wish to put my hands on Mr. Smith and make him tell me all. "I also had the idea of discovering if any large sums had gone missing when Joe took ship." I explained how Miss Townsend, Cynthia, and Bobby intended to go over old records and newspapers, trying to find out if there had been any significant heists in the docklands, or elsewhere, at the time.

"A chore, but helpful," Daniel said in approval.

"With several of us searching, we should be able to turn up something. I believe Cynthia has recruited Mr. Thanos. He is excellent at prying information from the printed page."

"Most excellent." Daniel's smile shone out again. "He will find the challenge entertaining and wonder why the rest of us groan at the tedium."

"Yes." Picturing it gave me a modicum of amusement. "I have also asked for Mr. Fielding's help."

I braced myself, waiting for Daniel to round on me and lecture me on the folly of trusting his brother. His smile did fade, but he continued walking calmly by my side.

"Ask a thief to catch a thief?" he said after a time. "I suppose there is some logic to that."

I decided to boldly broach the subject of his past. "You were a thief too," I said quietly.

"Errol told you that?" Daniel glanced at me, then away. "I will not deny it. Errol knows the worst of me."

"He told me you called yourself Daniel Carter."

Daniel stilled for a fraction of a second. "I did." He acknowledged this with a nod. "To honor Carter, and to let his killer know I would not soon forget what he'd done."

I raised my brows. "You taunted him? Daniel, the man you speak of—Mr. Naismith—is very dangerous." I had encountered the lieutenants of Mr. Naismith—who had killed Mr. Carter long ago—in previous adventures with Daniel. Even Naismith's underlings were terrifying.

"I did not care at the time," Daniel said. "As I

grew older and realized it was not very wise of me to, as you say, taunt them, I decided to resume the name McAdam and cease being openly defiant."

"Is that when you tried to join the police?"

Daniel sent me another long glance. "Errol told you much, didn't he?"

"We did have a long conversation."

Daniel grimaced. "I am not certain I want to know all of what he said, but yes. I decided that instead of trying to be worse than Naismith, I'd join a force of men who could catch him. I was naive. With my past, I had no hope to become a detective constable." He blew out his breath. "I promise I will tell you why Monaghan recruited me, but it's nothing I can say so near the Old Bailey and Newgate. Another day."

He often said he'd tell me things "one day," but it was never today.

I pressed aside my impatience with his secrets, as we had reached the street of Cheapside and the lane that opened from it, where the Millburns resided.

Daniel tipped his hat when I reached the door, a clear indication he would walk off and leave me to Grace. However, Grace, who'd been watching at the window, rushed to the door as soon as Joanna's maid of all work opened it.

"Uncle Daniel, I am so happy to see you," she cried. "Where shall we go today?"

14

Neither Daniel nor I had the heart to deny Grace the pleasure of Daniel's company that afternoon. He entered the house with me, Joanna welcoming us both.

"May we go to Primrose Hill again?" Grace asked when Daniel inquired what she would like to see. "It has such a lovely view. If I could paint, I'd paint it. It was ever so grand, Mrs. Millburn."

Joanna nodded and watched us with wise eyes.

"We might not have enough time this afternoon," Daniel explained to Grace. "We'd arrive and have to turn around and rush home again. But there are other fine places to see nearby."

Grace donned her coat and hat, and Daniel led us past St. Paul's to Ludgate Hill. At New Bridge Street, we turned south to the river, picking up the Victoria Embankment at Blackfriars Bridge.

We wandered along this wide thoroughfare, past the Temple Gardens where robed barristers and their students hurried about, past the large bulk of Somerset House, and to the strange obelisk called Cleopatra's Needle.

I remembered when the obelisk had been transported from Alexandria in Egypt to London with great fanfare and many newspaper stories, including the grim report of sailors who'd lost their lives during the journey. When the obelisk's special ship had nearly capsized, they'd had to abandon it, the obelisk floating free in its boat until found again by another ship.

The granite monument pointed to the sky, plaques commemorating the efforts of the men who'd brought it here mounted on all four sides. The Egyptian writing that was so many birds, snakes, and other marks meant nothing to me, but I enjoyed studying it.

The obelisk on its base sat quite alone on the edge of the river, the people moving to and fro on the street too busy to stop and marvel at it. For all the excitement at its arrival four years ago, it now rested in silence, the marks of the ancient Egyptians still plain.

"Thutmose the Third commissioned this," Daniel told us. "Nearly thirty-five hundred years ago. He had an inscription about himself cut down the middle." He pointed at the column of writing. "Then another pharaoh, Ramses the Great, added more words about *his* deeds."

"What do they say?" Grace asked eagerly.

"No idea," Daniel answered. "This is Mr. Thanos's area. I'm certain he could stand here and read every word."

"We should ask him to walk with us another day, then," Grace suggested.

"He is quite busy," I said. "He is teaching at

the new Polytechnic, which takes up much of his time."

"He'd be delighted," Daniel assured Grace. "He enjoys variety in his life. I wonder how long he'll be able to lecture on the same subjects before he grows weary of it and walks away," he added to me.

"Would he?" I asked in worry. "He'll not be steadily employed like that."

I had good reason for wanting that young man to keep a well-paying job. Mr. Thanos would never propose to Lady Cynthia until he could support her.

Daniel guessed my thoughts, the corners of his mouth quirking. "Thanos always survives—there are plenty who wish to pay him for his genius. If he could publish a few books, that might help."

"As long as readers could understand them," I said.

Daniel chuckled. "I suppose that is a point."

Grace sent each of us a reproving look. "I like Mr. Thanos. You should not make fun of him."

Her expression was so like my own, I wanted to weep, but I swept her into a hug instead. "I beg your pardon, my dear. We are very fond of Mr. Thanos, and we can't help teasing him a little."

Grace emerged from the embrace somewhat mollified. "Very well, but only tease when he is here to answer."

"I promise." I took Grace's hand. "I suppose we should go back now."

My feet always dragged when I had to return Grace to the Millburns'. Daniel tucked my arm through his, and the three of us strolled up the steps to the Embankment.

I turned to glance at the obelisk. It soared above the river with dignity, its point framed by a cloudless patch of blue sky. The writing on its face continued to proclaim its king's mighty deeds after thousands of lonely years.

Once I had Grace safely back with Joanna, I accepted Daniel's offer to return me to Mount Street in a cab. He rode with me, the two of us tantalizingly close.

I said little on the journey, because Joanna had taken me aside before I'd gone, Grace happily describing our outing to Joanna's four children, and told me that Grace was outgrowing her frocks and coats. She'd need new things for winter.

I thought of my small stockpile of funds that never seemed to grow. I paid for Grace's keep, of course, but there were always extra expenses—dresses, shoes, gloves, books for her schooling. Joanna was frugal, as was I, and we purchased Grace's things secondhand, but even those could be costly.

My husband's gains, no matter how ill-gotten, would be helpful.

I asked the cabbie to let me out on South Audley Street near Grosvenor Square so that I could walk the rest of the way. Daniel, understanding that I did not wish to be seen arriving with him, simply squeezed my hands after he helped me down, and said his farewells.

We parted cordially. I hoped that our discussion today meant we could return to being friends, though I knew some of the tension between us would linger.

The kitchen, when I reached it, was as warm and bustling as ever. Tess whipped eggs for a sauce, a bowl tucked under her arm. Charlie fed the stove, and Mr. Davis swept in to deposit two bottles of Burgundy I'd asked for before I'd departed.

Mr. Davis had been very pleased with Mr. Fielding's praise of the Bordeaux—"At last, a palate with good taste"—and had been inclined to surrender wines to me without fuss since then.

Lady Cynthia arrived after I'd immersed myself in roasting two hens and a pork loin, the red wines open and waiting for me to make the pork's drippings into a savory sauce.

"I've got them," she announced.

Cynthia carried nothing with her to enlighten me of what she meant. "You've got what?" I asked distractedly.

"The newspapers. And reports on anything unusual happening in London between April and

August of 1870." She dramatically clutched the back of a kitchen chair. "You wouldn't believe how many things did happen between April and August of that year."

"No doubt." I vigorously stirred potatoes I was roasting on the stove. "Newspapers must fill their pages day after day, so I imagine anything they can spin into a story is printed in them."

"You are a cynic, Mrs. H. But probably not far from wrong. I also have a few Home Office reports that Judith managed to coax out of whomever she tackled. We've been hammering at them all day, and thought you'd like to look at your share."

"I will, but after service." I gave the potatoes another toss. I wanted at that very moment to begin tearing through the information she'd turned up, but the supper was at a critical point.

"Of course." Cynthia took a prolonged sniff. "Smells wonderful. I'll be in the dining room, awaiting your creation with joy."

Tess watched Cynthia nearly dance out of the room, her butternut yellow frock complementing her hair and bringing out the blue in her eyes.

"Mr. Thanos needs to make known his intentions," Tess declared as she added a pinch of salt to the greens. "Our young lady shouldn't be stuck here when she has so much liveliness. I'd miss her, though."

I'd miss her as well—dreadfully. But if I could

convince Mr. Thanos to remain at the lucrative post at the Polytechnic and take Cynthia to wife, the two of them would be very happy. I'd sacrifice my own feelings for that.

Cynthia returned after supper, carrying a bundle of papers with her. She'd also brought Mr. Thanos.

Any other gentleman might be ill at ease to follow a lady of the house down the back stairs, through the passageway where footmen and maids flitted, and into the kitchen that had just been cleaned for the night.

Mr. Thanos, on the other hand, appeared to find nothing at all amiss. He beamed at everyone he passed, and greeted me cordially when he reached the kitchen door.

"An excellent meal, Mrs. Holloway. I always know I will eat well when Mr. Bywater invites me to supper. Much better than any restaurant."

I sent him a smile. "You are quite good for my confidence, Mr. Thanos. Thank you."

Mr. Thanos had very dark eyes that went with his neatly combed black hair. He was a bit nearsighted, but only liked to wear his spectacles for reading. "Not an empty sentiment, I assure you. You surpass the best chefs of London."

"*Very* good for me," I said warmly.

"Thought it best we work down here." Cynthia sent a surreptitious glance along the passageway and leaned to me. "Without Auntie interfering, or Uncle asking about Thanos's mathematics work. That is what they believe we are doing—researching for one of Thanos's papers. Here we can spread out, but be chaperoned, as it were."

Mr. Thanos appeared puzzled about why he and Cynthia would need a chaperone, but I understood why she'd brought him down to me. I'd not be able to join in if they worked upstairs.

"The staff has eaten their supper," I said. "And I am almost finished with preparations for tomorrow. We can work here in the kitchen, or in the servants' hall, which has a larger table. Or if you prefer more comfort, I can ask Mrs. Redfern if she minds if we use her parlor."

"Don't want to put anyone out," Cynthia said dubiously.

I forbore to mention that Cynthia could charge into any room she wished, hardly needing permission from the servants. But Cynthia was courteous, bless her, and she knew our jobs were made more difficult if she was in the way.

"I don't mind at all sitting in your kitchen," Mr. Thanos said. "It's wonderfully cozy and smells of good things."

I knew Mr. Thanos did not mouth an empty politeness—if he said he wished to sit in the kitchen, then he did.

Tess, who'd peered eagerly at the papers that both Cynthia and Mr. Thanos carried, began scrubbing off the table. I hastily removed my bowl of bread dough to the shelf above the stove and assisted Tess in wiping up flour.

Mr. Thanos waited until I waved him to a chair, but before he sat, he held out another chair for Cynthia. Once she was seated, he then escorted me to my chair, to the delight of Tess, who plopped down on her stool before Mr. Thanos could reach her. Only then did Mr. Thanos seat himself.

"What are we looking for?" Tess asked, reaching for a newspaper.

Mr. Thanos handed it to her without a qualm. "Any occurrence that could be tied with the ship, the *Devonshire*, or something out of the ordinary that happened between April and August 1870."

"Oh, is that all?" Tess unfolded a paper. "My reading's not as good as Mrs. Holloway would like it to be, but I can at least have a butcher's."

"She means a look," I clarified for Mr. Thanos.

"Ah yes, Cockney rhyming slang," Mr. Thanos said brightly. "I have made a study of it. I once told my landlady that my plates ached from walking home, and she thought I'd run mad. Scolded me that I shouldn't use such cant when I was a university gentleman." He chuckled.

"Is there anything you haven't studied, Mr. Thanos?" I asked in jest.

He gazed thoughtfully at the shadows beyond the dresser. "A good many things, I'm certain. There is always so much to learn." Mr. Thanos turned happily to the papers before him, documents that were covered in small, spidery writing.

"Records Judith procured," Cynthia said, noting my glance. "If there's anything to them, Thanos will find it."

I suppressed a smile and unfolded the newspaper that Cynthia had set in front of me.

As I turned the pages, scanning the tiny print, memories rose up and flooded me. I recalled the events of the days past, when what was in these newspapers was discussed on the corners, in the greengrocers, at the haberdashers, in the pubs. A fire at Hampstead Heath. A salvage worker in Islington killed by a falling building. A woman finally dying in her hundred and fourth year, the suicide of a housekeeper in Kensington.

I'd had little to do at that time but read newspapers and gossip about what was in them. I'd been unhappy in my marriage, having learned that Joe could be a brute, though he mostly left me on my own. I'd been lonely, missing my mother and also the business of cooking in a large house. Even with the drudging labor relegated to assistant cook, at least I'd been engaged in living and working.

About this time, I'd also felt Grace quickening inside me. I'd been flooded with joy but also fear. Joe never gave me much money—how was I going to raise a child?

I pushed aside the cascades of remembrance to focus on the stories in the newspaper and try to decide if the events were or were not significant in relation to Joe.

We'd been working steadily for an hour, Tess using her finger to slowly guide her eyes down the columns. She had to ask me about longer and more difficult words, but for the most part, she did well.

I had fixed us a pot of tea, and when I rose to refresh the kettle, I nearly ran into Mr. Davis.

"What are you all about?" he asked me, then cleared his throat and nodded at Lady Cynthia and Mr. Thanos. "My lady. Sir."

"Reading a lot of old newspapers," Cynthia answered him without hesitation. "A chore, really, but I thought I'd help Thanos."

Mr. Thanos tore his gaze from his documents and started, then caught on to Cynthia's ruse. "Oh, yes. Quite. A great help."

Mr. Davis looked over the newspaper spread open at my place with interest as I fetched the kettle. "What are you searching for? On April nineteenth of 1870?" He touched the date at the top of my issue. "Perhaps I can help."

He'd directed the question to Mr. Thanos, and both Mr. Thanos and Cynthia shot inquiring glances at me. When I gave Cynthia the barest of nods, she swept a wave of welcome to Mr. Davis.

"Of course. The more the merrier. Thanos is

writing a paper on events of 1870, so he's hunting for any unusual sorts of things—spectacular crimes, and incidents of that nature. Anything involving a large sum of money."

"Like robberies?" Mr. Davis removed his coat and hung it on a peg, then slid onto a stool and raked a newspaper from the stack. "Insurance fraud, embezzlement, large swindling schemes?"

"Exactly that," Cynthia answered.

Mr. Davis spread open his paper. "How does this tie in with mathematics?" he asked Mr. Thanos.

"Eh? Oh. Economy, don't you know." Mr. Thanos removed his spectacles to polish them and hooked them around his ears again. "How major crimes can hurt a country, even though most don't realize it. We might like to think that a bank missing some of its funds, or a fraud scheme that wipes out a company, is someone else's affair, but actually it affects us all."

"Mmm." Mr. Davis did not seem convinced by Mr. Thanos's explanation, though I thought it a clever one.

I poured Mr. Davis a cup of tea while he got stuck in. I was grateful for his help. Mr. Davis regularly read newspapers cover to cover, after Mr. Bywater finished them and tossed them to Mr. Davis to throw away. Mr. Davis could skim through a paper and find relevant articles quickly, digesting them without much effort.

By the time the rest of the downstairs darkened,

the staff stumbling off to bed to snatch what sleep they could before their early rising time, we had piled up several stories to investigate further, two found by Mr. Davis. Mr. Thanos, perusing the documents from the Home Office, had discovered a few items that matched the stories in the newspapers—the papers presenting much more sensational versions, of course.

Cynthia walked Mr. Thanos upstairs. I found it interesting that Mrs. Bywater thought nothing of her niece spending so much time with Mr. Thanos. She seemed to regard Mr. Thanos as a sort of eccentric and harmless friend, perhaps because he was a poor academic and not a likely prospect for Cynthia to marry.

Tess had fallen asleep with her head on a newspaper. She rose groggily when I roused her. "Did we find it?" she asked.

"Nearly." I patted her shoulder and walked her to the kitchen door. Tess yawned as she went out, her cap askew, her footsteps heavy as she made her way to the stairs.

Mr. Davis continued to neaten the papers and then helped me stack them on a corner shelf so that my table could be free for working.

"What is this really about, Mrs. Holloway?" Mr. Davis asked me as I scrubbed off the ink smudges. "Mr. Thanos's research in economy?" He eyed me skeptically. "I don't believe it."

15

I regarded Mr. Davis with some trepidation. He was a canny man, and Mr. Thanos's glib explanation had not quite rung true.

"Oh. I—"

Mr. Davis bent closer, engulfing me in a scent of silver polish and pomade. "Lady Cynthia is not in some sort of trouble, is she?"

My answer was swift and firm. "Good heavens, no. How could this be about her?"

"Good," Mr. Davis said, his tension easing. "I wasn't certain, but Lady Cynthia is involved with many interesting sorts of persons. I wondered if we were discovering if they had taken part in shady dealings of the past."

"Not at all," I said briskly. "She was simply willing to help, as you were."

"Well, that is a relief to hear. I worry about our Lady Cynthia."

"As do I, Mr. Davis."

I hoped he would bid me good night and waft off to bed, but Mr. Davis remained, one hand on the pile of newspapers he'd set on the shelf. "Then it's something to do with that McAdam chap."

Mr. Davis did not trust Daniel. Daniel was friendly to him, and Mr. Davis was courteous in return, but Mr. Davis had guessed that Daniel wasn't quite what he seemed. Also, Mr. Davis considered Daniel to be well beneath him and me in status. A butler and a cook far outranked a man-of-all-work. Mr. Davis could not understand my friendship with him.

"No, it is not." I could answer quite truthfully. "Nothing to do with Daniel." When Mr. Davis obviously did not believe me, I continued. "The problem is my own, Mr. Davis. And nothing I wish to speak about."

"Ah." Mr. Davis straightened the sleeves of the coat he'd resumed. "Are you after criminals again?"

"Something of that nature."

"I see." I wasn't certain he believed this explanation either, but to my relief he shrugged. "I do not mind lending any assistance, but I do hope you will not come to grief." He glided past me to the door, where he turned back. "If you decide to tell me any more of it, you are welcome to. I can be discretion itself."

Mr. Davis sent me a wise look, then continued out on silent feet.

I finished straightening the newspapers, wondering if Mr. Davis knew more than he let on. He'd come to my defense several times when I'd clashed with Mrs. Bywater, and I'd be forever grateful to him for that. But I wondered now if he knew my secrets and had chosen to help keep them hidden rather than expose me.

It gave me a warm feeling, a realization of friendship, but also a worry that I'd opened myself to far too many people. Once I'd done that, there'd be no going back.

Tuesday dawned, rainy and cool, the warm days of summer fading behind us. I welcomed the coolness, because London could become hot and sticky, the smell from the river unfortunate. A rain refreshed things beautifully.

I did not see much of this agreeable weather, because Mrs. Bywater had another of her charity teas, and Tess and I labored to make several cakes of currents and honey, dozens of macaroons, a batch of coconut biscuits, another batch of biscuits flavored with cinnamon, and a plum pudding made with a basket of lovely greengages I'd found at the market.

"Are they green plums, then?" Tess asked as she began cutting the fruit in half to de-stone them. "Not ripe?"

"They are their own variety and perfectly ripe," I explained as I mixed up a thick batter of eggs, milk, sugar, and vanilla seeds scraped from a vanilla bean. "They come from Persia—so I hear. Brought to this country many centuries ago."

"Persia," Tess said dreamily. "Where's that, then?"

"A long way from here. Beyond the lands of the Ottomans." I was a bit fuzzy on where exactly

Persia lay, but I was fairly certain it was east of the Ottoman Empire, which abutted the far end of Europe.

"Sounds ever so nice."

"I believe there is much desert there. Very dry."

Tess glanced to the high window that had fogged with the rain. "Even nicer. Do you think I'll ever go to Persia? Or anywhere else but England?"

"One never knows," I said philosophically. Travel was hideously expensive and very uncomfortable, but even I sometimes wistfully thought of the ladies I'd read about, who bravely sailed down the Nile or hiked across mountains in Italy. "Just get that fruit cut up, or neither of us will ever travel anywhere, because we'll be out on our ears and scrubbing steps for a living."

Tess grinned and returned to her slicing, singing under her breath.

I was not certain what Mrs. Bywater's charity was today, but the plates of our sweets came back empty, barely a crumb upon them. The greengage pudding had gone over well, Mrs. Redfern reported. We'd nestled the fruit Tess had cut into a pan half-filled with my batter, baked that, then covered it with more batter, and baked it again until the top crust was golden. I'd saved a few greengages and a cupful of batter to make a small pudding for Tess and me to share.

I put aside some of my portion as a treat for

after supper. Cynthia was assisting Mr. Thanos with a lecture tonight at the Polytechnic, so I would not have her help, but I was perfectly capable of going through what we'd found the night before and making notes in my book.

I asked Tess that afternoon to instruct Caleb to look for the particular cases we'd found last night while he was rooting around at Scotland Yard. Tess happily dashed out to find Caleb as he walked his beat, and she returned with a flushed face, I assumed from the brisk wind and rain.

Mr. Davis had said nothing more to me about his questions last night, and went about his busy day. His only conversation with me was regarding wines I needed, plus a brief rant about Mrs. Bywater's request for extra bottles of sherry for her guests.

The kitchen was quiet that night as I spread out the papers we'd set aside as the most relevant and took up my pencil to write in my notebook. A cup of tea, an intriguing problem, and half a greengage pudding, and I was content.

I was not expecting the knock on the back door, nor the way my heart sped when I heard it. I was across the kitchen lifting the bolt before I was aware of my actions.

"Thank heavens it's you," I said when I saw Daniel, then added hastily, "Not a burglar, I mean."

"I'd hardly have knocked," Daniel returned in

amusement. "If I'd truly planned to burgle the house, you'd never know I was here."

"That is *not* reassuring." I ushered him in, closing the door against the cool wind. "Why have you come?"

I expected him to scowl at my abrupt question, but Daniel only pulled his cap from his head, shaking the water droplets into the scullery's empty sink. "Thanos told me you'd found some enticing possibilities regarding your husband's fortune."

"Oh." I quelled my disappointment that he'd come only to investigate, then admonished myself for that disappointment. "Of course. I would welcome your opinion."

"Then I'm happy to give it."

Daniel left his hat on the edge of the sink to dry and followed me across the kitchen to the table. I saw his eye light on the chunk of pudding, but he did not ask for it. He did, however, manage to look hungry.

"I will fetch you a fork," I said, stepping to the dresser and pulling open the cutlery drawer.

"I don't always rush to your kitchen for your food, Kat."

Somehow, he was behind me, his warmth and the scent of rain touching me.

"No?" I asked, my voice a rasp.

"No." Daniel turned me to face him, took the fork from me, and laid it on the dresser. Then he cradled my face in his hands and gently kissed my lips.

I couldn't breathe. I had missed this after our quarrel, the easy way he'd kiss me, tender passion that demanded nothing.

I forgot about any uncomfortableness between us and returned the kiss, my mouth fitting to his, my fingers curling around the lapels of his woolen coat.

We stood thus for silent moments, no words to break this spell. No regrets for what we could not have, no hopes for what we could. I sank into Daniel, and he held me with strong arms.

After a long while, Daniel eased the kiss to a close. I am sorry to say it was not I who stepped away first.

"Do you mean you come to my kitchen for *that?*" I tried to quip, my voice shaking. "I ought to be shocked and incensed."

"I mean that my interest is in your good self," Daniel rumbled. "All of you—conversation, cooking . . ." He shot me a sly smile as he turned for the table. "And *that.*"

"Cheek." I was glad his back was to me so he would not see me clutch the kitchen dresser for support. When I could feel my legs again, I snatched up the fork and carried it to the table.

I clattered the fork to the plate. "This needs eating—it won't keep."

"I thank you most humbly." Daniel waited

until I'd taken my seat before he lifted the fork and devoured the remaining pudding in three large bites. He took his time swallowing the last mouthful. "This is the most wonderful thing I've eaten in a long time."

"Flatterer. You said that about the apple tart."

"And I say it now. This one is even better." Daniel laid the fork down reverently and wiped his mouth with the napkin I provided. "Now, what have you discovered?"

I tried to ignore the sensation of the kiss that lingered on my mouth as I laid out the papers for Daniel.

"We narrowed it down to three good possibilities," I said. "Each incident took place in late March or early April of 1870, not long before Joe took ship. Each involves large sums of money. I am waiting to discover whether these crimes have been solved and the perpetrators caught. I am afraid I have shamelessly recruited Constable Greene to look into the cases."

"I might be able to help as well," Daniel offered.

"If I will not offend you, I'd rather you did not. Caleb can search for these things without arousing suspicion, if he is careful. If you poke your nose in, everyone at Scotland Yard will wonder what you are up to."

Daniel raised his brows but nodded thoughtfully. "You could be right. Inspector McGregor notices everything I do from the moment I walk into the building until I slip out again. I have been avoiding Scotland Yard for that reason."

"He is an astute gentleman, Inspector McGregor. I have grown to admire him, though he terrified me when I first met him."

"He is good at terrifying. But I agree with you. He is a good copper, who worked hard to move through the ranks. No one handed him his position. He earned it, though his superiors are grudging about it."

I blinked. "Why should they be grudging? He has put away several very bad villains for them."

Daniel nodded grimly. "There are inner circles in every profession, and within them, those who want no one else to enter. Aristocrats and commoners, ladies and servants, chief superintendents and the rank and file."

"It is too bad." I spared a moment for disgust at those chief supers. "But I have faith in Inspector McGregor. He will become a chief inspector soon, I am certain."

Daniel seemed to find my optimism amusing but returned to my list. He rested his finger on the first entry in my notebook. "Insurance fraud—interesting."

"A warehouse fire, probably deliberately started," I explained. "Claimed as a loss worth thousands of pounds, but the police who investigated could not find the remains of the goods. They either burned to ash or had been taken out beforehand. The insurance firm paid a lot of money to an unknown individual. The company paid had a name—Armitage Shipping—but no one knows exactly who owned it."

"Clever. And Mr. Tuck, Charlotte's dear friend, is an insurance clerk."

"Exactly our thinking."

"Next, the Goldsmiths' Company. Hmm." Daniel's blunt finger paused. "If I understand aright, they assess the purity of goods made of gold and silver and hallmark it if it passes their standards. The customers can see the stamp of the assayers and know they've paid for excellent quality."

"Mr. Thanos told us they also test the coins for the Royal Mint," I said. "The Mint apparently sends over sample coins—a whole heap of them—so that the Goldsmiths' Company can make sure they are made correctly. Or something of that nature."

"Ah yes, the Trial of the Pyx."

"I beg your pardon? The trial of the what?"

"The Pyx. It is an actual trial with a judge and jury—the jury are members of the Company. The process dates back centuries. Coins pressed by the Royal Mint must be a certain weight and have a certain amount of precious metals in them. This court at the Goldsmiths' Company assesses the coins and decides, in effect, whether the Mint has done its job."

"So men at the Mint can't pocket the gold they're given and turn out brass sovereigns," I concluded for him.

"Precisely. What was stolen from the Goldsmiths?"

"Apparently, some of the coins they were assessing," I said, checking my notes. "They are carried from the Mint to the Company in special chests, Mr. Thanos said, but that year, a few chests went missing. The chests each hold quite a lot of coins."

Daniel's eyes lit. "If someone got their hands on one of those, they'd certainly have a fortune. But the thief couldn't spend them, could he? I have no doubt that those particular coins are well accounted for. As soon as he tossed one to a landlord for a pint, he'd be found out."

"He could spend them in Antigua," I pointed out.

"Yes." Daniel ran his fingers over his chin, his gaze becoming remote. "Exchange coins for goods or land far from London, say, a plantation in Antigua. Sell that after a time and return to England with money to buy a house in Kent, with funds that have nothing to do with coins from the Royal Mint."

"A canny scheme," I said. "I'd never have believed Joe a clever swindler, but he did manage to keep two families without either of us knowing about the other."

I had to wonder, at that moment, whether Joe had yet another family elsewhere? In the West Indies, perhaps? What if Charlotte herself wasn't actually his wife, but this third woman he'd married before either of us? I'd found the record of his marriage to Charlotte, but perhaps there was another in the Antilles. Or anywhere else Joe had traveled. What was to stop him having a wife in every port?

I pushed those ponderings aside. I'd get nowhere with such a circle of thinking.

Daniel closed his hand over mine, warming my fingers. "He did a cruel thing to you, Kat. Crueler because I suspect it was thoughtless. He strikes me as a man who did as he pleased without realizing or caring who he hurt."

"That is true." I swallowed a lump in my throat. "He truly cared for no one but himself. I am ashamed it took me so long to realize that."

"You have nothing to be ashamed of. No one wants to believe they are unimportant, especially to the person they care about."

Mr. Fielding had said much the same thing to me regarding Joe. I searched Daniel's eyes, fearing he meant I was being as cruel to him as Joe had been to me, but I found only sympathy and understanding.

"Thank you," I said softly.

I thought Daniel would speak, make a quip, or continue our discussion about the pair of us, but he released me and turned back to my list.

"Finally, we have an embezzlement at the Bank of England." Daniel pursed his lips. "I remember this—a huge scandal at the time. I believe Inspector McGregor worked on it when he was still a detective sergeant. One of the cases that helped his career."

"Then he solved it and found the money?" I asked. We could cross it off the list in that case.

"The case was never closed." Daniel's interest rose. "McGregor was commended not because he caught the embezzler and recovered the money but because he exposed the corruption and incompetence of those who first conducted the investigation. The case cost several detective inspectors their jobs, and the chap who embezzled the money was later found murdered, the cash gone."

16

My excitement grew as well as my dismay. Had Joe killed a man for this cash? Getting into brawls was one thing, but going as far as taking a person's life was quite another.

"We might have to consult with Inspector McGregor after all," I said.

"Cautiously." Daniel set aside the notebook and leaned his arms on the table. "We don't know if Bristow had anything to do with any of this. We have to establish that he was acquainted with the embezzler, or knew about or committed the robbery of the Goldsmiths' Company, or helped with the insurance fraud."

"Mr. Tuck might know about the insurance scam," I said with conviction. "He was nervous about speaking to me, as though trying to carefully choose his words. I wager he left out much."

"Could you arrange for me to speak to Mr. Tuck, do you think?"

"I can try. I'll have to visit Charlotte at her boardinghouse and ask if he's returned from his jaunt to Reading, though she's not keen on me seeing too much of her Mr. Tuck." I smiled wryly. "She fears I'll steal him away."

Daniel's brows rose. "Is her concern well-founded?"

I sent him a disparaging look. "I am not the flirt you believe, Mr. McAdam." I ceased my teasing. "They are besotted with each other. Is it odd that I am glad for them?"

"Not at all. Bristow was cruel to her as well. Both of you are far better off without him."

"Would I had realized that the day I'd met him." I let out a sigh. "No use crying over it now. It was a long time ago." My voice softened. "The only reason I will forgive him—and me—is Grace."

Daniel's smile comforted me. "She is a gift."

"A most precious one. Grace taught me that love can be selfless, not needing or grasping."

Daniel's hand found mine again. "James also taught me that." He paused. "And so have you. It is something I never knew before."

For a moment we sat in silence, the past forgotten, our old regrets and heartbreaks gone. Forgotten too was Joe and the prospect of his money—a fortune that the police would never let us keep, if we were to find it. Such things were not for us, something inside me warned.

But in this now, it did not matter. I had love, and friendship, and caring in my life, more than I'd ever had before. For that moment, as I sat in my warm, quiet kitchen, Daniel beside me, our hands entwined, it was enough.

As I predicted, Charlotte did not want me to meet with Mr. Tuck again.

"He's told you all he knows." She glared at me where we stood in the tiny parlor of her boardinghouse on Thursday, the landlady blatantly watching through a slit in the doorway.

"Yes, but now *my* friend wishes to speak to him," I said, holding on to my patience. "He might have questions none of us thought to ask, including Mr. Tuck himself."

"He?" Charlotte's gaze turned sharp.

"Yes. Mr. McAdam." I lifted my chin. "I am walking out with him." This was the first time I'd admitted such a thing, even to myself. I felt oddly light for a moment.

"Oh?" Charlotte looked me up and down, as though surprised any gentleman would wish to squire me about. "Why should I trust this bloke?"

"Because he is very clever and has assisted me often in the past. You asked for my help because I had discovered solutions to crimes, remember? Well, Mr. McAdam helped me with those."

I decided not to mention Daniel's association with the police, because I knew Charlotte would not want the constabulary involved. I did not want them involved either, but as Daniel and I discussed the other night, it would become inevitable.

Charlotte at last reluctantly admitted that Mr. Tuck had returned to London and agreed to consult him about speaking to Daniel and me later today. I left her after we'd said a cursory good-bye, the landlady gazing at me in suspicion as I marched out of the house.

Charlotte's boardinghouse lay near Smithfield, the stench of the meat market heavy in the air. I took Aldersgate Street straight south toward Cheapside, but on a whim, I ducked down a lane that took me to Gresham Street and its intersection with Foster Lane.

There stood the Goldsmiths' Hall.

It was a massive edifice, with six giant columns topped by lavish capitals and an ornate cornice. Enormous coats of arms hung above the windows of the second floor, sculpture in plaster and stone. The center emblem was of two rearing unicorns flanking a woman who resembled Elizabeth I holding a set of scales.

For all the grandness of the building, the only entrance was a small door between the center set of columns. It was a structure meant to impress, not to welcome people inside.

I walked slowly along the street, just another passerby blending in with hansom cabs, goods' wagons, and carriages. A turn down Gutter Lane took me along the side of the building, which was just as ornate as the front. More columns, only four this time, soared above me. An iron railing separated the Hall from the lane, and another small entrance, closed, waited up a flight of stone steps.

On the opposite side of the lane was the livery

hall of the Wax Chandlers, a smaller brick building that seemed much friendlier. I wandered between these halls of ancient guilds as though I had business there, and scanned the windows of the Goldsmiths' Hall.

I could not imagine anyone having the audacity to steal chests of gold coins from the men inside this grand establishment, but I supposed it could be done more easily than I imagined.

In spite of the pomp of these companies, they were run by men who had much pride in themselves and in their traditions. They paid so much attention to the details of their rituals that they might miss something as ordinary as a man picking up a few boxes and walking off with them.

Gutter Lane ended at Cheapside, and I resumed my walk toward the Millburns'. This entire area had been gutted by the Great Fire more than two centuries ago, but no one observing it would guess that fact. Shops did a lively business on the ground floors of buildings that rose seven or more stories, awnings like sails over almost every door. Men hurried toward the financial center of the City, and delivery wagons and omnibuses crowded the road.

Cheapside segued into a street simply called Poultry, at the end of which sat the Bank of England. Even more imposing than the Goldsmiths' Company and several times as vast, the bank reared above its surroundings like a temple to an ancient god.

Two structures that held the wealth of nations lurked within an easy walk of Bow Lane, where Joe had lived with me.

I passed the Church of St. Mary-le-Bow as I retraced my steps to the turnoff to the Millburns'. The church's bells tolled the hour, the music reaching down Cheapside toward the Goldsmiths' Company on one side and the Bank of England on the other.

Grace was disappointed that Daniel hadn't accompanied me today, but she readily donned her hat and coat for a walk with me.

I took her to Bow Lane. I'd never considered bringing Grace to my old street, as the memories pressed upon me too hard, but today, I wanted her to see it. I wanted her to know the house and the lane where I'd been a child, where I'd had innocent dreams and no idea what troubles the future would bring.

The wind was brisk, but the clouds were scattered and puffy, not gathering as they would in a storm. Bow Lane was busy today, with women scurrying to shops, men delivering goods, builders repairing a house on the corner of Bow Lane and Cheapside, opposite the church.

I walked Grace to Watling Street and stopped before the unassuming brick house that contained the rooms my mother had let. The ground floor held a tobacconist's shop, where a woman sold not only tobacco in many forms but newspapers, magazines, and a few books. My mother had borrowed books from here to teach me my letters.

The lady behind the counter today in the tiny, cluttered shop filled with the earthy odor of tobacco was a stranger to me. The previous owner had either passed away or sold up, but this woman was of a similar sort—stout of build, red of face, and sharply watching that no one walked away with a newspaper or a pouch of tobacco without paying.

I purchased a small packet of sweets for a farthing as a treat for Grace and me. As the woman was weighing out the candy, I asked her, "Are the rooms on the second floor let?"

"All the rooms here are taken," the woman said brusquely. "People need somewhere to lodge, don't they?"

"Indeed, they do." I would not let her short temper dissuade me. "I lived in this house once, in those very rooms I inquired about."

The woman stilled, the paper cone in one hand, the scoop of sugar drops in the other. "You ain't never Elizabeth Holloway?"

I smiled. "I am her daughter, Kat."

"Oh, my good Lord. Look at you, the spitting image of her." The woman's rancorous expression fled, and she quickly finished pouring the sweets into the cone. "I was a charlady like herself, love.

She were a dear friend. When my husband died, I moved back here to Bow Lane, but she'd gone."

"She passed on, I'm afraid," I said, my sadness sharp. "She was the best of women."

"She was indeed. Oh, poor Lizzie." The woman sighed, dropping the scoop back into the bin. "We scrubbed at several places together—the school at St. Paul's and the police office on Gresham Street. Tiny place that was, with the constables tramping in all sorts. Lizzie talked a lot about *you*. My name's Alice, dear. Alice Taylor."

Alice looked me up and down, as though trying to see the little girl my mother had gone on about. Mum had always been proud of me, an awkward child who must have given her nothing but trouble.

"And is this your daughter?" Alice's eyes lit as she moved her gaze to Grace. "My, my, I see Lizzie in her too. Such a lovely thing, Lizzie was. Too good for charring."

I had always thought so. My mother had been a comely woman, too soon weary and worn by the labor she'd had to perform to feed us.

"She taught me well," I said. "I'm a cook now, in Mayfair."

Alice appeared impressed. "Well, then you've done all right for yourself. Fancy that. What about your husband, dear? Does he mind you cooking in a great house instead of for him?"

"He's gone," I said, but felt nowhere near the

sorrow that I did for my mother's death. "He'd been at sea."

"Oh, how sad. Poor duck," she said to Grace. "You keep your mum company, do you?"

"Yes, ma'am," Grace responded without hesitation. "Whenever I can. My father has been gone a long time now."

"Well, that is sweet of you, dear," Alice said approvingly. "But you know." She switched her attention to me and grinned. Half her teeth were missing and her face sank into a mass of wrinkles. "You are young and pretty, Kat, dear. Another man will come along."

I saw Grace open her mouth, as though to proclaim that one already had. I nudged her. With a quick glance at me, Grace closed her mouth again, but she sent me a sly look and a tiny smile.

"Do you know, the tenant upstairs has gone out for a time," Alice was saying. "Off to visit his sick granny. I can let you have a peep at your old rooms, if you like. It will be clean—I see to that."

I was not certain if Alice was the landlady of the building or simply managed it and this shop, but if she'd worked with my mother, she'd be a stickler for cleanliness. I felt a slight qualm about walking into a man's rooms without his leave, but my curiosity proved too great.

"If it won't be any trouble . . ." I said with just enough hesitation.

"Not at all, dear. Let me turn the sign around and fetch the keys."

She bustled off to lock the door and root in a drawer until she fished out a key ring that clanked, reminding me of the chatelaine Mrs. Redfern kept on her belt.

"This way, loves."

It gave me an odd feeling to approach the familiar door with its peeling green paint, and the narrow stairs between brick walls beyond it. I'd run up and down these stairs and through this door many, many times in my young life.

In some ways, as I stepped through the door, it was as if no time had passed. I'd dash upstairs on light feet, singing, *I'm home, Mum!* And she'd look up from whatever she'd been busy about and send me the smile that made me know I was loved. My mother would never let anything bad happen to me, no matter what, and I'd been secure and comforted in that knowledge.

At the same time, it had been far too many years since those happy days. The stairway was silent, the door to our flat repainted a dull brown—it had been a brilliant but fading blue in my childhood.

Alice thrust one of her many keys in the lock and opened the door. It swung on the same creaky hinges it always had and bumped into the same wall, leaving a scuff mark on top of all the others.

Mum and I had lived in two rooms. The front

chamber held a dresser full of crockery and foodstuffs, a table and two chairs, a bench under the window, and a fireplace that had been converted to hold a small cookstove. An open door showed a small bedroom beyond, containing the very bedstead I'd shared with my mother.

The dresser was the same too, though the chairs, table, and bench were different, and the cookstove was newer than the one in my mother's day.

I could scarcely breathe as I stood in the room I'd cavalierly hastened from to go to my post as assistant cook in Grosvenor Square, scarce knowing that my mother would not live much longer. I recalled even more clearly the last time I'd been here, after my mother's funeral, tears on my face as I clutched the small bundle of her belongings.

I'd treasured her things ever since, and even now my mother's prayer book, keepsake locket, and precious ribbons she'd bought as a last gift to me reposed in the bureau drawer in my chamber in Mount Street.

As I stood, transfixed, Grace's hand stole into mine. Even through our gloves, her warm, firm touch lent me strength. I wished with all my heart that my mother would patter out of the bedroom, a smile on her face, delighted to meet her granddaughter.

"Take as much time as you like, dear." Alice's

voice was subdued as she slid out of the room and quietly closed the door.

Grace squeezed my hand. "How old were you when you lived here, Mum?"

I drew a calming breath. "Oh, I was a wee lass. My first memories are of this place, though my mum might have lived elsewhere when she bore me. My old dad died very soon after. I don't much remember him. I lived here until I became a kitchen assistant when I was fourteen."

"Not much older than me, then."

I started and gazed down at my daughter, whose head was on level with my shoulder. Had I really thought myself grown-up when I was only two years older than she was now?

I pulled her to me in a rough embrace. "Very nearly. But you are ever so much cleverer than I was at your age."

Grace's expression held surprise when the embrace ended. "You are one of the cleverest people I know, Mum. I think maybe only Mr. Thanos is more clever than you."

I laughed. "How flattering you are. I shall tell all my friends I am nearly as clever as Mr. Thanos."

"Don't make fun," Grace admonished. "I know you say you're just a cook without much book learning, but book learning doesn't always make one wise."

She sounded like Joanna in that moment, which made me hug her again.

I took one last look about, remembering the days I'd peer out the front window to the street, waiting for my mother to return from whatever job she had on at the time. I'd rush down the stairs to meet her, hanging on to her hand, as Grace did to mine now, to guide her home.

My mother would have been exhausted, I realized now, ready to put up her feet, but she'd always taken the time to fix a bite of supper for us both and read with me.

I wanted to linger in my memories, but I made myself go, towing Grace into the hall and closing the door. It was someone else's flat now.

Downstairs, Alice handed me the wrapped sweets and waved away the farthing.

"You enjoy, dears. For Lizzie's sake."

Grace and I left the shop, and we continued our stroll up the lane. I deliberately did not pause at Mr. Miller's haberdashery or even glance at the rooms above it. Fond memories were far preferable to bad ones.

We reached Cheapside, walking in the shadow of Bow Bells. I studied the church with its slender, elegant steeple, remembering the last service I'd attended there, which was to say good-bye to my mother forever.

One of our favorite tea shops was around the corner from Cheapside, on King Street, and I led Grace there. I sank gratefully to the chair, and the plump-cheeked waitress brought tea and cakes.

I gladly exchanged the melancholy memories of the past for the cheerfulness of now, and Grace.

We downed our tea and cakes, our appetites strong. When we finished, I inquired of Grace where she'd like to go on our next outing, on Monday.

"Can we see Bow Lane again?" she asked eagerly.

I felt a pang as I sipped the last of my tea. "There's not much to it."

"But I want to know all about it. About where you played and who with. Mrs. Millburn has told me a little about when you were a girl, but I want to know everything."

Nonplussed, I set down my empty cup. "Are you that interested in what your old mum got up to?"

"Of course I am. And I want to know about my father as well."

I'm sure Grace saw me flinch. "Do you?"

"I am old enough now to know the truth, Mum," Grace said in reproach. "I'm not a child anymore."

"No?" I patted my coat pocket, the packet of lemon sweets rustling. "Then I will eat all these myself."

"Don't tease." Grace flowed into her ready smile. "I truly do want to know. Please, will you tell me?"

She was correct; she did deserve the truth. "I

will. But perhaps not today." I sounded like Daniel, but I acknowledged how difficult it was to explain certain topics.

"No," Grace agreed. "Not today."

We finished the last of the tea and departed the shop, sharing the lemon drops as we strolled back toward the Millburns' home. It was early afternoon, and we'd spend the rest of my day out in Joanna's cozy parlor, perhaps stuffing ourselves with yet another tea.

As we walked, the sensation came over me that someone was observing us. I turned my head, expecting to find Daniel sauntering along with his hands in his pockets, but I saw no one who remotely resembled him.

I tried to convince myself that I was imagining things. A crowd of people walked the same way we did, and perhaps someone only indulgently watched a mother and daughter amble together while they nibbled sweets.

But when we turned into the lane that led to Joanna's home, the back of my neck tingled, and I hurried Grace to the safety of my friend's front door.

17

Later that afternoon, once I had said good-bye to Grace, I made my way to the same insalubrious tavern in Soho and met Mr. Tuck and Daniel. Charlotte had come as well, of course.

Mr. Tuck eyed Daniel askance as Daniel took his seat, observing his worn coat, trousers, and thick boots with a superior air.

Once we had ale on the table—in my case, tea—Daniel became his usual disarming self and soon had Mr. Tuck opening up to him. Even Charlotte grew less fractious. She clearly could not understand why Daniel had taken up with me—I saw her eyeing me and then Daniel and shaking her head ever so slightly—but she became almost amiable.

Mr. Tuck, however, had little to add to his story. He repeated the fact that Joe had returned from Antigua by other means than the *Devonshire* and then had met his death in the old London Dockyards.

"Why those dockyards?" Daniel asked him. "When he usually sailed from Gravesend?"

"I wish I knew," Mr. Tuck said. "He was likely meeting some nefarious person, probably Thomas Smith. Joe was tough. He thought he could best anyone."

Yes, Joe had certainly had an overweening confidence in himself. He thought himself impervious to everything, and he had been, until the end.

"You said he showed you coins," Daniel went on. "Gold ones?"

"Yes. As I told Miss Holloway."

Again, I did not correct him about my name. Daniel leaned his arms on the table, hands around his pint. "Did he give you any?" He was eager, interested, a workingman fascinated by the aspect of gold.

Mr. Tuck started, his beard jerking. "He did, as a matter of fact. Just one. A souvenir, he told me. And as a promise of more."

"I assume you spent it?" Daniel asked. "What couldn't a man buy with a gold coin?" he finished wistfully.

"I kept it," Mr. Tuck said, affronted. "To remember him by. And as a sort of good-luck charm."

The coins hadn't brought Joe much luck, I reflected.

Daniel leaned closer to him, his eyes alight. "You couldn't let me have a butcher's, could you? The only metal I ever see is copper." He chortled. "If you have it on you, that is."

Mr. Tuck glanced about the tavern's snug, but today, we were its only occupants. Once satisfied no one was watching, he pulled out a tiny pouch, such as one for keepsakes. He withdrew from this a coin, about an inch across, that caught the light. Gold spangles fell across Daniel's fingers as he reached for it.

"Now that's a lovely sight." Daniel's backstreet accent grew as he laid the coin on his palm. "There's the queen, plain as day. And a pretty design on the back." He flipped the coin and squinted at it. "Chap on a horse, fighting some beast."

"St. George and the dragon," Mr. Tuck said, pained.

Daniel turned the gold piece to the front again. *"Victoria,"* he read painstakingly. *"Britannia Reg.* What's that bit mean?"

"Reg is *Regina."* Mr. Tuck's mouth tightened. "Latin for *Queen.* Britannia is Britain, as you know."

"Course it is. Course it is." Daniel continued to admire the coin, then deftly flicked it across his fingers. "And Mr. Bristow had a whole bag of these?"

"I don't know how many he had." Mr. Tuck reached for his coin. "He never told me."

Daniel took the velvet pouch from the table, slid the coin into it, and dropped the pouch into Mr. Tuck's coat pocket, patting it as though assuring Mr. Tuck it was safe. The sudden absence of the gold made the drab room appear shabbier still.

"Would be nice if we could find out, eh?"

Daniel said. "For Mrs. Bristow's sake, that is." He grinned at Charlotte, who nearly simpered under his smile.

"I would like to help her, yes," Mr. Tuck said coolly, clearly displeased at Daniel's flirtatious manner. "If you discover anything, you must tell me immediately."

"Course I will." Daniel's eyes went wide. "You can count on me. Any fee I get out of this comes from Mrs. Holloway." He sent me a wink, which I pretended to ignore.

Mr. Tuck rose, and Charlotte hurriedly leapt up beside him. "Then good day to you," Mr. Tuck said to Daniel, who politely got to his feet, as did I. "You may send word to me at Lime Court, just off Leadenhall Street."

"I make deliveries near there, so it's no bother. Good evening, sir." Daniel stuck out his hand, which Mr. Tuck shook firmly.

Daniel bowed to Charlotte, who shot him a hesitant smile, then me a wary glance, before she left the snug, arm in arm with Mr. Tuck.

Daniel finished his pint without hurrying, while I sat in silence, not bothering with the bitter dregs of my now-cool tea. Once his glass was empty, Daniel gave the barmaid a few coppers—Mr. Tuck and Charlotte had left us to pay up—and escorted me out.

A sharp whistle from Daniel brought a hansom cab, driven by Daniel's friend Lewis. "Mount

204

Street," he said, after cordially greeting the cabbie. "Let us convey Mrs. Holloway home on time."

Lewis had the cab moving at a smart clip north toward Oxford Street as soon as we'd settled in.

"Was it real?" I asked as the cab swept along, Lewis's abrupt left turn causing me to lean into Daniel.

"The sovereign?" Daniel's arm seemed to find its way around my shoulders. "Oh yes." He pulled a coin from his pocket, the flash of gold stunning me.

"Daniel." I snatched it from him and studied it. Sure enough, I held the very sovereign that Mr. Tuck had showed us. "You took this? He'll come after you."

"I switched it," Daniel answered calmly. "I gave him back a gold sovereign, one very much like this one. He won't know the difference unless he studies it closely, and in any case, its value is the same. And the one he has now isn't part of a stolen cache. I've saved him from imprisonment, or at least from close questioning by a magistrate."

"You should not have done it," I began.

"Why not? It's stolen goods he shouldn't have. I'm the one who's out a quid."

"Which you prepared specially for this encounter?" I studied the coin, an entire pound in beautiful gold. If Joe had acquired even a dozen of these, he'd have been a rich man. "This is why you wanted to speak to Mr. Tuck. Not to drag more information from him, which he did not have anyway."

"I prepared for the opportunity," Daniel said. "He told you he'd seen the coins, and I wagered with myself that Bristow would have let Tuck keep one, either to boast or to prove he had the gold, so Tuck would insure it. Tuck seems wise enough to realize that if he flashed a stolen coin, he'd be arrested, so I guessed he had hung on to it. Waiting to reunite it with the others."

I handed the sovereign back to Daniel with some reluctance. What I couldn't buy with that—the clothes Grace needed, a new frock for myself, with money left over to go into my fund for the tea shop.

"He wouldn't be able to spend any of it," I said. "A bag of stolen coins is worse than a single one."

Daniel slid the coin out of sight. "I am thinking he and Charlotte will try to abscond with their share—if we find it—to the Continent. I imagine the Royal Mint will want the coins back, so no, you won't be able to keep any of them either. But, there might be a reward for their return."

His confident expression made me more hopeful. If anyone could pry a reward out of the tightfisted Mint, it was Daniel McAdam.

"What will you do with that?" I gestured to his pocket.

"Take it to a chap I know." Daniel patted his coat. "He can put me in touch with a man in the Goldsmiths' Company."

"What about the insurance scam with the warehouse fire?" I asked. "Have you looked into that? And the embezzlement?"

"I have," Daniel said as the cab rocked along Oxford Street. "Especially the insurance, as Mr. Tuck's job could put him close to it. But the firm he works with is not the one who insured the warehouse, and this coin has me thinking we've found the correct case with the Goldsmiths."

"I walked by their building today. It's impenetrable," I said gloomily. "One small door, which is guarded. People hurried past but none tried to enter."

"It's a closed club, like all guilds are. Not much different from gentleman's clubs in St. James's. You are either sponsored and accepted or blackballed, the door barred to you."

I peered at him. "Have you been in a gentleman's club in St. James's?"

Daniel contrived a modest demeanor. "One or two. As a guest, of course. Terribly honored, and all that." He briefly took on the tones of an upper-class gent. "No matter how good my guises, I'd never be admitted as a member. The boards of these clubs know everyone's lineage without fail. Only the pedigreed allowed. I can only invent so much."

"What are they like?" I asked with interest.

"Stuffy. Full of prideful gentlemen who've known one another from boyhood. But valuable information flows there—financial, political, international. Nations have risen and fallen by what men discuss in the clubs, even more than what they say sitting on their rumps in Parliament." His eyes twinkled. "The food, though, is nothing to what you cook."

"Very flattering." I tingled with his nearness, though I tried not to. "Why are you helping me?" I asked abruptly.

Daniel sat up straight, removing his warm arm from around me. "Pardon? I always help with your investigations. Happy to."

"But this is about my life. There is no lady being poisoned, or antiquities going missing, or a young woman killed—nothing you'd be sent to investigate. This is my deceased husband, who was not my husband, and money he might or might not have come to possess, a very long time ago."

Daniel studied me quietly. "I am helping you because it *is* about your life. And I know that poking into the past can be dangerous, especially when it involves large sums of money. I can't let you do that alone."

"I am thinking of our quarrel. You were angry at me for not . . . wanting what you want. I thought you'd be finished with me."

I didn't mean to say those words—I hoped we could return to the way we'd been, comfortable together, exchanging tenderness when the time called for it, laughing together when it did not.

But I could only be honest with myself, and with Daniel. I had to understand his intentions.

Not quite honest, I chided myself. I did want what Daniel wanted, intensely so. And yet, that longing terrified me. I'd given myself up once and had paid an awful price.

I knew Daniel was *not* Joe, nothing like him at all. But when a woman married, she was bound to that man, whether he was good for her or not. There was no way out, except through scandal so great I'd never work again, and my daughter might be taken from me as a consequence.

I did not know who Daniel truly was. Mr. Fielding told me he'd been many people, taking a different name when it suited him. Violent with the frustration of youth, and then when he grew older, beguiling and coercing at the same time.

I knew him, and I did not.

"I'll never be finished with you, Kat," Daniel said, answering my statement. "I know I should walk away from you, but I can't seem to do so. I understand your objection to me, and I do not blame you for your mistrust. I can only promise—" He broke off. "No, I can't promise anything. I have no right to. But know this, Kat Holloway." He took my hands, pressing them firmly. "I will look after you and do my best to keep you from the danger you run headlong into. I ask for nothing in return. I'll do it, because I love you."

All breath left my body. Had he said what I'd just heard?

I opened and closed my mouth, trying to form an answer. *Nonsense,* I ought to say, and scoff at his sentimentality. *Don't go on so.*

Or I could say, *I love you too.*

No sound came out of my parched throat. I could only stare at him, lips parted. I must have looked like a gaping fish.

"You do not have to care for me in return." Daniel's voice hardened. "You wanted an explanation for why I stay. That is it. I will not press my attentions on you. What I'd do for you is what I'd do for my son, what you'd do for your daughter. For the same reasons."

I stared at him in silence as Lewis shot us around the corner to Duke Street, making his way to Grosvenor Square. The hansom rocked, but I braced myself this time so as not to be thrown against Daniel.

Instead, I took his face between my gloved hands and pressed a firm kiss to his lips.

18

Daniel started under my assault. For a moment, he did nothing, then abruptly he grasped my arms in a fierce embrace and kissed me with an intensity I'd never felt from him. My lips parted, and all propriety left me.

If any other man had kissed me so, I'd have struggled away and boxed his ears. But this was Daniel, his passion as strong as mine. Who knew what fires might blaze if we let ourselves ignite them.

Daniel, as he had in my kitchen, eased away first. I continued to cup his face, gazing into his eyes, dark like blue lakes, and he brushed my cheek with his fingertips.

"Kat," he said in a profound whisper.

I realized he brushed away my tears. I don't know why I cried—because of the joy I felt that I'd finally admitted to myself what he meant to me, or because of worry that I'd done so?

The cab halted. "We're on Charles Street, Mrs. Holloway," Lewis called to us.

Lewis knew I liked to alight from the hansom before it reached Mount Street, so I could walk the rest of the way home. Mrs. Bywater did not approve of her staff riding around in hansom cabs. The omnibus or our two feet should be good enough for us.

Daniel released me. His face like stone, he helped me descend, then sent me off with a quiet good-bye. Lewis waved to me, cheerfully unaware of the drama that had just occurred in his cab.

I hastened toward Mount Street, wiping the tears from my face, wetting my lips to cool them. The imprint of Daniel's kiss did not leave me, and I doubted it would for a very long while.

Tess was so busy with the dinner preparations that she barely noticed me pass through the kitchen on my way to change my frock. By the time I descended in my gray work dress, I'd pasted on a neutral expression, hiding the turmoil I felt within.

My mouth had not been swollen, as I'd imagined it would be, though perhaps my lips were a little more pink than usual. I'd patted them with a wetted handkerchief in my chamber, but they did not cool much.

Once back in the kitchen, I settled my apron and began to chop onions, as though I were the apprentice and Tess the cook.

Tess sidled to me, halting a safe distance from my rapidly moving knife. "Caleb came to chat today," she murmured. "He couldn't stay, but said that the three cases we chose were never closed. The money was never found, nor the thieves arrested." Her eyes were round. "Maybe your husband done all three?"

The absurdity of this remark broke through my confused thoughts. "Absolutely not. Joe could never have been the mastermind of three sensational robberies. If he was able to pull off *one,* it was only with great good luck."

Or much help, I amended to myself. Daniel had said that no one entered the Goldsmiths' sanctum without permission. I doubted a rough sailor like Joe would be admitted there, or to the Royal Mint either. That pointed to someone giving him a leg up, either working for the Goldsmiths or the Mint. Perhaps one man in each place? Agreeing to split the takings?

"That is excellent information, Tess," I told her. "Please convey my thanks to Constable Greene."

"He can poke around some more if you like. Find out who investigated what, and if they know anything more. He's interested."

"No," I said quickly. "He has done enough. I do not want to find Inspector McGregor on my doorstep again. That man unnerves me." Inspector McGregor had investigated the embezzlement, Daniel had told me. I doubted he'd thank me for looking into it.

Tess shuddered. "Me too."

"But he is honest, at least," I added. "Unlike some other coppers I've had dealings with. If I do find out what happened to the money stolen from any of these places, I will tell Inspector McGregor first. Or have Daniel tell him."

"No," Tess wailed in distress. "Don't let on to *him*. He won't let you keep any of whatever coin you turn up."

"I was never going to be able to keep it." I'd thought I could for one wild moment, but I knew the world had other ideas. "It doesn't belong to me, nor to Charlotte, and it never belonged to Joe. There might be a reward, Daniel says, which is all we can hope for."

I tried to be philosophical about this, but I admitted to disappointment. The thought of having enough put by so Grace and I could achieve our dreams had been pleasant.

Even in my disappointment, however, I still did want to know what Joe had done and why, and who had dealt the blow that ended his life. Perhaps if I discovered all this, I could truly put his memory behind me.

"But the Bank of England and the Mint and those insurance men don't need all that money," Tess protested. "*You* do. Why shouldn't you have it?"

I set aside the now-diced onion and pulled several carrots to me. "I'm certain many a criminal thinks that very thing. *Why should the duchess have so many diamonds when I only have a few pennies in my pocket?* Perfectly reasonable to steal them, he thinks, no matter how special they are to her. A gift from her mother, perhaps. Or from her son."

"I think the criminal's got a point, Mrs. H." Tess moved back to the capon she began to stuff with bread and sweetmeats. "Why shouldn't he have the diamonds? She has heaps, and maybe his family needs to eat."

"Please tell me you have no desire to rob our mistress." Mr. Davis's voice slid over Tess's as he entered the room in his silent way. "Not that I've caught her wearing diamonds. Too frivolous for her."

Tess reddened. "No, no, Mr. Davis. We were just passing the time of day."

"Conjecturing," I said. "On the motives of the less fortunate. I will need a Côtes du Rhône tonight, please, if it is not too much trouble."

"No trouble at all. I anticipated it when I saw that you planned to make a braised beef dish. I have decanted it."

"Thank you," I said in true appreciation.

"I have come to give you word of that vicar, Mr. Fielding. He was here today, to leave you a message. I am reasonably certain he is sweet on you, Mrs. Holloway. He'd not come around here so often otherwise."

Tess laughed. "He ain't."

"I sincerely doubt it," I said without amusement. "What was the message?"

Mr. Davis handed me a folded paper. "I did not read it. It is private."

I wiped my hands and opened the note. In a few scrawled words, Mr. Fielding indicated he wanted to meet me, tonight, at Grosvenor Chapel. The vicar there was a friend of Daniel's, I knew, and perhaps Mr. Fielding had befriended him, too.

"Never fear, Mr. Davis." I crumpled the paper, marched to the stove, opened its door, and consigned the note to the fire. "He is only reminding me of a charitable donation I promised him. He is persistent."

"I'd had hopes of him," Mr. Davis said. He'd in the past wished that I'd succumb to Mr. Fielding rather than to Daniel. "But I am not certain he is good enough for you either. He is rather unctuous."

"The consequence of having to wheedle money out of people for repairs to the church, I imagine." I returned to the table and my carrots. "I will fend him off with a small token."

"I'm certain you will." Mr. Davis sent me a nod, then floated out of the kitchen.

"What did Mr. Fielding really say?" Tess asked in a low voice after the door of Mr. Davis's pantry had closed.

"He wants to meet me tonight." My knife tapped the board as I chopped the carrots into bits. "I am certain he has news."

Tess's eyes sparkled. "Exciting. I'll fend off anyone who comes looking for you, Mrs. H."

"I doubt they will." I scraped the diced carrots into a nice, neat pile. "Once the house retires, they think very little about me. Now, I must fetch that Côtes du Rhône."

I waited until everyone had gone to their beds except Tess, who was busily preparing the kitchen for tomorrow's breakfast, before I slipped out in hat and coat. I opened the back door and nearly collided with a slim figure in a man's suit scurrying in.

"Lady Cynthia," I exclaimed. "I beg your pardon."

Cynthia swayed a bit unsteadily, and I smelled whiskey and cigar smoke on her breath. Bobby's influence, undoubtedly. That young woman did love her whiskey and tobacco.

Cynthia regarded me with narrowed eyes. "Where are you off to, Mrs. H.? Meeting McAdam?"

"No, indeed." I tried in vain to stem the flooding memory of his kiss in the hansom. "To meet Mr. Fielding, in fact. He says he has news."

Cynthia immediately took my arm. "Then I shall go with you. Can't have a young lady of your reputation out and about unescorted."

She laughed at her own humor and climbed the outside stairs at a pace faster than her apparent inebriation should allow. As she'd hooked her arm firmly through mine, she nearly dragged me along with her.

Fortunately, she let me lead the way once we reached the street. I did not like walking in the dark, and I was rather relieved that Cynthia had come in when she had.

Mount Street was quiet, but when we rounded the corner to South Audley Street, we were met with light and noise from one of the tall houses there. Carriages choked the road, and guests streamed into and out of the house, from which music poured, a lively tune for waltzing. A viscount and viscountess lived in that house, which I knew from my occasional chats with their cook, and Mrs. Bywater followed their social life with interest.

The guests ignored us as we hastened by, heads down. "That's what my aunt wants for me," Cynthia said after we'd passed. "For me to be a grand lady, with soirees every night. Heaven help me."

"You have many friends," I pointed out. "Surely, it would not be a bad thing to invite them to your home for balls and that sort of thing."

"Ha. My closest friends are eccentric blue-stockings. My friends who *have* become society ladies are miserable, holding their heads high while their husbands rush off to their mistresses every night. It is why the viscountess dances so

218

fervently in her ballroom, to fend off the sting of knowing the viscount will slip away to his actress lover when the festivities are done."

"Your views are very cynical. At the same time, you are encouraging me to settle myself with Mr. McAdam."

I again recalled the kiss as I spoke his name, and in my heady state, I nearly missed her answer.

"You and McAdam are a different thing entirely. Marrying for love and friendship is a damned sight better than making a match with a man of the correct lineage and fortune so your relations will cease tormenting you. Your class is far better off than mine in that regard, if you don't mind me saying so."

"You have a blurred view of the working classes, then," I said. "We blunder into unfortunate marriages as readily as you lot do. Only in our case, our husband may not leave us enough to pay for the heating when he runs off to his bit on the side."

"Ah, you'd be amazed at how many aristocrats are nearly penniless, Mrs. H. Land rich and cash poor, as Uncle says. Frantically keeping up appearances while their servants go hungry, and their children shiver in the nursery."

"Mr. Bywater can be very wise," I agreed. "Perhaps we should both strive to remain as we are, then. A happy medium."

"As though either of us has a choice," Cynthia growled. "Here's the church. I suppose we simply go inside?"

The door at the back of the chapel, near the iron gates to the churchyard, stood ajar. A faint light streaming from the crack illuminated the brown brick of the building's facade.

I tentatively pushed open the door and slipped inside. Mr. Fielding turned at my step, revealing a tall and thin man behind him, who wore a parson's collar and dark suit. I recognized him as the vicar of this chapel, who preached gentle sermons from the pulpit every Sunday.

Cynthia recognized him as well. She hunched her shoulders, bowed her head, and backed quickly into the shadows. I wasn't certain the vicar would betray her night wanderings to her aunt and uncle, but she apparently did not want to take that chance.

"Mrs. Holloway," Mr. Fielding exclaimed in delight. "Thank you for coming. The vicar is a friend of McAdam's, and has kindly offered this as a safe place for us to speak."

I curtsied to them both. "It is very kind of you, sir."

"Not at all," the vicar said smoothly. "I know Mr. McAdam well, and he has told me much about you. You may speak freely—I will step into my office and finish my business there. There is a pot of tea for Mrs. Holloway and the young gentleman, though it might be rather cool now. Let me know when you depart, Mr. Fielding, and I will lock up."

So saying, the vicar glided to another door, but his backward glance before he went through it held plenty of intelligence. He knew full well who the "young gentleman" was with me, but he'd chosen to say nothing.

As the vicar closed the door softly behind him, I realized that if he had to let Mr. Fielding into and out of his church, then Daniel, whom I'd met here alone on several occasions, must have his own key.

"Lady Cynthia." Mr. Fielding pressed his hands together and bowed in her direction. "I am honored."

"I'm only escorting Mrs. Holloway," Cynthia said, unfolding herself. "Making sure she comes to no harm."

"Very good of you." Mr. Fielding's eyes danced. "I have discovered much about your deceased husband, Mrs. Holloway. His cronies in Stepney were most forthcoming, especially when I was liberal with the ale. Also, I found the man purporting to be his devoted follower, one Thomas Smith."

"Ah." My heartbeat quickened. "Excellent work, Mr. Fielding."

"She praises me." Mr. Fielding moved his

clasped hands to his chest. "Dear lady, I will treasure your approbation."

"Don't be daft." I'd said those words often enough to Daniel, but with a different inflection. With Mr. Fielding, I could only be exasperated. "Where is he?"

Mr. Fielding left off his obsequious pose and became somber. "There is more. What I discovered about Joe Bristow, Mrs. Holloway, is that his name was not actually Joe Bristow."

19

"Not . . ." I gaped at Mr. Fielding, and Cynthia stared at him in surprise.

"Good Lord," she said. "Then what the devil was it? And why did he tell everyone, including Mrs. H., that he was called Joe?"

Mr. Fielding kept his eyes on me, as though wondering how much he should reveal. I couldn't speak, but I managed to nod at him, hoping he'd understand he should proceed.

"He changed his name because he did not want the shipping company he joined as a sailor knowing that he had spent several years in Australia, courtesy of Her Majesty and a High Court judge."

My mouth went drier still. Mr. Fielding was saying, in his roundabout way, that Joe had been transported as a criminal to one of the penal colonies on the other side of the world. When he'd returned to England, he'd decided to become someone else.

"Jove." Cynthia moved closer to me, her hand on my wrist, as though she feared I'd collapse. I stood rigidly, unable to fall, speak, or do anything else. "Did he come back before he should have?" Cynthia asked. "Was he hiding from the police?"

A convicted person who escaped a penal colony

before his sentence was up would be executed. England had ceased sending convicts to Australia and Tasmania a dozen or so years ago—shortly before I'd met Joe, in fact—but those men and women had still had to finish their time there. Many stayed in Australia once their sentence was done, I'd heard, settling down and working, often for the very plantations they'd labored on as prisoners.

"As far as I can discern, he did finish his term," Mr. Fielding said. "He'd been sentenced to five years labor in Western Australia. His pals told me that when he returned, he vowed he was done with thieving, but he was too well known to find any useful work. So he became Joe Bristow."

"What was his name before?" Cynthia asked. "Do not leave us hanging, Mr. Fielding."

"William Glover."

Mr. Fielding pronounced the words like an omen. He waited, but neither Cynthia nor I reacted. The name meant nothing to me, but I had the feeling Mr. Fielding believed it should.

"Who the devil is William Glover?" Cynthia asked. "Or was, I should say."

Mr. Fielding regarded our ignorance in surprise, then he shook his head. "I am glad you don't know the name, because it means both of you have led blameless lives. Billy Glover was a feared name on the streets when I was growing up on them. Even as a youth—he'd been perhaps a few years older than Daniel and me—he was known as a bully and a brute, but a strangely congenial one. He stole whatever he pleased and persuaded men not to take him to court for it. Beat them if he couldn't talk them into letting him get away with it. No one took Billy lightly. The big criminals—like Naismith—tried to recruit him, but Billy ran his own gang of mates. He was tried and convicted because he robbed the wrong person, did over a well-to-do man of the City who had friends in high places. Threats and coercion did not sway this man, though they must have swayed the judge. Instead of hanging, Billy was sentenced to a penal colony and only given five years."

Now my legs gave way. I found myself sitting on a chair that had suddenly appeared under me, Cynthia hovering anxiously. Mr. Fielding shoved a cup of tea into my hands.

"Not the best stuff, but you'll need it. And this." He removed a flask from his pocket and poured a large dollop into the tea.

I drank obediently, and coughed. It was foul—cold, bitter tea laced with stinging brandy—but I was able to draw a breath.

"I thought I could not have been any more a fool," I said in a hoarse whisper. "You are telling me I married a criminal, one even you stayed clear of, Mr. Fielding."

"I stayed clear of most of them. I wanted my

bones whole." Mr. Fielding put his hand on mine, and his voice turned kind. "Not your fault, dear lady. Glover was a liar through and through, but a very persuasive one. He could be like honey, his old mates say. Also, they claim that when he returned from Australia, he was a different man. The colonies broke him. He declared he'd given up his old ways, wanted to take a regular job and settle down. No one believed him at first, but he did it. Turned to sailing because he'd gotten a taste for it in his travels and wasn't afraid of ships."

"I suppose he did give it up." I took another gulp of the tea and did not cough this time. "I never saw a sign that he stole anything when he was with me. He gave me some of his pay packet—if reluctantly." I sighed. "Until he robbed the Goldsmiths' Company, that is."

"What is this?" Mr. Fielding stared at me. "The Goldsmiths' Company?"

"Have you decided that's the one he did?" Cynthia asked at the same time.

While both watched me worriedly, I disclosed what Daniel and I had discussed after meeting Mr. Tuck. When my speech faltered, Cynthia filled in Mr. Fielding about the three large—and unsolved, according to Caleb—robberies we'd pinpointed from news stories and documents of the day.

"So Billy Glover did the Goldsmiths' job,"

Mr. Fielding mused when I'd finished. "Bloody cheek of him."

"You knew of it?" I asked. I'd never heard of the Goldsmiths' robbery before our investigation. But then, in April of 1870, I'd been preoccupied with worrying about my marriage and the child I carried.

"Was a right hullabaloo," Mr. Fielding said. "Police horribly embarrassed, the Royal Mint and the Goldsmiths' Company enraged—and also humiliated. Many theories were put forth, including that of porters or members of the company itself pulling it off, but nothing came of those ideas. And all this time, it may have been a sailor, late of the penal colonies."

"If he did it, he must have had help," Cynthia declared. "Whoever assisted him might well still have the money, or know what happened to it. Or even killed the man for it."

I could only sit and listen to her ask the questions I ought. I reeled from the knowledge that Joe hadn't truly been Joe. But the calm voice that lurked inside me told me I shouldn't be surprised. Joe had always had quite the gift for lying.

That voice also told me that Daniel changed his guise and his name from time to time as well. I tried to argue that Daniel had his reasons, but Joe obviously had had them too.

Was it my lot to fall for liars and deceivers?

Joe had been a criminal, sentenced to hard labor on the other side of the world. Daniel, according to Mr. Fielding, had committed crimes in his youth and had to change his name to work for the police.

I felt wrung out and limp. I needed time to think through all these things, but Cynthia and Mr. Fielding had gone on discussing the robbery.

". . . Thomas Smith," Mr. Fielding was saying when my awareness swam back to me. "He must have helped, but I doubt he has the money anymore, no matter what Charlotte Bristow claims. I found him in a run-down boardinghouse in the middle of a rookery, an unhappy man. No sign of any cash. I had to drop a few names before he'd even speak to me—before I could enter the rookery at all. Terrible place." He shuddered.

"Will he see Mrs. Holloway?" Cynthia asked him. "He must have a nice lot of information about Mr. Bristow—er, Mr. Glover—and the robberies."

Mr. Fielding shrugged. "I stood him an ale and left him with a donation for his upkeep. I also paid off a moneylender he owed, who decided to send some bullyboys around while I was there. For the sum of one guinea, I was able to clear his debts."

"Then you must be right that he has none of the money," Cynthia said glumly. "Or else he spent it long ago."

"If I had known about the Goldsmiths' job when I spoke to him, I'd have pried more information out of him," Mr. Fielding said. "But I have oiled him enough to go back for more, I think."

"Or else he swindled you." My voice was a croak. Both Cynthia and Mr. Fielding swiveled to me in surprise, as though they'd forgotten my presence. "The bullyboys might have been his mates," I went on. "Touching you for coin, which they split when you were gone."

Mr. Fielding's lips twitched. "A plausible idea, but for two complications. First, as a former swindler myself, I can smell a hoax a mile off. Second, Mr. Smith was truly afraid of these men, no feigning it. I know the moneylender he owed by reputation. Nasty bit of goods."

"Does that moneylender work for Mr. Naismith?" I asked.

"Everyone in Stepney and Bethnal Green works for Naismith," Mr. Fielding said grimly. "He wouldn't tolerate them otherwise."

"Then perhaps *he* took the money from the robbery."

"That is possible, I suppose. Glover never worked for anyone but himself, from what I understood. Preferred to make himself scarce rather than answer to a boss. But if Naismith had got wind of the robbery, he might have beaten the money out of Glover, or Smith."

Cynthia thrust her hands into her coat pockets.

"If Mr. Bristow—I will have to keep calling him that—planned to buy a plantation in Antigua with the proceeds, then he was not worried about sharing the money with anyone else."

"Unless Naismith instructed him to purchase it, but that's wrong for Naismith," Mr. Fielding said with conviction. "He likes to keep his underlings close at hand, where he can intimidate them and have them beaten on a whim. I doubt he'd allow Glover and the money to flee all the way to Antigua."

"But supposing Mr. Bristow actually *did* work for him," Cynthia argued. "What if, after the robbery, which was done at Mr. Naismith's direction, Bristow decided to keep the money for himself? He boards his ship and flees to the islands, well out of Naismith's reach. Bristow buys his plantation then decides to return to England—perhaps to fetch Mrs. Holloway or— I beg your pardon, Mrs. H.—Charlotte. Mr. Naismith gets word that Bristow is back, and in anger, has him killed. The money, if there is any, is in Antigua, invested in a plantation. Unless it can be proved it was bought with stolen funds, I doubt the law could touch it."

Cynthia brightened, as though all I had to do was set sail for the Antilles, claim Joe had left me the plantation, and be rich. She was forgetting that not I but Charlotte, as Joe's legal wife, would reap the benefits. Once Charlotte had this mythical money, would she conveniently forget that she offered to pay me part of what she recovered?

"Lady Cynthia, are you suggesting Mrs. Holloway should benefit by crime?" Mr. Fielding laughed. "I do admire you, my lady. You have a practical bent most aristocrats lack. How is your dear father?"

Their words streamed past me as I lost sense of the conversation. My past and present were tangled together, and I felt sick. I must have faltered because Cynthia's arm was around me before I realized she'd moved to my side.

I felt Mr. Fielding's gaze hard upon me. "Do *not* blame yourself, Mrs. Holloway. As I said before, your husband's lies and double life were not your fault. Men like that leave a trail of victims in their wake and care nothing about it. The fact that you believed in him proves that you are a good person, and not the contrary."

"I agree," Cynthia said in quiet sympathy. "I bless the day my half-mad sister hired you to cook for us. And though I don't like the idea of chaps murdering one another, I'd say this husband of yours, whatever he called himself, got his comeuppance."

Her words warmed some part of me under my numbness. "I must go home," I said.

"Of course you must." Cynthia's strong hand under my elbow helped me to my feet. Mr.

Fielding leapt to my other side to steady me. "A strong cup of tea and a good night's sleep will help you immensely. We'll make sense of it all in the morning."

They walked me to the door. Before Cynthia opened it, I saw Mr. Fielding pass her his flask. As I suspected some of my numbness came from the brandy he'd poured into my tea, I'd have to prevent Cynthia from dosing my cup at home.

"I thank you for your assistance, Mr. Fielding," I managed to say. "Also, please thank the vicar for allowing us the church."

"I am happy to help, my dear Mrs. H. You did me a great service in the past, and I will not ignore that debt. I will look into the Goldsmiths' Company robbery—I know men I can ask about it."

"Daniel is already doing so," I said. "You really have more important tasks, back in the East End."

"Yes, and that is where I plan to investigate. Daniel rubs shoulders with the police, while I keep in touch with the underworld. Someone is bound to know how it all happened, even if it's nothing more than a good story to pass around the pub."

"Do take care," I said in sudden concern. "A robbery like that must involve dangerous persons. Perhaps one of them will not like you raking up the past."

"True, but I am also a dangerous person." Mr.

Fielding grinned as he ushered us out. "I will leave no stone unturned, and I will make that Smith fellow open up to me. He already admires me for showing his creditors the door."

At the cost of a guinea, he'd said. Mr. Fielding did not seem to feel the loss of the money, which a vicar of a poor parish should. I dimly wondered why he could shrug it off.

Cynthia towed me out, and Mr. Fielding, with a final farewell, closed the door behind us. The night was brisk, the wind cooling my skin and awakening me from my stupor.

"I am confounded," I began.

"It is a confounding situation." Cynthia locked her arm through mine, her compassion lending me strength. "Let us get you home."

I feared I'd not sleep a wink, even though Cynthia did slip a drop of brandy into the tea she steeped for me before I could stop her. However, I was so exhausted by it all that I dropped into deep slumber almost before I pulled the covers over my aching body.

I woke with a slight headache and a feeling of unreality. Had I truly learned that my so-called husband hadn't even been the man he'd told me he was? Had his change of name been legal, or had he married Charlotte under false pretenses as well?

My mind spun with questions. I was not

bothered about the money anymore—I doubted the police or the Royal Mint would let me have a penny. Even if Joe had indeed purchased land in Antigua, any funds from it were likely out of my reach. I had made my peace with this knowledge.

Breakfast went as usual. Tess, who'd been abed when I'd arrived home with Cynthia, wordlessly baked bread and chopped herbs for the omelets Mr. Bywater had asked for. We could hardly discuss Mr. Fielding's revelations in a busy kitchen with everyone scurrying in and out. I'd have to tell her all later.

Once Mr. Bywater had departed for the City, and Mrs. Bywater readied herself to make calls, Mr. Davis strode into the kitchen.

"A policeman called and asked to see you, Mrs. Holloway," he announced. "But never mind. I turned him away. He came to the *front* door, if you please. Cheeky sod."

20

I ceased scraping flour from the table and stared at him. My eyes were dry and aching, which told me that in the future, I should avoid brandy in my tea.

"What policeman?" I demanded.

"It weren't Caleb, were it?" Tess broke in anxiously.

"If it had been Constable Greene, I'd have indicated so," Mr. Davis said with his imperious air. "*He* is a polite young man and knows his place. He'd never be so gauche as to ask for Mrs. Holloway at the front door. No, it was a plainclothes person. A detective."

"Inspector McGregor?" As much as I admired the inspector's shrewd competence, I was not inclined to face him so early in the day, while my throat was dry, my tongue thick.

"I did not ask his name, and he did not offer a card. But it wasn't McGregor. I'd have recognized him."

"Perhaps you ought to have inquired why he wanted to see me before you sent him away," I said with a touch of impatience. Daniel, or Caleb himself, might have discovered something and sent a detective with word for me. Or perhaps that detective had worked on one or more of the cases we'd decided to look into.

"I didn't have the chance," Mr. Davis replied, affronted. "I told him to go around to the kitchen, though I said you were very busy, and he should make an appointment. Off he went in a huff. Marched down Mount Street and around the corner, and was gone. Rude bugger."

Having delivered his news, Mr. Davis glided out of the kitchen, back to his own demesne.

"Think this detective will come back?" Tess asked worriedly as we returned to the luncheon preparations.

I shrugged as though it was no matter. "Who knows? Perhaps he was busy as well, and will speak to me another time."

"Suppose." Tess knew better than to continue asking about a matter when I took on my brisk tone. She lowered her voice to a whisper. "Can you tell me what Mr. Fielding said now?"

"Later," I murmured as Sara, the upstairs maid, sailed in, requesting barley water for the mistress.

I did tell Tess all when time allowed, though I did not much want to speak of it. She sensed my unhappiness and curtailed her questions.

I did not hear from either Daniel or Mr. Fielding that day, nor the next, nor on Sunday. I assumed they would seek me when they turned up any new information. I refused to let myself worry about the danger both put themselves in by digging into these crimes for my sake. These thoughts did not bolster my spirits.

The police detective never returned. I wondered about him, but as the weekend wore on and Tess and I were run off our feet preparing meals for the mistress and her charity groups, I forgot about him.

I did manage, however, to speak to James.

That lad turned up, as he often did, eager to run errands for me for extra coin. I remembered Cynthia's admonition that I should interview him about Daniel. I was reluctant to now, as Daniel and I had come to a better understanding—so I hoped—but I found myself studying him as he waited for my instructions.

James had brown eyes instead of Daniel's blue, and his hair held red tints, but his face and expression were much the same as his father's. I invented the necessity for extra potatoes and walked James upstairs with me, a coin for the purchase in my hand.

"How is your father these days?" I asked tentatively.

James's brows went up. "Dad? He's all right."

The typical answer from a youth with his own life on his mind.

I held on to the coin a little longer, while James waited, puzzled. "I mean—what is he like as a father? Do not say *he's all right*. More details, please."

James's grin, so like Daniel's, began to spread across his face. "He's sweet on you. You not

237

falling at his feet came as a blow, the poor man."

My face warmed. I had to wonder how much Daniel had told him. "You're very impertinent."

The grin didn't waver. "You want to know if he's good enough for ya. Don't blame you. I don't think he is, but in truth, he's not a bad bloke, my dad. He's always looked after me, at least, once he knew I was alive. I remember when I met him—he was shocked. Could see it in his face. I mean bowled over, like he'd lost his footing and would never get up again. I was just a tyke, not sure who this geezer was who'd turned up for me. But he was kindness itself from the start. Got me clothes and all the food I wanted— you know I love me victuals, Mrs. H. Found me a place to stay with a good-hearted lady. Told me he was my dad and that he'd look after me now. No question, no denial. I know some lads whose dads won't even admit they're their dads, but mine took me on without turning a hair."

"I'm glad," I said warmly.

"Course, it meant he thought he could tell me what to do." James's eyes lit with amusement. "We had some rows about that. But he was never harsh. His commands were for me own good—I see that now." He spoke with the superiority of a seventeen-year-old looking back on a misspent youth.

"Thank you." I took James's hand and pressed the shilling into it. "Whatever's left from the potatoes, you keep. But find good ones, mind." I pointed a finger at him as he tossed the coin into the air and whooped.

"Right you are, Mrs. H." James sprang away, sprinting down the street with his usual exuberance.

I cared nothing for the potatoes, and I'm certain James knew that. What he'd told me settled some things inside me. A man suddenly saddled with a lad could easily pretend he had nothing to do with siring him.

James resembled Daniel enough that I knew they were father and son, but Daniel could easily have ignored the responsibility to look after James. I knew little about James's mother, or what she'd meant to a very young Daniel, but the fact that he'd taken James in without hesitation spoke much of him.

I returned to the kitchen more at ease than when I'd left it.

On Monday afternoon, I happily climbed out of the stuffy kitchen and made my way to see my daughter.

"May we go to Bow Lane again, Mum?" Grace asked me.

"Wouldn't you rather have a walk somewhere more beautiful?" I replied nervously. "The Embankment Gardens are rather nice. We could find a tea shop nearby for afterward."

"There are tea shops near Bow Lane," Grace pointed out. "Like the one we went to on Thursday."

"But we might see elegant ladies and gentlemen in the Embankment Gardens . . ."

I broke off as Grace studied me shrewdly. I realized I was treating her like a simpleton, because I was uncomfortable with my own past. But now that I knew her father had been even worse than I'd suspected, I was that much more reluctant to talk about him.

I knew, however, that I could not give her excuses forever. "Very well," I said, trying to sound cheerful. "Bow Lane it shall be."

The day was cooler, and both of us buttoned our coats against the wind. It was not far to my girlhood home, and soon Grace and I turned onto the narrow lane.

I decided today to lead her to Mr. Miller's haberdashery. I'd not wanted to go on our last visit, but Mr. Miller was kind, and perhaps visiting his shop would be a good way to ease her into the larger picture of my past.

A lady I did not recognize exited with a parcel as we made to enter. She nodded at me cordially and was gone.

Mr. Miller turned from a shelf behind his counter as the door banged and smiled widely when he beheld me with Grace.

"Welcome, Miss Holloway," he said. "And Miss Bristow."

I winced even as I kept my polite smile. *Bristow* was Grace's registered surname, the one written on the parish record at her christening. If Joe hadn't legally made it his, then Grace's name would be a lie as well. Joe had harmed so many with his machinations, blast him.

"Good day, Mr. Miller," I managed. "Grace and I are revisiting all my old haunts. I lived in rooms above this shop once upon a time," I told Grace.

"Do you think we could see them?" Grace addressed her question to me, having been taught never to directly ask an adult she didn't know for a favor.

"Someone else lives there now," I said at once.

"I could inquire," Mr. Miller offered congenially, and I hid another wince. The last thing I wanted to see were the walls that had enclosed my younger self while I waited for Joe to return, both longing to see him and fearing to.

"I am certain we don't have time today," I said firmly.

"I will inquire." Mr. Miller's helpfulness was determined. "Then whenever you return, I can tell you if the tenants are congenial to it."

"That is very kind of you," I had to answer.

Mr. Miller rested his thin hands on the counter. "Oh, and I must mention, there was a chap here asking after you, Miss Holloway, on Friday it was. Seemed to believe I would know where to find you. I didn't like the look of him, so I was rather terse, I am afraid."

Unfortunately, there were plenty of chaps who could have asked after me that he wouldn't like the look of. Daniel? Mr. Fielding? The elusive Mr. Smith? Another of Joe's mates? Or the mysterious police detective Mr. Davis had turned away?

"Can you describe this man, Mr. Miller?"

"Of course. I never forget a face. He was tall, thin but not spindly, wore spectacles—" Mr. Miller broke off, his eyes widening. "Jove, there he is now."

He pointed through the dusty window to the road, where I saw, to my great alarm, the lean form of Mr. Monaghan, Daniel's cold-eyed guv'nor.

My first instinct was to flee, to plead for Mr. Miller to let us out through the back, no matter how insalubrious the passageway behind this building. Had I been alone, I'd not have been so inclined to run—in fact, I had long wished to say a few things to Mr. Monaghan—but I did not want the man anywhere near my daughter.

But he'd already caught sight of us. Mr. Monaghan started for the door with a long stride, and I leaned to Grace.

"Stay here with Mr. Miller a moment, darling."

I sent Mr. Miller a pointed look, which he understood, bless him.

"Of course," Mr. Miller said breezily. "I have

some new hair ribbons in, Miss Bristow. Let us see which colors you like best."

Grace was not deceived. "Who is that man, Mum?"

"Daniel works for him," I babbled, not wanting to lie. Before Grace could hold me to an explanation, I rushed out the door and onto the lane.

"Mr. Monaghan?" I stepped straight into his path.

Monaghan halted, obviously nonplussed that I'd spoken his name. I felt slightly more confident. He had found out about me, but he hadn't realized I knew all about *him*.

"Katharine Holloway?" he asked. "Or do you call yourself Katharine Bristow?"

"Mrs. Holloway will do." I met his gaze behind the glass lenses, though it was difficult. His eyes, a clear gray, held much anger, subdued under an ice floe. "Are you arresting me? If so, I must know upon exactly what charge, and I will engage the services of a solicitor."

Those eyes flickered. "Should I arrest you?"

"There is absolutely no reason to, but policemen have arrested people erroneously in the past, including myself on one occasion. I will also ask that you include Inspector McGregor and Mr. Daniel McAdam in my interrogation."

"I have read your record, Mrs. Holloway." Monaghan did not move, blocking my way into Bow Lane, and subsequently anyone who might want to enter Mr. Miller's shop. "You were arrested for the murder of your employer and held over for trial, but released for lack of evidence. Did you ever wonder how you were so easily let go?"

"I was innocent," I said with all the dignity I could muster. "Another was proved to be guilty of that crime."

Monaghan's jaw moved in irritation. "McAdam insisted you be released. But *I* was the one who signed the order. You owe your freedom to me."

I fell silent, my breath tight in my chest. I'd known Daniel had procured my liberty, but I'd not thought through who he'd had to convince to make it possible. Daniel had not told me about Monaghan at that time, not until I'd spied him with Daniel at the scene of another crime.

"Then I must thank you," I said stiffly after a moment. "But you see my point. I was wrongly arrested. I would not wish to be again."

"I have not come here to take you to the Yard, if that worries you," Monaghan snapped. "But I do need to speak with you."

He was highly annoyed—I imagine he'd expected me to be cowed and terrified of him. I was, indeed, terrified, but I'd never give him the satisfaction of showing it.

"Should I fetch a solicitor?" I asked in calm tones.

"No." His lips pinched. "Or McAdam either. In fact, this interview should be kept between you and me."

"I see." I of course would go straight to Daniel with this tale, but I kept that to myself. Also, in spite of my worry, I was curious as to what Mr. Monaghan wished to say. "There is a tea shop around the corner in Cheapside. Perhaps we could sit down there."

I thought he'd tell me to go to the devil, perhaps seize me and drag me to some dingy nearby cellar to put me to the question. But after a moment of giving me his icy stare, Mr. Monaghan swung on his heel and began marching up Bow Lane, fully expecting me to follow.

I signaled to Mr. Miller that he should keep Grace occupied for a time, then I lifted my skirt from the muddy street and hurried after the swift form of Mr. Monaghan.

21

In less than a quarter of an hour, I faced the man who was not supposed to know of my existence across a small table in a tea shop.

The middle-class ladies and the respectable poor who'd come in for tea and cakes glanced in puzzlement at the tall, bespectacled man in a crisp black suit, his bowler hat placed on the empty chair beside him. They looked from him to me, whom they recognized as a regular, and then pretended to ignore us, but I could see they wondered. They wondered very much.

The woman who brought the tea and a three-tiered tray of cakes did not hide her disapproval of seeing me with a gentleman who was not Daniel. Perhaps she believed me fast. She slammed down the teapot and clattered the tray to the table, not caring that tea sloshed and one of the petits fours fell to the floor.

"Is she yours?" Monaghan asked after the waitress had stomped off.

I understood whom he meant. "Yes, she is my daughter," I said coldly. I would never give him Grace's name. I lifted the pot of cream to offer it, and when he declined, I trickled dark tea into his cup. "Sugar?"

Monaghan dragged his teacup toward him

without answering. I took my time adding cream to my cup, then tea, and a small lump of sugar. I stirred carefully until the sugar dissolved and the cream turned my tea a uniform pale taupe. Then I tapped the spoon once, twice, three times to the cup and set it quietly on my saucer.

Monaghan watched every tiny move as though affronted by each one. "Is she McAdam's?"

I hoped my expression was withering. "Not that it is your business, but no, Mr. McAdam is not her father." I let my chill gaze tell him what I thought of his assumption that Daniel and I had borne a child together out of wedlock.

"Everything McAdam does is my business." Monaghan took a noisy slurp of tea.

I leaned to him. "And before you ask such an indelicate question, no, I am not his paramour. Mr. McAdam and I are friends." I sat up straight and sipped my tea, which was too strong, but I pretended it was fine. "Now, why have you sought me? And how did you know of my existence at all?" I held up my hand before he could speak. "I know you said you signed the order to have me set free a few years ago, but I do not believe that is all there is to it. I think you did not know my name until very recently."

Daniel had told me that Monaghan knew nothing about me and that he wanted to keep it that way. He feared Monaghan would use me against him. I reasoned that if Monaghan *had* realized Daniel and I had a friendship, no doubt he'd have hounded me before this.

"I did sign the order," Monaghan said waspishly. "I did not know the name of the person McAdam insisted be released."

"But you do now." I set my teacup onto the saucer with a sharp click. "How did I come to your attention?"

Monaghan did not make a show of glancing about the tearoom to see who might be listening, but I could tell he assessed the shop without turning his head. His gaze went to the mirrors on the wall behind me, which reflected the entire room. No doubt, the view was why he'd chosen that seat.

"I lately discovered that someone was very interested in the robbery of the Goldsmiths' Company in the spring of 1870," he said. "The box of papers on the case was recently obtained by a constable. As soon as I was told he'd fetched it, I sought out his sergeant to find out why. Turned out, the sergeant knew nothing of it, nor did Inspector McGregor, whom you, interestingly, wanted present at your interrogation. When I finally had the constable brought to me, he pretended that he was simply learning the police business and interested in old cases—perhaps one day he would try for detective. I can smell a lie a long way off, Mrs. Holloway. He was very good—very, very good—but in the end, he let slip your name."

Oh dear. Poor Caleb. "You must not blame the lad," I said. "Yes, I did ask him about it. But he is a police constable, looking into police business. Surely he should be commended for his initiative."

Monaghan remained ice-cold. "I have no power to dismiss Constable Greene, if that worries you. His sergeant will deal with him." He flicked his fingers dismissively. "I decided to discover who the devil was this Mrs. Holloway, and learned you were a cook, of all people. McGregor filled in the rest—a bothersome woman, he said, but one who sometimes discovered the identities of thieves and murderers. He named culprits you'd helped bring down, even if you are not listed in the reports of those cases. McGregor was surprised I'd not heard of you, since you were such a good friend of, and worked closely with, McAdam."

I thought of Inspector McGregor—a sharp, bad-tempered but intelligent man, who did not like superiors who waved their authority about. He'd likely had no idea that Daniel did not want Monaghan to know about me and had been exasperated by all Monaghan's questions.

While I could not scold him too much about betraying us, I would have to speak to Inspector McGregor. Bothersome woman, indeed.

One thing McGregor had not imparted, and Monaghan hadn't known about, was Grace. Her name was on the parish record of St. Mary-le-Bow, but Monaghan hadn't checked it. Which meant he hadn't looked or realized he needed to. Doubtless he would now.

"Very well, Inspector McGregor told you all he knew," I said. "Then why come to me?"

I sounded composed, but my body quivered. I forced my hand not to shake as I reached for a tiny cake and placed it on my plate.

"I want you to tell me everything you know about the Goldsmiths' robbery, about the two boxes of coins stolen on their way back to the Mint. Who did it, and where are they now?"

I paused in the act of lifting my fork. Mr. Monaghan had just given me two pieces of information I hadn't had before—there had been two boxes of coins stolen, and they'd gone missing on the way out of the Goldsmiths' Hall, not on the way in.

"You have wasted an afternoon following me, Mr. Monaghan," I said. "I don't know who committed the robbery, where those robbers are, or what became of the money. I asked Constable Greene to look at the records precisely because I *didn't* know."

Monaghan's mouth hardened. "I know you believe yourself a clever woman. But I am more

250

clever, Mrs. Holloway. There was a reason you told the constable to help you—ordered him to. Why?"

I tried to shrug. "Curiosity?"

He leaned across the table, tapping it, his long finger coming a little too close to my petit four. "You will tell me everything." His eyes behind his spectacles held cold fire.

I pondered as I deliberately lifted the cake and ate it, dusted off my fingers, and took another sip of tea.

If I mentioned Charlotte, Mr. Tuck, or Mr. Smith, Monaghan would swiftly find them and interrogate them. As much as I disliked Charlotte, I could not bring the wrath of this man down on her, and neither Mr. Tuck nor Mr. Smith deserved it either.

If I told him I believed my husband had been involved, adding who my husband truly had been, he might decide I knew a great deal more than I admitted to. He might even assume I had the money stashed away somewhere. This pleasant tea truly could end with me being escorted to Newgate.

I set down my cup. "I believe you must ask Mr. McAdam."

Monaghan sat up straight in his chair, his rage threatening to destroy his coldness. "McAdam will answer to me, do not worry. Stealing from the Royal Mint involves great penalties, madam. Including ones that will leave your child motherless as well as fatherless."

I lifted my chin, though watery fear laced my heart. "Please do not threaten me, sir. I vow I know nothing of the robbery."

Monaghan went silent a moment, his finger brushing the curve of his cup's handle. I saw him realize that he could not browbeat me for information. He must've counted on me crumpling before him.

His voice was a touch calmer when he spoke again. "You see, Mrs. Holloway, I am always interested when large sums disappear and the police are stymied as to where it went. As you probably know, given what cases McGregor tells me you were involved in."

"I know very little," I said truthfully. Daniel kept his secrets, and Monaghan's too.

"McAdam does try to be discreet," Monaghan said, to my surprise. "But when it comes to a woman, many a man turns into a fool."

I clutched my teacup. "Are you speaking from experience?"

"No." The word was sharp. True, I could not imagine him softening enough to have any feeling akin to caring. "I will tell you this—vast amounts of gold fall into the hands of terrible people, ones who assassinate rulers and overthrow governments. The world teems with such people who, either through misguided idealism or complete madness, will stop at nothing to carry out their plans." He leaned to me again, his voice going deadly quiet. "They murder, they maim, and they hurt innocents such as your daughter, believing their cause justifies it all."

I recalled those few situations I'd found myself in that had clashed with Daniel's work—the gang out to kill the queen, the brutal murders in Dublin, the stolen antiquities scam that had Daniel pretending to be a pawnbroker to catch the thieves—and had turned deadly dangerous. I thought of Grace, waiting fearfully at Mr. Miller's, and mindless mobs, who did not care who they trampled.

"I understand," I said, subdued.

Monaghan tapped the table once more. "The barrier that stops these people is *me*. To do it, I need as much information as possible. I want to know what happened to that money, who took it, and what they intended."

"It was so long ago," I tried. "What does it matter now? Surely, it's long gone."

"Plots can simmer for decades." Monaghan sat up, reaching for his tea, looking almost like a human being. "Trust me. They fester, they build, like a sleeping volcano. The mountain might seem calm on the outside, but inside, it churns and seethes, until one day, the magma bursts forth and destroys all in its path."

It was an apt metaphor, and I shivered. As far

as I knew, Joe had wanted the money purely for selfish reasons, and not to overthrow the British Crown or any other government. He'd been a crook and a liar, but not an anarchist.

But Mr. Monaghan was correct that such people existed, even among London's most respectable citizens, as I'd come to know. A pool of gold would help them buy loyal followers, as well as weapons with which to carry out their schemes. Such men could very well have found a willing dupe in Joe Bristow, or Billy Glover, or whatever name they'd known him as.

I set my defiance aside. "I can honestly say, sir, that I do not know what became of this money. I happened upon the story of the robbery in an old newspaper, and I grew curious. I wondered if the money had ever been recovered or the robbers caught, and so I asked Caleb—Constable Greene, whose beat is on the street where I work—to look up the case. It is the sort of thing that intrigues me, and I wanted to see if I could discover what happened. As Inspector McGregor says, I am a bothersome woman."

It was a glib explanation and very close to the truth.

Monaghan watched me a moment, took another loud sip of tea, and clattered his cup to his saucer. He rose, shoving back his chair, but I remained seated. I would not leap up as though intimidated by him.

He rested both hands on the table, his loose sleeves brushing the backs of his fingers. "You are a liar. Though I think for your own reasons and not because you are a traitor." He lowered his voice. "But I will find out. And if you turn out to be involved in this, God help you, because no one on this earth will be able to." Monaghan fixed his icy gaze on me, then straightened to his full height.

"I look forward to learning what you discover," I said, as though my heart wasn't hammering, my stomach not roiling. "Please relay it to Mr. McAdam. Good day to you, sir."

Monaghan did not answer. He merely stared at me as though he could squash me with a look alone, then turned silently and left me. He pushed open the door, nearly running down a pair of ladies intent on entering, and strode into the street without looking at them.

I exhaled through shaking lips and gulped my too-strong tea. I smiled weakly at the other patrons, and when I simply reached for another petit four and did not seem too upset by the man's abrupt departure, they returned to their own conversations.

I made myself finish the cakes and the tea, then I rose and made my way out after settling up with the still-disapproving waitress. Mr. Monaghan, the snake, had left me to pay the bill.

• • •

As soon as I neared Mr. Miller's shop, Grace burst from it and dashed to me. She threw her arms around me, and I gathered her close.

Grace soon pushed away, scraping straggling hair from her face. "Are you all right, Mum?"

"Yes, indeed. Nothing to be alarmed about." I tugged Grace back to me, wanting my arms around her. "The man only wished to speak to me."

Grace was skeptical, but she did not argue. I saw the reason for her silence when I beheld not only Mr. Miller behind her but several of his customers, and unhappily, Nettie Sheppard the greengrocer, who'd trotted up the lane to see what the fuss was about.

"He didn't look like no gentleman to me," Nettie declared. "Can't be up to any good lurking around here."

Nettie could barely have seen the man, even if she'd been peering hard from the doorway of her shop.

"He works with the police." I wasn't certain why I imparted that information, but perhaps it would make Nettie cease her loud speculations.

"Mum sometimes helps them," Grace said proudly.

Nettie did close her mouth. In fact, she paled, took a step back, and then turned on her heel and marched back down the lane toward her shop.

Mr. Miller raised his brows after her swiftly moving form. "Perhaps she's a thief on the run," he joked.

I doubted that Nettie, with her prim and prissy ways, would ever stoop to thieving. But her sudden alarm made me wonder why the mention of the police unnerved her so. I watched her slam the door to her shop as though shutting out the world.

I took Grace back to the Millburns', trying to explain to her on the way that everything was fine. She knew it was not, but she let me rattle on.

"You should talk things over with Mr. McAdam," Grace said as I took my leave of her. "He will know what to do."

Yes, I would indeed speak to Daniel. And Inspector McGregor. I wondered why Inspector McGregor had told Monaghan all about me, though I suppose he had not seen any reason not to.

Daniel could not have kept the secret of his friendship with me for long, in any case. We'd been together much more often this summer, and he'd accompanied me on most of my days out with Grace. Monaghan would have found me out sooner or later.

What incensed me most was not that Monaghan had sought me or accused me of being Daniel's paramour. I was furious with him for confronting me when I'd been with my daughter.

After tea with Joanna, during which neither Grace nor I spoke of what had happened in Bow Lane, I boarded an omnibus to take me west. I hopped out on Piccadilly and walked northward through narrow lanes to Curzon Street, then to South Audley Street and on to Mount Street. Grosvenor Chapel was quiet as I passed it, no one lingering on its porch on a Monday evening.

I'd hoped for a quiet moment to compose myself when I reached my kitchen, but I found it in turmoil. Mrs. Bywater, Mrs. Redfern informed me testily, had decided at the last minute to host a soiree this evening.

It seemed that one of the ladies in her charity group to train girls to service had begun a rival group, hosting a large party in her home without inviting Mrs. Bywater. Incensed, Mrs. Bywater had decided she'd have a larger do, inviting all the aristocrats she knew through Lady Cynthia and her family. She'd not only wheedle donations from them but have them lend their names to her cause.

Tess gazed imploringly at me from the work table, where she was surrounded by heaps of vegetables, bowls of dough in various stages, and a mountain of chopped fruit bits.

"I apologize for leaving you to it, Tess," I said as I surveyed the result of her labors.

"I'm managing," Tess said faintly. Her hands were covered in apple and berry juices to which flour and cinnamon had adhered. Her apron was stained with streaks of green from the pile of peppers, brown from the apples, and red from cranberries, the last of which would never come out.

"You've done well." I held in my disquiet at walking into a mess, as Tess appeared on the verge of collapse. "We'll have plenty for the soiree with what you've done here."

Tess did not brighten. "I know how to chop it all up, but I don't know what to *do* with it." Her voice held the hint of a wail.

"Of course you do. It's nothing we haven't cooked before. You've made enough dough for an army—clear off the table and start rolling it out. We'll make fruit tartlets and galettes, and form some of the dough into little bag shapes that we'll stuff with meat hash. Beggar's purses, they're called. Put on a clean apron, and we'll begin."

Tess sagged in relief that I'd taken charge, and I left her to move all the cut fruits and vegetables while I went up to don my work frock.

I changed myself from one person into another, I reflected as I shook out and hung up my brown gown and slid into my daily gray one. I moved from the Kat who had a beautiful daughter and faced down policemen, to the Kat who created the best dishes she could in a dark, hot kitchen at the beck and call of the feckless lady of the house.

Which Kat was the real one? Would I one day become completely one of them, and the other would fade? I did not like that possibility.

Whoever I became, the constant in my life would be Grace. I would take her with me wherever I went, no matter what.

When I returned to the kitchen, Tess had calmed somewhat. She'd donned a laundered pinafore and rolled out dough on the now-clean kitchen table.

She and I worked hard the rest of the evening, cutting the dough and shaping it into tarts in small pans or folding it around meat filling.

"Beggar's purses," Tess said delightedly as we removed the finished pastry bags from the oven. "I bet beggars would be chuffed to find purses like these."

"Indeed, they would," I agreed.

I baked up pieces of leftover dough, basted with butter and dusted with cinnamon, as a treat for later. Not long after that, the footmen and maids carried up tray after tray of our creations to set in the dining room for the guests to feast on.

"I have to tell ya something, Mrs. H." Tess stepped next to me as I began gathering up the remains to make into the servants' supper. "Didn't want to distract you when we was working so hard."

"Mmm?" I turned out the tray of cinnamon pastry scraps to cool, tasting one to make sure it had baked well.

"Caleb came to see me today. He was a bit distressed. He'd been called out by one of the policemen for digging into those old cases."

"Oh," I said, stricken. I set down the warm, buttery, cinnamon-infused pastry. "Tess, I meant to—"

"Funny thing, though," Tess said, not heeding me. "Caleb said he'd never seen the bloke before, didn't even know he was with the police. Anyway, Inspector McGregor hears the ruckus, and he goes in and tells this bloke to stop haranguing his constables, when that constable was only trying to do his job. The pair go at it, with Caleb sitting there trying not to make a sound. Then off they go into an office, where there's more shouting. What do you make of that?"

22

What I made of Tess's story was that Inspector McGregor was a fine man. I almost forgave him for his *bothersome woman* remark.

"Sorry, Mrs. H.," Tess said, winding down. "What were you trying to tell me? I'm always interrupting."

I snatched up the sweet pastry and decided to enjoy it. "Only that I too heard Caleb was caught helping us. And to apologize."

Tess's brows went up. "Why should ya? Caleb thought he was for it, but then Inspector McGregor came back to him and told him he was doing a fine job. The inspector seemed very pleased that Caleb upset the other policeman. He has no idea why."

I crunched the pastry and caught up another piece. "It goes to show that there is as much jostling in the ranks at police stations as there is below stairs in houses."

"I suppose that's true." Tess observed the mess of the kitchen and let out a happy sigh. "You saved the day again, Mrs. H. Or rather, the evening."

"It is only a matter of experience," I replied modestly. "And you were an immense help."

I left Tess to congratulate herself and me as she

helped Elsie carry dirty pans and platters to the sink, and I turned to scrub up the table and shut down the kitchen for the night.

When I emerged from the house much later with my basket to hand out food scraps to the hungry men and women who waited for me, I thought I saw a figure across the street, one that flitted out of sight as soon as I turned my head.

It was not Daniel, and I wondered if Mr. Monaghan had sent a spy to watch my comings and goings. He must have done, to know I'd go out today to see Grace. I recalled how I'd felt a prickle on the back of my neck when I'd walked Grace home on Thursday, and I knew he or an underling must have been following me then.

If I discovered he had put people to watch Grace and the Millburns' house, I would have something to say about it. I'd face down that cold man again if he dared put my daughter in danger.

I set aside my anger to hand out the food to the less fortunate, wrapped in scraps of cloth they could use to wipe their hands and faces after. I knew some of them by now and greeted them by name and asked after their families, if they had them.

When I returned to the kitchen, I found myself quite tired after my afternoon facing Mr. Monaghan and then having to hastily prepare for the soiree. Mr. Davis reported that the guests had swooped upon the trays and devoured every morsel, like starlings going after the best fish. And, he added gleefully, they'd drunk up every drop of Amontillado. "Beastly stuff," he finished. "I'll discourage Lord Rankin from laying any more in."

Though I was exhausted, I sat up alone after Tess retired, making notes on the pastries, and feasting on leftover beggar's purses and more tart crust. My notebook, splotched and stained from years of jottings, was why I'd been able to assess what Tess had prepared and decide quickly what could be made with it all.

When the knock came on the back door, I laid down my pencil and cautiously made my way to answer it.

My relief when I saw Daniel was great. I pulled him inside quickly, closing and locking the door behind him. He sent me a quizzical glance but said nothing as he followed me to the table. Silently, I pushed a plate with a galette and a beggar's purse on it at him, along with a fork.

"Something has happened." Daniel sat down with me, but he did not lift the fork and tuck in, a bad sign. "I can see it in your face. Please tell me what."

The words were delivered evenly, a command rather than a plea.

I closed my notebook and folded my arms on the table. "I met Mr. Monaghan today. In Bow Lane, where he had followed me and Grace."

Daniel went utterly still. "He *what?*" he asked quietly.

"I left Grace with a friend and agreed to speak to him in a tea shop."

"A tea shop." Again, Daniel had no inflection in his voice, though I heard the slightest hint of incredulity.

"Please inform him it was a shilling for his share. He rudely neglected to pay up."

I rose to fetch the teakettle, my hands shaking so much that I had to wait a few moments before I dared carry the steaming thing to the table.

Daniel watched me. "What happened?"

I poured the hot water into the teapot, returned the kettle to the stove, and sank down into my seat. As the tea steeped, I related what Monaghan had said to me and what I'd said to him.

"He is convinced I have something to do with the missing gold," I finished. "He believes I will give it to anarchists to bring down the queen or some such nonsense."

I poured tea into the cups I'd brought from the dresser and pushed Daniel's in front of him. He did not reach for it.

I'd seen Daniel angry once or twice, but the rage that rested upon him now was nothing I had ever beheld. He sat very still, his face like thunder, as he uttered a string of foul and low-voiced words.

When Daniel ceased his tirade, he regarded me steadily. "He will not trouble you again."

I blew across my tea to cool it, and sipped. Much better stuff than the tea shop served. "I believe he might. He seems a very powerful person."

"After I speak with him, he will not come nigh you. This I promise." The words were stony, final.

"Please, say nothing, Daniel," I said in worry. "I have already plunged Caleb into trouble. I do not want you to answer for my meddling as well. I know Monaghan holds your life in his hands."

"Nothing as dramatic as that." Daniel drew a sharp breath. "*I* might be paying off a debt, but *you* are not. You have nothing to do with any of this, except for an unfortunate connection to me."

"I do not consider it unfortunate." I lifted my cup.

Daniel stopped, his throat moving the slightest bit. He remained silent a few moments, and I self-consciously sipped tea.

"You say the most astonishing things at the strangest moments," he said in a hushed tone.

"I see no reason for my statement to be astonishing. My connection to you is not unfortunate. It has brought me much happiness."

That was the stark truth. When Daniel had stepped into my kitchen a few years ago on his delivery rounds and sent me his warm smile, something in me had awakened.

I wasn't inclined to send that part of me back to sleep. Once I'd come to know him, after a few shocks resulting from him disguising himself to do jobs for the police, our friendship had deepened, understanding growing.

Very different from what I'd had with Joe. Both men had practiced deception, but Joe had done it to advance himself, and Daniel to protect others.

Daniel shoved back his chair and rose. Startled, I scrambled to my feet, wondering why he moved so abruptly.

He glared at me, his blue eyes hot. "Damn you, Kat."

I blinked at him, my lips parted in confusion. "What on earth is the matter?"

Daniel leaned his fists on the table, coming close to me, while holding himself away at the same time. "You say such words to me, as though they are nothing. Then you wonder why I assume you care for me."

He continued to glare as I gaped at him, then he turned and strode to the scullery and through it, boots loud on the flagstones. He wrenched open the back door and banged it behind him as he went.

The draft scurried across the kitchen, making my hair dance before it faded.

I sat down hard on my chair, hands shaking as I reached for my teacup.

"Daft man," I whispered.

In the morning, Tess and I cooked breakfast as usual. I said nothing to her about Daniel's visit, as I was still unnerved by it. Daniel had been very, very angry about Monaghan approaching me, and I fretted about what he would do.

The day proceeded quietly. Mr. Bywater went off to his office. Mrs. Redfern told me Mrs. Bywater would be out all day, calling on her friends. She was gathering them to oppose the group that had formed without her, Mrs. Redfern finished in amusement. Only a light luncheon for Lady Cynthia would be called for.

It was a relief after the scramble the previous evening. I confess we prepared a luncheon of leftovers for Lady Cynthia.

I took the opportunity after the luncheon went up to step out of the house and walk along Mount Street. I presently found Caleb, who was walking his beat—strolling along, touching his hat to ladies, and keeping an eye out for undesirables in the neighborhood.

Caleb's was a fairly easy beat. Few burglars wanted to tackle the immense houses in this busy district in broad daylight, each with a dozen staff ready to beat them off.

Caleb touched his helmet and nodded a greeting as I approached him.

"Constable Greene," I said. "I wish to apologize to you. Tess told me what happened with Inspector McGregor yesterday."

Caleb had a round face nearly hidden between the helmet that pressed down on his forehead and the thick chinstrap that held it in place. The bit of face I could see flushed. "Makes no difference, ma'am. The cases were interesting, and Inspector McGregor is pleased with me."

"That is true, though I am distressed you had a dressing-down. But no matter." I held up my hand as Caleb seemed about to apologize to *me*. "Will you do me another favor? This one is less onerous. I would like to speak to Inspector McGregor. Can you inform him?"

Caleb's gape told me he thought I'd run mad, then he closed his mouth and swallowed. "Do you want him to come here, ma'am?" He gazed at the house behind me in trepidation.

"I can attend him in his office if it is more convenient." I disliked visiting Scotland Yard, but needs must. "On Thursday morning, say at nine o'clock. But he must be prompt, because I have much to do on Thursday."

Caleb listened in consternation. "I will ask him, ma'am."

I summoned a weak smile. "You can tell him that the bothersome woman would appreciate him letting her bother him once again."

Caleb backed a step. "I don't think I can say that to the inspector, Mrs. Holloway."

"I am teasing, do not worry. If nine on Thursday is impossible for him, he may visit me here today or tomorrow, but he must come to the back door." I did not want to risk Mr. Davis sending him away or disdainfully pointing out he should have descended the outside stairs.

Caleb nodded hastily. "I will give him the message. But I can't until four. My beat's not over until then."

"That is no matter. Here." I removed from my pocket a wrapped packet of galettes from last night and handed them to him. "In case you get hungry."

Caleb brightened as he took the cakes. "I shouldn't but . . . Thank you, Mrs. Holloway." His face grew redder. "Will you . . . um . . . give Tess—Miss Parsons—my regards?"

I resisted the urge to pat his arm. "I will indeed. Thank you, Caleb. I promise I will cease getting you into trouble."

His grin flashed. "I don't mind. I like helping Tess. I mean you, ma'am."

"You are a good lad. Now, carry on."

I left him then, and he began to whistle as he continued his amble along Mount Street.

When I entered the kitchen again, Mr. Davis was waiting for me rather impatiently. "Having a stroll, Mrs. Holloway?" he asked. "In the rain?"

It had barely begun sprinkling. "Fresh air never does a body any harm."

"The air in London is not fresh," Mr. Davis pointed out. "Smoky and smelly." He sniffed. "Mr. Thanos has come to call. Lady Cynthia is giving him lunch, but the master and mistress are not home. It might be best if you went up to chaperone."

"Chaperone?" I repeated. Tess had been bringing out the supplies for supper's preparation, and I would have much work to do, as much as I enjoyed Mr. Thanos's company. "Mrs. Redfern or one of the maids can chaperone."

"Mrs. Redfern is quite busy—Mrs. Bywater wants all the linens gone through and mended or replaced. The maids are helping her, and besides, those young ladies might look the other way if there were any goings-on. They are romantic." Mr. Davis gazed heavenward.

"I doubt Mr. Thanos would instigate any goings-on," I said. "But very well, I take your point. If Mrs. Bywater heard they met alone in her house, she'd be incensed."

"Maybe he'd have to marry her," Tess put in happily. "That would be wonderful. Stay downstairs, Mrs. H., and let them kiss if they like."

Mr. Davis snorted. "The mistress would be more inclined to pack Cynthia back to the country and have Mr. Thanos dismissed from his post

271

than let them marry. Off you go, Mrs. Holloway. Save the young people's reputations."

I agreed with Mr. Davis that Mrs. Bywater would more likely try to prevent the match than force it. I certainly did not want Mr. Thanos in trouble for behaving immorally—in Mrs. Bywater's opinion—or Cynthia sent to Hertfordshire, never to be seen in this house again.

I hung up my apron, smoothed my frock, and went up the back stairs.

The house above was silent, save for a clock ticking in hushed tones somewhere on a landing. Mrs. Redfern and the maids must be going through the cupboards upstairs, diligently performing Mrs. Bywater's inventory of the linens.

Cynthia and Mr. Thanos were seated in the dining room, a footman just serving them the last of the pudding. Mr. Thanos leapt to his feet as I entered.

"Mrs. Holloway. I must say, I've never had a finer feast," he said. "I thank you from the bottom of my heart."

Mr. Thanos made me a gallant bow, to the amusement of the footman. I sent the lad away and closed the door.

I didn't have the heart to tell Mr. Thanos he'd been fed only the extras from last night's soiree. I thanked him politely.

"I invited Thanos for a chat today," Cynthia said. She wore a frock this afternoon, one of the simpler garments Miss Townsend had recommended she have made. The trim lines and flowing dark blue skirt suited her. "First, because he's fed beastly meals when he dines at the Polytechnic, and second, because I wanted him to speak to you."

"Ah." I hid my disappointment that Cynthia had not sought time alone with Mr. Thanos—even chaperoned—and turned my gaze to him. "What about, Mr. Thanos?"

"McAdam," he said promptly. "Cyn—I mean, Lady Cynthia—says you want to hear everything I know about him."

23

I remained awkwardly in the space between table and door, my fingers curling to my palms.

"Please, do not trouble yourself, Mr. Thanos," I said.

"It is not a bother." Mr. Thanos seemed surprised I'd think it would be. "Lady Cynthia told me that you and McAdam have had a misunderstanding." His face reddened, but he regarded me resolutely. "I agree he can be a bit unfathomable at times, and also dashed stubborn."

Mr. Thanos's exasperation when he uttered this last was sincere. I relaxed a bit and sent him a tiny smile. "Indeed, he can be."

"Do sit down, Mrs. H." Cynthia jumped to her feet and pulled out the chair beside her. "No one is about."

After checking the hall to make sure the footman had truly gone, I pulled forward an extra chair that rested next to the sideboard, ignoring Cynthia's offered one. If Mrs. Redfern, or heaven forbid, the mistress, entered and saw me sitting familiarly at the dining room table, I'd be, at best, subject to a tedious lecture about knowing my place, or at worst, sacked on the spot.

I understood my place quite well and seated

myself on the chair a good foot from the table. "This is most comfortable."

Cynthia was not pleased with me, but restored the other chair and resumed hers.

"I asked Thanos if he'd mind telling all about McAdam," Cynthia said, her voice light.

"It really is not necessary, Mr. Thanos," I tried again.

"I believe it is." Mr. Thanos surprised me with his answer, delivered somberly. "McAdam is a good friend—one of the best I've had—and he is a good man. I am also fond of you, Mrs. Holloway, if you do not mind me saying so. I do not like to see the two of you falling out."

"We have restored our friendship," I said. "I believe." Daniel had not been happy when he'd rushed off last night, but he hadn't intimated he'd not return this time.

"Even so." Mr. Thanos rested his elbows on the table and twined his fingers together. Several plates remained near him, but they were quite empty, not a crumb gracing their surfaces. "I met McAdam at Cambridge, as you know. He wasn't a student—he had a job in the gardens at King's, always with a pleasant word for anyone who passed. I met him in a typical fashion for me— I'd dropped an armload of books while I was hurrying along a path, and got tangled in my own robe. McAdam helped me retrieve all the books, and he organized them better than I ever could.

I was astonished when he read the titles and started talking about what was inside the books, including ones in Latin. I grew interested in him, and I invited him to my rooms."

Mr. Thanos would, without realizing anyone would express horror that a gardening assistant was admitted to a student's quarters.

"Did he come?" I asked.

"He did. We had a jolly good chat about Newton and Faraday, and new studies in electromagnetism, which is a favorite subject of mine. I asked where he'd studied all this science, and he laughed and said 'in books.'"

I imagined it, the brilliant Mr. Thanos and the affable Daniel, chattering about sciences. While Daniel did not have the genius that Mr. Thanos had, Daniel was interested in all sorts.

"I encouraged him to attend lectures," Mr. Thanos continued. "Even if he had to sneak in through the back door. I'd spy him in a shadowy corner or up on a balcony, absorbing it all, the way he does. He'd come to my rooms after and we'd discuss the subject. Occasionally, we'd meet at a pub in town where we could speak long into the night. Our friendship grew from there."

"That is a very nice story, Mr. Thanos." I spoke honestly—I liked picturing the two men, ten years younger, earnestly discussing points of learning as they nursed pints. Daniel had once told me he'd been at Cambridge, but roguishly finished the statement by declaring he'd never said he'd been a student there.

"Oh, I'm not finished." Mr. Thanos blinked. "Have I gone and left out the most intriguing part? I have, dash it. I was enjoying the memories."

"Spit it out, Thanos," Cynthia advised him. "Briefly and clearly."

Mr. Thanos sent her a fond glance. "Dear Cyn tells me this quite often. But she is correct—I do tend to be verbose. My lectures have improved since I've taken her advice."

Cynthia flicked her fingers at him, but I noted the happy flush on her cheeks.

"I nearly had to leave university," Mr. Thanos said. "My family is not wealthy, and the money had simply run out. I tried to live frugally, but books, even secondhand ones, are expensive, and one does have to eat once in a while. I was a year from reaching my degree. With it, I could be eligible for good posts, such as the one I have now, but without it—I wasn't certain what I would do. I was at the very top of my class, with the best marks and the most potential, or so my tutors told me. They were very upset when I informed them I could not pay for my last terms, and while they attempted to help, there was little they could do. They tried to find me some sort of post, but I was hopeless at office work." He chuckled.

I'd visited Mr. Thanos's office at the Polytechnic, which had been at sixes and sevens. I hoped Cynthia had made some better sense of it by now.

"What happened?" I prompted. Obviously, Mr. Thanos *had* finished the degree.

"McAdam paid his fees." Cynthia broke in, unable to stop herself.

My eyes widened. "Pardon?"

Mr. Thanos nodded. "He did. Knocked me over with a feather. McAdam noticed my moroseness one day and commanded me to tell him everything. After that, I did not see him for a time, and I feared I never would again—not every man wants a friend who is in penury. Then he visited me in my room and said that all my fees had been paid. I was flabbergasted. I asked him who had been my benefactor. He tried to put me off with some evasive answer, but I ground him down at last. He'd paid the fees himself."

I sat in open-mouthed disbelief, but deep down inside, I was somehow not very surprised. It was just like Daniel to quietly solve a person's direst problems and then try to pretend innocence. He'd done this for me in the past, and I could not be amazed that he'd done it for others.

What I wondered, of course, was where Daniel had obtained the money. A young man's schooling at a Cambridge college was expensive, and I knew that even the best families scrambled to place their sons there. I'd worked for a gentleman who'd mortgaged his estate and hocked everything he could lay his hands on in order to send his son to Jesus College.

Mr. Thanos was pleased with my reaction. "Indeed, I was blown over. I told McAdam he must do no such thing, and to take back his money, but he said it was too late. The deed was done. Where he came into such a fortune, I could not say. I have always hoped that he did not spend the entirety of some inheritance on me, but he always seems to have funds, even if no one would guess it."

Cynthia seemed less worried about this. "McAdam is a clever chap. He might have finagled your stay without having to hand over a thing. I know plenty of titled families who haven't got two ha'pennies to rub together, yet they manage for their sons to have Oxford degrees and a grand tour, and dress to the nines and go to Ascot every year. Not to mention throwing lavish parties. It's a question of leveraging one's connections."

"True," Mr. Thanos said. "But I am a nobody from a forgotten family, and McAdam is no aristocrat."

Daniel, however, did know how to survive and thrive in a world that was decidedly against anyone not from the correct level of society.

"I'm sure he managed," I said. "He always does."

"Very true," Mr. Thanos agreed. "Cyn—er, Lady Cynthia—wished me to tell you that tale. McAdam swore me to secrecy, of course, but we are all friends here."

Cynthia had wanted to prove to me how generous Daniel was, I understood. I was, in truth, quite touched by this benevolence to Mr. Thanos.

"I am glad he helped you," I said with conviction. "Now here you are, a respected tutor at the Polytechnic, famous for your mathematics and your brilliant mind."

Mr. Thanos turned a bright shade of red. "I don't know about all that. But I am dashed grateful to him."

Cynthia had an eye on me, as though expecting me to clasp my hands and declare that Daniel was a wonderful man who had my heart.

"Thank you for telling me, Mr. Thanos," I said without any sign of such melodrama.

"Not at all," Mr. Thanos said cheerfully. "I of course told him I'd pay back every penny, but McAdam won't hear of it. He told me I could repay him by letting him borrow my brain every once in a while." He chuckled.

As I had observed Daniel do on several occasions. He had recruited Mr. Thanos to help on problems we'd faced in the past—Mr. Thanos had used his mathematical skills to illuminate aspects of the cases we hadn't unfolded ourselves.

"I do hope he doesn't feel he's bought and paid for you," I said in some worry.

Mr. Thanos's eyes widened. "Gracious, no. McAdam is an honorable chap. I happily look over problems for him in my gratitude, and even then, he always tries to compensate me for it. When I remind him that he's already done plenty for me, he shrugs, as though he's forgotten about it. Confound him." Mr. Thanos beamed.

"He has been a good mate to you," I said. Daniel, as did Mr. Thanos, liked or disliked people on their merit alone. It was a trait that warmed me to both of them.

"A damned good mate," Cynthia put in. "Now, before we grow too maudlin about the poor man, please, Mrs. H., tell us how the investigation into your husband's missing money is proceeding."

I was happy to change the subject. Cynthia went on that she'd already told Mr. Thanos how Daniel strongly suspected that the Goldsmiths' Company robbery was the one Joe had become involved in, as I'd revealed to her and Mr. Fielding at Grosvenor Chapel.

I added the story about how Daniel had lifted the coin from Mr. Tuck so he could discover its origins. I had not heard what he'd learned about the coin—I wondered if Daniel would have revealed that to me last night before I'd blurted out the news that Monaghan had confronted me.

Cynthia had also told Mr. Thanos about Mr.

Fielding's discovery of Joe's past identity. We discussed that, as well as how we should go forward.

"I have a few things I wish to ask Inspector McGregor," I said. "I bade Caleb to make an appointment with him for me."

"McGregor?" Cynthia repeated, startled. "Are you certain you wish to bring him into this?"

I was not, but I knew I needed to be practical. "He will have information from the police files that we lack, though whether he will tell me anything remains to be seen. I cannot ask poor Caleb to do any more than he's done."

"But if McGregor discovers what you are investigating, the police will take over," Cynthia declared. "If the money is found, I wager you won't get a penny."

"I've rather given up on the idea of receiving any compensation." I toyed with a fold of my skirt. "There is more to this situation than Joe amassing a fortune that was then stolen from him. Joe was a lifelong criminal who possibly robbed coins from the Royal Mint, and then was murdered. It will become a police matter, as it should be."

"I suppose." Cynthia let out a breath, resigned. "I'll accompany you to see Mr. McGregor, if you like. I'll wear a sensible frock and dare him to be rude to a lady."

"He will be rude regardless." I smoothed the

fabric I'd wrinkled. "But it is true he might be less belligerent if you were with me."

"And me," Mr. Thanos said stoutly.

He was right that men, even Inspector McGregor, were most respectful to other men. "I would be pleased to have you there," I said. "But I can only go on Thursday morning."

Mr. Thanos began to agree, then his face fell. "Dash it all, I have a meeting, and I cannot put it off. Another time?"

Cynthia clasped his arm fondly. "Never worry, Thanos. Mrs. H. and I will take Scotland Yard by storm. I will be every inch the earl's daughter, and we will prevail."

Mr. Thanos was not happy he could not gallantly escort her, but he was realistic enough to concede the point.

I noted, as we continued our discussion, going over what we knew, that Mr. Thanos gazed admiringly at Cynthia whenever she spoke, probably not realizing he did it. His affection for her was stronger every time I observed them together.

Cynthia was doing her best to shove me and Daniel together, not noticing that her own romance was progressing as rapidly.

Daniel did not return that evening, nor did he show himself the next day. I told myself that fretting and worrying did no one any good, but

I could not cease picturing Daniel confronting Mr. Monaghan and perhaps being arrested for his pains. Or told to leave England on the moment, or something else dire.

I wished he'd send word, but perhaps he was unable to. I could only stew while I tried to cook to please the family and their guests.

I was tiring of it, I realized. Cooking dish after dish, waiting to learn whether the master and mistress would praise me or dismiss me. Or, worse, come into the kitchen and instruct me exactly what to cook and with which ingredients.

All cooks faced this dilemma, and if I went to another house, it would be the same. The mistress might adore my dishes at first but then tire of them and crave novelty.

I continually put money by for my fantasy of owning a tea shop, but realistically, I doubted I'd ever reach that dream. Leasing a shop in London was costly. We could always leave London for a more pleasant clime, but a shop thrived on custom, and a small village might not provide enough. Villagers were notoriously hesitant to accept outsiders as well.

Besides, London was my home. I'd grown up on its streets and knew every facet of it. It was a city of deep history and much character, a colleague and an enemy at the same time.

I'd stay here, and I'd work, and someday I would be with Grace. I vowed it.

On Thursday morning, I dressed in my best frock and hat, and ventured out to find Cynthia waiting for me next to a hansom around the corner on South Audley Street.

She wore a dark gray gown with a loose skirt and a bodice that fit snugly but not tightly. Absent were bustles and stiff fabrics—instead, the gown flowed around Cynthia's slim form, covering her modestly but not hampering her with ruffles, laces, ribbons, and other things ladies piled onto their clothing.

"Auntie says I look like a nun," Cynthia said as she hopped, unimpeded, into the hansom. White stockings and black lace-up, high-heeled boots flashed before she settled on the seat. "But she's happy I'm in a frock instead of a gentleman's suit."

I climbed into the hansom less exuberantly. "You are lovely. The gown suits you."

"Judith has excellent taste. No one would ever tell her *she* looks like a nun." Cynthia lost her good humor. "I do wish I had her freedom of life. I'd wear any ridiculous gown in exchange for that."

"A fortune, coupled with a strong will, can work wonders," I said. Miss Townsend was a very wealthy young woman.

"I have strong will, but no fortune, alas." Cynthia left off with her moroseness. "Let us see if we can find *you* a fortune. Then I'll live with you wherever you go, and you can tell your friends I'm a poor relation. Ha!"

So cheered, Cynthia shouted for the cabbie to take us to Scotland Yard, and we careened into traffic.

When we entered the large, solid brick building from the lane called Great Scotland Yard, we learned that Inspector McGregor was in and waiting. He received us, rather grudgingly, in his office on the second floor.

He rose when we entered and gave Cynthia a respectful bow. "Your ladyship. Mrs. Holloway." His scowl at me was less respectful, but he gestured to two chairs drawn up before his desk—I suspected he'd put them there for us specially.

As Inspector McGregor continued to frown at me, Cynthia began. "Thank you for seeing us, Inspector. We are interested, as you know, in a few old cases that have taken Mrs. Holloway's attention."

"So I have heard," Inspector McGregor answered with his usual growl. "You want me to explain to you all about the Goldsmiths' Hall robbery in 1870, so says McAdam. Though why you believe you can solve a case a dozen years old, I don't know. If you do have new information about it, I want it."

"I haven't come about that," I said calmly. Both Inspector McGregor and Cynthia started,

Cynthia's brows rising. I looked directly at Inspector McGregor without flinching. "I want you to tell me everything you know about a criminal called Billy Glover."

24

Inspector McGregor's stare intensified, and Cynthia's mouth popped open.

"Billy Glover?" Inspector McGregor demanded. "Why the devil do you want to know about *him?*"

His bluster unnerved me as usual, but I steeled myself. "Do take care with your language, Inspector. There is a lady present. I want to know who Mr. Glover was. What did he do? What became of him?"

McGregor gazed at me a moment longer, then answered in clipped tones.

"William Glover was a bone-breaker and a thief of the worst sort. Robbed people in broad daylight, and had many a man under his thumb, including constables, inspectors, barristers, and judges. Being shipped to a penal colony was too good for him. As far as I know he's still out there, unless someone even harder than he was found him tiresome and killed him. Again, I ask you— why do you wish to know?"

"He did not remain in Australia," I said. "He returned to England once his sentence was finished. He became a man called Joe Bristow. And I married him."

If I'd ever wanted to see Inspector McGregor dumbfounded, I'd have been rewarded now. His jaw dropped, his eyes widened, and his face drained of color.

"I believe you have amazed the inspector," Cynthia said mildly.

"*Married* him?" Inspector McGregor's breath wheezed through his nose. "But your name is Holloway." The words emerged feebly.

"Holloway is my maiden name. I resumed it on Joe's death. Did you not know that fact, Inspector?" I should not have needled him, but after all the times he'd tried to browbeat me, I was enjoying myself.

"No, I did not." Inspector McGregor popped his mouth closed, resuming his usual bad-tempered expression. "Billy Glover became Joe Bristow?" He frowned. "Wait. I know that name."

"Possibly because Joe was killed twelve years ago, in a shipwreck," I said. "Near the same time as an unknown man was murdered in the London Dockyards, that crime unsolved."

Inspector McGregor snarled. "Bloody . . ." He shot a chagrined glance at Cynthia, rose swiftly, strode to the door, and jerked it open. "Anderson," he shouted. "Bring me all the notes on a fellow called Bristow. Christian name Joe. Died about twelve years ago. And all the information we have on Billy Glover."

"Sir," came the response. Inspector McGregor closed the door with a bang and returned to his desk.

"While we wait, you can tell me everything you know." Inspector McGregor seemed pleased he could browbeat me once again.

"That is very little," I said. "I was young when I married him, and quite naive. The reason I wished to speak to you today is because I know barely anything about my former husband at all."

"You lived with the man," Inspector McGregor snapped. "Didn't you?"

"Yes, in a flat in Bow Lane, above a haberdashery. But Joe was not home often, as he'd become a sailor and was gone for months at a time. What little I have learned is that when he returned from serving his sentence in Australia, he considered himself reformed and decided to change his name so he could earn an honest wage. I did not know any of this at the time we married—I only found out this week."

"Reformed," Inspector McGregor repeated skeptically. "Billy Glover wouldn't have reformed if Christ himself came down to him." He peered at me, enraged. "How could you not know you were married to a notorious criminal?"

"Do not admonish her, Inspector," Cynthia broke in. "This is difficult enough for Mrs. Holloway. She is not at fault for anything that man did."

For a moment, I saw a flicker of contrition in the inspector's eyes. "I beg your pardon, Mrs. Holloway. I imagine you were as much a victim of his ways as any other. But, I ask again, how could you not realize?"

I twined my nervous hands in my lap. "I never met any of his old friends. He insisted we take rooms in Bow Lane, where I'd lived as a girl, instead of in his haunts. At the time, I only thought he wanted to please me." My fingers tightened. "If he did any thieving, I never saw sign of it. Mostly, when he was home from his ship, he met his mates at the pub downstairs. I didn't see much of him at all."

"Hmm." Inspector McGregor lifted a charcoal pencil from a tray and scribbled notes on a clean sheet of paper.

A discreet tap on the door was followed by a uniformed man with a thick mustache and matching head of dark hair. Without glancing at me or Cynthia, he laid a shallow wooden box on the inspector's desk.

"Thank you, Anderson," Inspector McGregor said with only a hint of a growl. "That will be all."

"Sir." Anderson came to attention, then turned and departed as silently as he'd entered.

Cynthia and I waited without speaking as Inspector McGregor opened the box and leafed through the papers inside.

"Not much on Joe Bristow," he announced. He peered at me over a lifted sheet. "Says here that he died at sea. Went down on the *Devonshire* in the western Atlantic. A tragedy."

Cynthia answered before I could. "We've discovered that he was actually not on that ship when it sank, but had conveyed himself to London some other way. Then he was found in the London Dockyards with his head coshed in."

Inspector McGregor glared at the form in his hand as though willing it to confirm her statement. "This says nothing about him being killed in the dockyards."

"He was not identified," I said. "Perhaps you ought to check the death of an unknown man there in August of 1870."

Another growl issued from the inspector's throat. "Anderson!" he bellowed.

In a very few moments, the thick-mustached Anderson opened the door. "Sir?"

"Pull records from August 1870. Deaths. Docklands. All of them."

If Anderson was surprised by this request, he made no sign of it. "Yes, sir." He noiselessly closed the door.

Inspector McGregor returned his irritated attention to me. "Might take him a few days to sift through all that. I suggest you go home, and I'll look over what he finds."

I noticed he did not say he'd send word about his conclusions. "He was my husband, Inspector. I would like to know what truly happened to him."

Inspector McGregor made a noise like a grunt. "You will be informed."

"Excellent. Now then, before we rush away as you would like us to, I want to ask you about Mr. Monaghan."

Cynthia shot me a puzzled look, but Inspector McGregor stilled. "Where did you hear that name?"

"From himself." I straightened in my chair. "He approached me and asked me all sorts of questions."

"Questions regarding the Goldsmiths' robbery?" Inspector McGregor's face was like thunder. "Why the devil is he so interested in that?"

"Because I am." I regarded him as calmly as I could. "Because I asked Constable Greene to look into it, unaware that Mr. Monaghan would have his eye on the case. Mr. Monaghan fears the money might be used to fund anarchists."

"He sees anarchists everywhere," Inspector McGregor muttered.

Cynthia broke in. "But who is this Mr. Monaghan?" she asked in bewilderment.

"I regret to say I do not know." Inspector McGregor clearly did not like to admit this. "But I'm only a detective inspector." Too low a rank to know the secrets of the upper echelon, he meant. "Not," he added sternly, "that I would tell you everything about him even if I did know."

"I am merely curious, sir," I said. "He frightened me, and I did not like it." I kept to myself that he'd also frightened Grace, because I did not want to mention her name in this place.

"He has McAdam working for him." Inspector McGregor folded his hands on the desk. "Ask *him*. Now, I am extremely busy, so I would be obliged if you'd go." He flushed as he glanced at Cynthia. "I beg your pardon, your ladyship."

"Not at all." Cynthia brushed aside his rudeness as she rose. "Thank you for taking time to speak to us."

Inspector McGregor sprang to his feet, a follower of polite convention, even if it annoyed him. "Mrs. Holloway, if you discover anything more about the death of Joe Bristow—Billy Glover—or anything about this Goldsmiths' business, you are obligated to report it to me."

"Of course," I said. "But I will ask that you give Constable Greene some credit if the crime is solved. He has been trying to help."

"Just so you report it," McGregor snarled. He went so far as to escort us to the door and open it, likely to hurry us out.

"Anderson," he called to the long-suffering sergeant as Cynthia and I made our way through the outer office. "Bring me everything you can find on the Goldsmiths' robbery."

Cynthia was not content to let the matter lie. As soon as we were heading up Whitehall in another hansom, her questions began.

"Who is this fellow Monaghan? McAdam works for him? Never heard of him. You do play your cards close to your chest, Mrs. H."

I waited until her breath ran out before I answered her quietly. "He accosted me Monday when I was visiting Grace. I know little about him except that he sends Daniel to do dangerous jobs." I fixed her with a gaze. "This must stay a secret, my lady."

Cynthia's fair brows shot together. "As though I parade about London shouting everything you tell me. I would have thought you'd trust me by now."

"My apologies." I knew part of her annoyance was that I'd addressed her formally. I could not bring myself to simply call her *Cynthia,* as she wished. There were lines I would never cross. "Daniel does not want him discussed. I believe what Daniel and this man do is terribly important, even if Mr. Monaghan is ill-mannered and harsh. So please, say nothing."

"Thanos must already know," Cynthia said, subsiding. "McAdam recruits him often enough, the two of them whispering in corners."

Mr. Thanos using his brains to pay his debt to Daniel. "I imagine Mr. Thanos must know some of it. But we should proceed cautiously."

"Agreed." Cynthia folded her arms and said no more. I could see she was annoyed with me, but I knew by now that she was canny enough to understand the dangers Daniel let himself in for.

The hansom reached Trafalgar Square and the jam of carriages and carts in the streets that led to it. The square was more a large open space with several wide thoroughfares spilling from it, large fountains in the center, and, of course, the massive column with Lord Nelson on top, surveying the roads that led south to the river.

Cynthia called for the cabbie to stop, and he pulled to a halt the best he could close to St. Martin-in-the-Fields. "I'll leave you here. I told Judith and Bobby I'd meet them in the National Gallery. Judith loves to stare at old paintings. She'll do it for hours."

She alighted in a flurry of skirts, tossed a coin to the cabbie, and waved a farewell to me. Before I could object to her running off by herself, she had sprinted across traffic to the wide square, heading for the long, ponderous building that housed the National Gallery.

Miss Townsend would look after her, I comforted myself, so I instructed the cabbie to take me on to Cheapside.

I had a pleasant day with Grace, though my thoughts were troubled. She wished to walk to Bow Lane again. I understood her fascination with the place, but I was uneasy, remembering how Mr. Monaghan had accosted us there. I promised Grace nothing and told her we would simply walk.

Our route took us north past the large edifice of the Goldsmiths' Hall. I gazed at its facade, windows neatly pedimented, the doors shut. An uninviting place.

As we passed the front entrance, a well-dressed gentleman was just exiting the building, escorted by several other gentlemen and a uniformed doorman who darted a glance about as though his duties included guarding the place.

The gentlemen spoke to one another a few moments, and the departing man tipped his hat, revealing a thick head of dark hair. A smile flashed in the sunshine, then Daniel turned away and walked in the opposite direction from us along Gresham Street.

Drat the man. I could not hurry after him without drawing attention to him or myself and Grace. Obviously, he'd been visiting the Goldsmiths' Hall purporting to be . . . who knew? Someone from the Royal Mint? Or a bank? Or a collector wanting his gold valuables appraised?

Daniel raised his hand to a cabbie and leapt inside the slowing hansom. The cab turned on the tight street, and the horse trotted off eastward to the heart of the City.

"Was that Mr. McAdam?" Grace leaned to me. "In disguise?" she whispered.

"Apparently." I tried and failed to keep the irritation from my tone. "Shall we walk to the cathedral?"

We soon strolled about St. Paul's Churchyard, admiring the architecture that had been familiar since my childhood. The boys in the nearby school ran behind the fence that blocked it from the road, screaming and shouting at the top of their lungs.

"Are boys always so noisy?" Grace asked with a touch of hauteur. "Matthew and Mark sometimes burst like pent-up teakettles. Mrs. Millburn becomes exasperated."

"They are." Joanna's two sons were bright boys but restless with the energy of sprouting lads. "I am afraid they never grow out of it. Would you not agree?" I called to the man who approached us, the cab he'd descended from rolling away into the traffic.

Daniel tipped his hat to me. "Would I agree with what?"

"That boys are rambunctious for life."

"I would indeed." He fell into step with us but did not take my arm. That would look odd—a gentleman escorting a working-class woman in too friendly a manner.

"You are very handsome today, Mr. McAdam," Grace said admiringly when Daniel greeted her and asked how she fared. "It is a fine suit."

"Thank you, my dear." Daniel pressed his hand to his heart. "Kind words."

"You should dress so every day," Grace went on.

Daniel grinned at her. "Difficult to haul sacks

of flour in a costume like this. I'd be covered in white powder from head to foot."

Grace laughed, covering her mouth as her eyes danced. "Mum would enjoy seeing that, I think."

"I might," I said with good humor. "But I agree that such clothing would be most impractical for honest work."

Daniel sent me a wink. "Yes, I dress well for *dis*honest work."

The question of his abrupt departure from my kitchen and whether he'd confronted Mr. Monaghan hung between us, but it was nothing we could discuss here. Daniel's cheeriness was for Grace's sake, but I spied the anger smoldering in his eyes.

"I presume you went to the Goldsmiths' Hall for a reason," I said.

"I did." Daniel strolled along with us, but kept his head tilted at a pompous angle as though he condescended to speak to one lesser than he. It would have the correct effect for anyone studying us. "I wanted to question someone who knew more about the Goldsmiths' robbery, instead of relying on a police report."

He slanted a glance at Grace, who made no pretense at not listening.

"You may speak freely," I said. "Grace is old enough to know something of this case. Unless there are grisly facts," I added quickly. "Those you may leave out."

I had debated what to tell my daughter about this mess, especially since her father was involved. But Monaghan seeking me out had made up my mind. I would not frighten Grace by hiding things from her. Better she know than for her to lie awake at night, imagining all sorts.

"Very well." Daniel checked his watch as though he had an appointment soon, and returned it to his pocket. "The police had no suspects for the robbery. They did round up several known criminals for questioning, but they couldn't pin it on any of them. According to the reports I have managed to read, the criminals they pulled were astonished, admiring, and envious of whoever had actually done it. But the police were looking in the wrong place."

They'd been searching for thieves they knew, not a man who'd returned from a penal colony and changed his name.

"Did you discover whether someone in the Goldsmiths' Company helped with the robbery?" I asked. "There must have been a man in the know there—someone who could tell the thieves where the boxes would be, or had a key to the strong room where they were kept, or some such thing."

Daniel frowned as though disappointed he couldn't announce this revelation himself. "That is exactly what I was confirming today. The gent I met who is one of the Goldsmiths' Company was happy to talk about their sensational robbery. They suspected a clerk who kept track of valuables that went into and out of the building, claiming he must have given the thieves a duplicate key or let them in, or set aside the boxes for them to take."

My interest quickened. "Did the police question this man?"

Daniel shook his head. "The Goldsmiths sacked him and said nothing. They did not want either the police or journalists getting hold of the fact that someone at the Goldsmiths' Hall might have betrayed them. Their reputation for hundreds of years has been one of absolute trust. One of their own being questioned by Scotland Yard or on trial at the Old Bailey would not have been the thing."

Grace tugged on my hand. She wanted to ask a question, but she'd been taught to never interrupt her elders.

"What is it, love?" I asked.

"Didn't the police ask all the Goldsmiths if someone could have helped?"

"A very apt observation, miss," Daniel said, sending Grace a smile. "The answer is no. Inspector McGregor tried to interview those in the Company, but his superiors refused to let him. McGregor wasn't an inspector then, only a detective constable without much power."

"Why wouldn't they let him?" Grace asked.

"The same reason the Goldsmiths sacked the clerk without telling the police," Daniel answered. "The guild is a very old institution, far older than the police as they are now—the metropolitan force has only been running fifty or so years, and the criminal investigation division less than that. The guilds like to keep their problems private."

"Did the clerk they sacked do it?" I asked. "Shall we speak to him?"

"He's dead, poor chap." Daniel went somber, clasping his hands behind his back. "Went to live with his sister and died of a weak heart a few years later. My Goldsmiths' acquaintance believes he never lived down the shame of his dismissal. Whether he was truly guilty or not, I suppose we will never know."

"Of course we will know," I said stoutly. "We will ask until we discover all."

I had grown annoyed with myself for my former despondency. It was a fine day, Grace was holding my hand, and Daniel did indeed look very handsome walking beside us. I would find out what my husband had done, who had coshed him in the dockyards, and where the blasted money had gone, and hand all the information to Inspector McGregor. He could solve the case and rub Mr. Monaghan's nose in it.

Daniel's brows lifted, but he grinned. "I commend your spiritedness. You are right, my dear Kat. We will find out the truth and clear the poor man's name—if he was innocent."

"As it should be," Grace put in, sounding very like me.

Daniel halted and regarded the pair of us, taking in mother and daughter. His smile widened, and I had the impression he wished to open his arms and embrace us together.

He checked himself, as though remembering he was in disguise, and did no such thing. He laughed, spun in place, recovered his dignity, and led us on.

Daniel left us not long after, and Grace and I continued our outing at one of our favorite tea shops.

Though I was disappointed Daniel could not join us, I pushed aside all thoughts of the police, robbery, and murder to simply enjoy being with my daughter.

We spoke of her studies, and Joanna and her husband, and the games Grace played with Joanna's children. She'd become very close to them, speaking of them as she would brothers and sisters, for which I could be very glad. I'd been an only child myself, and was happy Grace had lads and lasses of her own age to grow up with.

Grace somehow turned the topic to Daniel.

"Mr. McAdam should marry," she announced.

"He is very unsettled, and should have a wife to look after him and James."

I paused, my teacup hovering at my lips. "James is nearly grown. He might object to a new mother who admonishes him to eat his vegetables and put on clean clothes." I sipped.

"Not if that mother was you."

I nearly spit my tea. I gulped it instead, then coughed and buried my face in a napkin. "Grace." I wiped my eyes. "Love."

"It is true." Grace carefully split the last petit four in half with her fork and laid one piece on my plate, the other on hers. "James likes you very much, and so does Mr. McAdam. Mr. McAdam needs a permanent home and looking after, and you are a wonderful cook. Mrs. Millburn says *Mr.* Millburn was nothing remarkable until she took him in hand. Now he's a clerk in the City with a pay packet and a nice home."

I hastily sipped more tea to clear my throat and patted my mouth with my napkin.

"Joanna is a very determined lady," I croaked. "Hers is a different circumstance."

Grace regarded me wisely. "I think you should speak to Mr. McAdam about it." She popped her tiny piece of petit four into her mouth, finished with her declaration.

Grace's clarity of thought astonished me sometimes, but this idea flattened me. I finished the tea and cake, though they now tasted like dust.

"I shall do nothing of the sort." I tried to sound stern—children should not instruct parents what to do, I implied.

Grace paid my admonishment no heed. "I think you ought to, Mum. Once you and he have finished this investigation, of course." She took a serene sip of tea.

I could think of no way to answer her, so I said nothing at all. Grace, thankfully, switched the subject to books she was reading, and soon it was time to return her home. But while she did not continue the topic of me looking after Daniel, I saw her watching me, hope in her eyes.

I thought much about what Grace had said in the next few days, though I tried to keep busy enough to avoid having to ponder too much. The situation was not as simple as Grace, Cynthia, Mr. Thanos, or even Daniel himself wanted me to believe.

I did not see much of Daniel, in any case, the rest of the week, or Lady Cynthia, for that matter. They were pursuing what they needed to pursue, I decided, and made myself use the time to perfect a butter cake with strawberry fondant I was creating to thank Miss Townsend for her help.

On Sunday, Mrs. Bywater peremptorily summoned me upstairs when she returned from church—Mrs. Redfern directed me to the lady's sitting room on the first floor, to which I nervously went. A summons from Mrs. Bywater could mean anything from a lecture to a request for currant tea cakes.

The chamber was small, located in the front of the house. The tall windows were hung with lace curtains that blocked the view of the street without obstructing the light. A sofa with cushions reposed under the windows, a side table strewn with magazines next to it, and a desk and chair graced the wall opposite.

This was not the same sitting room I had entered when I'd first interviewed for my post here two years ago—this was smaller, with a connecting door to Mr. Bywater's study. The other sitting room, belonging to the deceased Lady Rankin, had been shut up at her death, and no one used it now.

Mrs. Bywater rose from the desk, whose surface was bare but for a pen tray and inkstand. She had a letter in hand, a smile on her face.

"Of course you shall go, Mrs. Holloway," she said without preliminary. "At once."

25

"Go?" I asked in bewilderment.

Was she sending me to one of her friends, perhaps to cook for them for the day? For the rest of the year? Ridding herself of me altogether?

"To the East End," Mrs. Bywater said. "So kind of the vicar, and so kind of you to help the bishop in his work for the poor lost souls of the slums."

"Bishop?" I repeated, the answer dawning on me.

Mrs. Bywater flushed with pride. "When I was leaving Grosvenor Chapel this morning, the vicar asked me to wait. I couldn't imagine what for, though I thought he'd ask my opinion on the flowers, which are never quite right, in my view. But when everyone was gone, he stepped to his sacristy and returned with a letter to give to you." She flourished the paper.

I started to reach for it, but Mrs. Bywater held the letter in front of her, preparing to read it out.

Mr. Errol Fielding, suffragan bishop of the East End, commends you, Mrs. Holloway, on your work and donations toward the charities of the parish. To that end, you and Lady Cynthia Shires, also a supporter of our charities, are invited to partake in a luncheon this Sunday at All Saints Church in Shadwell, commencing at one o'clock precisely.

I remain,
Your humble servant,
E. Fielding

Mrs. Bywater beamed as she finished. "Is that not splendid, Mrs. Holloway? I am surprised at Cynthia's contribution, but I believe it was your influence that prompted her. I am afraid I misjudged you, and for that I beg your pardon. Mr. Fielding is such a kind gentleman, so caring of his parish, and he is always singing your praises. So, of course, you must have your luncheon. If you go now, you will arrive just in time."

The only way I could respond to this monologue was to curtsy and try to hide my astonishment.

Mrs. Bywater had made it clear in the past that my friendship with Lady Cynthia must be curbed at all costs. Mr. Fielding, with his devious charm, had now convinced her I was a paragon who, instead of leading Cynthia astray, was guiding her to the path of righteousness.

Mrs. Bywater shooed me out, and I hastened up to my small room to change into my Sunday frock—Mrs. Bywater insisted on that. I kissed my fingers to the small photograph of Grace on my bureau, and went downstairs to find Cynthia waiting for me outside, a hansom halted at the front door.

Cynthia was in high spirits as she climbed in, me barely getting my foot past the wheel before the cabbie started.

"Good old Mr. Fielding," Cynthia crowed. "We should let him settle all our little problems."

"We should not invite such a thing," I said darkly. "We might regret it."

"Rot." Cynthia laughed. "Why not enjoy our lunch?"

I was more interested in the real reason Mr. Fielding had contrived our presence, but I said nothing of that as we rode through the metropolis. It was a lovely September day, and I let myself enjoy the journey.

The buildings changed from lovingly painted and well-trimmed red brick to gray blocks with peeling paint on doors and windows as we headed east. At Whitechapel Road, we turned south and eventually arrived at Mr. Fielding's church in Shadwell.

All Saints was a simple brick building with clear glass windows and a tall steeple reminiscent of Grosvenor Chapel and Bow Bells. Once we descended from the hansom, Cynthia opened the gate in the iron fence that surrounded the church, and we headed for the vicarage behind it.

Mr. Fielding emerged from a door on the side of the church. "Welcome, dear ladies. So good of you to answer my summons."

"Good of you to summon us." Cynthia stuck out her hand, and Mr. Fielding, amused, shook it.

I kept my arms at my sides, and Mr. Fielding, with still more amusement, ushered us on.

A lad burst out from behind the church, slammed into Mr. Fielding, then dodged him and sprinted past us for the gate. Not one of Mr. Fielding's urchins, I saw. The boy was painfully thin in his threadbare clothes, his face smeared with dirt and soot.

"I see you, Arthur Shaw," Mr. Fielding called after him. "Cease running pell-mell before you come to grief."

The lad swung around and nearly ran into the railings. "I wasn't doing nuffink," he shouted.

"You certainly were. That was a valiant attempt at a dip if I ever saw one. An excellent effort but a fruitless one." Mr. Fielding held up his pocketbook in one hand, his watch in the other.

The lad's eyes widened, his expression too innocent. "I wasn't trying to nick nuffink from *you,* sir."

"Never lie, Arthur. Always stick as close to the truth as possible, which will serve you much better." Mr. Fielding returned his belongings to his pockets. "You come to evensong tonight, and I'll forget all about it. After, there will be a large supper for the congregation. Why not bring your whole family?" He held up a finger. "But no nipping out for a smoke during my homily, mind, or it won't count."

Arthur grinned with delight. "Yes, *sir*." He leapt into the air, came down, and dashed through the gate, skimming past a rolling cart with the ease of long experience.

Mr. Fielding shook his head. "That boy will end up in the dock, if he's not careful. Transported far from home, and that will break him."

"It was kind of you to offer him the supper," I said as I watched the lad disappear into the smoke-filled lanes.

"No one in that family gets enough to eat, but they are too proud to take charity," Mr. Fielding said, leading us on. "Five of them live crammed in one room, eking out an existence on whatever factory work they can find. I always host a supper on Sunday nights in the parish hall—at least some of my congregation can have one good meal a week. Their payment, to soothe their pride and mine, is sitting through my service." Mr. Fielding quickened his stride. "I have much to do. I'd never have guessed when I was Arthur's age that Sunday would be my busiest day of the week."

I followed, keeping both my compassion for Mr. Fielding's parishioners and my approbation for Mr. Fielding's actions to myself. He'd known enough deprivation as a lad to understand what his people needed.

Mr. Fielding's housekeeper, Mrs. Hodder, opened the door of the vicarage for us.

"I made him wash, and got him into a clean suit," she confided to me. "One from the charity barrel."

As Mr. Fielding was dressed in his usual tailored and pristine clothing, this declaration puzzled me, but I understood once Mr. Fielding led us into the small dining room.

A small, grizzled-haired man sat at the table, idly examining the fork at his place. I had the notion he'd have slipped it into his pocket, if not for Daniel, who sat across from him in a respectable workingman's suit.

Daniel rose to his feet when he saw us, but the other man remained seated, switching his absorption to the teaspoon. Checking its hallmark, I saw.

Mr. Fielding swept a wide gesture to the man. "My lady, Mrs. Holloway, may I present Mr. Thomas Smith."

"Pleased t' meet yer," Mr. Smith said as he peered more closely at the spoon's handle. "Won't stand up. Half me right leg is missing, and it's a right chore to be getting up and down."

The man could not yet be forty, but his hair had gone gray, his face weathered. His hazel eyes were those of a younger man, but his body was hunched, the hand that clutched the spoon gnarled.

"Do not trouble yourself, sir," Cynthia assured him. "It is quite all right."

She greeted Daniel and sank into the chair he'd pulled out for her, then Daniel slid out another for me.

Mr. Fielding, as he passed Mr. Smith on his way to the head of the table, yanked the teaspoon from Mr. Smith's hand and laid it back on the tablecloth.

"Mr. Smith knew your husband, Mrs. Holloway," Mr. Fielding declared as he took his seat. "In all his manifestations. Tell her, please." He sent Mr. Smith a stern look and signaled Mrs. Hodder to begin serving.

Mr. Smith at last raised his head and directed his gaze to me. In his eyes I read hatred so dark and deep it startled me.

"Tell her what?" Mr. Smith demanded. "This is the bitch what killed me mate."

I froze in the act of taking my seat. I felt Daniel's hands on the back of my chair become dangerously still.

"Now, look here . . ." Cynthia began.

At the same time, Mr. Fielding rocketed from his chair and closed on Mr. Smith. "You keep a civil tongue or I'll put my foot up your backside—I don't care about your bloody leg."

I did not look away from Mr. Smith, who was unaffected by the others' admonitions.

"I beg your pardon?" I asked him. "I killed no

313

one. Joe—or Billy, or whatever you prefer to call him—was struck down at the docks."

"I know," Mr. Smith snarled. "And you did it."

I thumped into my chair. Daniel left me to crowd Mr. Smith on his other side.

"Reconsider your words." Daniel's rumbling command was far more chilling than Mr. Fielding's threats.

Mr. Smith's bravado faltered, and he glanced at Daniel uncertainly. "She must have done it. Because of him lying to her and having another wife, and all."

"Oh, I often considered wringing his neck," I told him. "But at the time of Joe's death, I had no idea he was in England—I believed he'd gone down on the *Devonshire*. I was living in a women's boardinghouse at the time of his true death. I had grown very large and was barely able to move." When Mr. Smith looked blank, I added, "I was expecting a child."

Mr. Smith's mouth puckered as though he found it painful to rearrange his ideas. I reasoned that if Mr. Smith had spent all this time believing I'd gone with Joe to the docks for some odd reason and bashed him over the head, then he himself must be innocent of the deed.

"Ye could have hired someone to do it," he persisted.

"I could have, yes. But I did not. As I say, I thought Joe was already dead at the time. Is that

314

mushroom bisque, Mrs. Hodder? It looks lovely."

Mrs. Hodder readily ladled the brown-gray soup into the bowl in front of me, at the same time shooting an angry scowl at Mr. Smith. Cynthia, by rights, should have been served first, but I realized this would be a rather unconventional meal.

Daniel murmured something into Mr. Smith's ear. Mr. Smith paled, but Mr. Fielding sent Daniel a grim smile. I decided I did not want to know what Daniel had said to him.

Daniel and Mr. Fielding took their seats as Mrs. Hodder filled our bowls in silence. Once she withdrew, Cynthia, as the highest-ranking lady present, took up her spoon, a signal that we could all begin.

I forced some bisque into my mouth. At any other time, I would consider it excellent, but I was far too unnerved to enjoy it.

Mr. Smith slurped without compunction. He even lifted the bowl and drank from it as it grew empty. Mr. Fielding held a napkin to him at arm's length as the man began to wipe his mouth on his dirty sleeve.

Cynthia pretended not to notice. "Well, now that we have all calmed ourselves," she said, "why don't you tell us, Mr. Smith, what Mr. Fielding brought you here to say?"

"He wants me to talk all about Billy Glover. Me best mate." Mr. Smith mopped soup from his lips with the napkin, then blew his nose into it. "We grew up together, Billy and me. Friends since we was tykes."

"Partners in crime," Mr. Fielding suggested.

"Oh aye, Billy were a genius at nicking things," Mr. Smith said, brightening. "Taught me all I knew. That's all I'm saying about that. I know you're all right, Vicar, but I don't want these others rushing to the police trying to fit me up for a job what was over and done with years ago."

"The only job we're interested in is the Goldsmiths' Company robbery," Daniel said. "And how Billy, now known as Joe, did it. We want to know why he went off to Antigua, what he did there, and why he came back, letting people think he'd gone down in his ship. Finish by giving us an account of his last day."

Mr. Smith's eyes widened. "Oh, ye don't want much, do ye? I already told the vicar here, I don't know as much as you'd like me to."

"Tell us what you do remember," Daniel said. "I promise not to fit you up for the Goldsmiths' job—it was many years ago, as you say—but I need the truth. We only want to know what happened."

"What happened to all the money, you mean," Mr. Smith said. "I know some say *I* took it and went off to live life in a palace." He spread his arms. "Look at me. I've barely got a farthing in me pocket, and this is me best suit. The lap of luxury, that's me. Wherever that gold is, I never saw a ha'penny of it."

He finished with a bitterness that made me believe him.

"It was an admirable feat," Mr. Fielding said in admiration. "Two boxes of gold coins from the Royal Mint disappear from under the noses of their guardians, and to this day, no one knows who took them or where they ended up. Brilliant."

Mr. Smith's sour countenance turned pleased. "It were, weren't it? But simple. That was key."

"The best heists are," Mr. Fielding agreed. "None of the shenanigans of the magazine stories or stage productions."

"You're right there." Mr. Smith chuckled. "It were Billy who thought it up. He'd come back from Australia a changed man—sober and broken, ready to work for a living, straight up. He tried Bristol, married a woman there and all, but he loved London. He'd already changed his name before leaving the penal colony, and he decided to risk people in London recognizing him. He looked me up first thing—Billy never kept nothing from me. Besides, he needed a place to stay."

Joe had been quite congenial when he'd wanted to be. I imagined it had been a friendly reunion.

"Did anyone recognize him?" Cynthia asked. "Or was he so changed by the hard labor he'd done?"

"Oh, he weren't much different, not to look at. Brown as a nut and thinner than he'd been, but his old mates knew him. They understood why he'd changed his name, and they weren't about to peach. I'd taken to being a sailor meself, which is how I lost the leg—caught in a winch, it was. Billy needed work, and so I went with him to the docks to recommend him to me old crew, who were in at the time."

"Good of you," Mr. Fielding said.

"That's me. Full of good deeds." Mr. Smith chortled. "Billy'd had experience on the ship back from Australia—when they ran into bad weather, they appreciated all the help they could get, even if it were only watching that the ropes didn't come loose. So Billy, now Joe, became a sailor. Liked it for a while. Told me he'd met a wench in London who wouldn't let him touch her for nothing until she had a ring on her finger. So he pretended to wed her. That were you." Mr. Smith pointed a stubby finger at me.

I sopped up the remains of my soup with a piece of bread and ignored him. Of course I'd insisted on marriage with Joe. I'd had no intention of becoming his tart.

"Billy were content," Mr. Smith went on. "Would nip to Bristol to be with his other family then come back to be with his London missus before he'd hop ship again for foreign parts. But once a thief, always a thief, eh? One day Billy

318

comes to me and says he can get us more money than we'd ever seen, and we'd never have to drudge another hour."

"How did he come by this idea?" Daniel interrupted. "Happened to stumble upon the opportunity, did he?"

"No." Mr. Smith scoffed. "Billy were careful. He'd been nabbed once, but that had been bad luck and a stubborn witness. He never wanted to be sent to the nick again.

"He'd become acquainted with a gent, he told me, who had a cousin what worked in this place called the Goldsmiths' Hall. Gent tells him a story one day, about how every year, the Royal Mint sends off coins to be looked over by some toffs who sit stiffly in their chairs and decide whether the coins are rightly pure enough. They send near fifty thousand of these coins, all locked up in boxes, to lie about in the Goldsmiths' Hall until the men there decide they're all right. Then off they go back to the Mint.

"Billy says, why not help ourselves to some of these coins? Not all of them, mind—every copper in the land would be up in arms about that—but a few could go missing, couldn't they? Billy said he'd take them across the ocean, on his ship, which was heading for Antigua, and buy some land with them. Then when he sold that land, the money would be free and clear, and all ours."

"Hang on." Cynthia pushed aside her soup

bowl. "Wouldn't whoever he bought the land from be suspicious when he handed over pristine gold coins as payment?"

"Billy thought through all that. He'd made friends with men out in the islands who wouldn't ask questions like that. They'd make an investment account for him and then draw up the land agreement, paying the owner in clean money from their funds. Billy would own the plantation fair and square, and do whatever he liked with it."

"Did he actually buy the plantation?" I asked, amazed my voice was so calm. I hadn't been able to speak once Mr. Smith began his story, having to let the others ask the questions.

"He said so." Mr. Smith's petulance returned. "Hadn't sold it yet, though, when he was offed. Like I said, I never saw tuppence from it."

Daniel broke into Mr. Smith's complaint. "I had a telegram yesterday from Antigua confirming that Mr. Joe Bristow had purchased a plantation of two hundred acres not far south of St. John's. The deed was registered by a firm of investment bankers in the town."

"Did the firm know he'd died?" I asked.

Daniel's gaze held mine. "They did. Claimed they were managing the plantation for his heirs. I suspect that this shady investment company— very likely the one that exchanged the money for him—is pocketing whatever they are receiving from renting the place. I requested a copy of the deed, and I believe I've made them nervous."

"Serves them right," Mr. Smith growled. "Keeping the money that should be mine."

"And Mr. Bristow's children's," Cynthia said indignantly.

Mr. Smith's frown deepened. "Aye. Poor tykes."

"So all the money really is in Antigua," I said. "Though the original coins must be long gone."

"Seems like." Mr. Smith sniffed. "Billy might have had some in his pocket when he died—I don't know."

"Let us return to the robbery," Mr. Fielding broke in. "I am interested in the details. You said Bristow learned about the gold coins from the cousin of one of the Goldsmiths. Did that friend's cousin become his inside man?"

"Aye." Mr. Smith nodded. "Had to be talked into it—both of them did—but yes, the cousin of the friend helped Billy set it up. When the boxes were to go back to the Mint, this gent at the Goldsmiths' made certain two were kept back—*after* they were checked off the sheet by the guard who was to load them into the cart. Guard walks out, man hides boxes behind a tapestry and fetches 'em later. Easy as spitting."

"And then handed them over to Bristow?" Mr. Fielding asked.

Mr. Smith nodded, his soup spoon clutched in his hand. "That night, Billy and me came by, and the gent shoved the boxes at us out the back. We were pushing night soil carts—loaded one box into each. Then we just trundled 'em off. Weren't any shit or nuffink in the carts, but who was going to look, eh?" Mr. Smith guffawed, proud of their cleverness.

"The name of this inside man?" Daniel asked in a mild tone.

Mr. Smith shrugged. "I suppose it don't matter now. He never got nuffink for it neither except what Billy tossed him that night. Man by the name of Birkett. Alan Birkett. He were a toff, but not an aristocrat or anything like that. He was respectable by then, but he grew up in the backstreets out Hatton Garden way."

Hatton Garden was not far from Farringdon Road and Clerkenwell. The area was not as desperate as some slums, but it was far from affluent, even if the street of Hatton Garden itself housed jewelers and dealers in diamonds.

"Was Birkett the name of the clerk who got the sack?" I asked Daniel.

He shook his head. "No—his name was Gouldon, and wrongly accused, it looks like, poor chap. I will have to find out if this Birkett is still one of the Goldsmiths or in happy retirement, courtesy of Billy Glover."

"He might be," Mr. Smith said grudgingly. "Like I said, Billy could have had some of the money with him when he came back here.

Don't see him trusting *all* of it to those agents in Antigua. Billy liked to fence his goods here and there, not in one place, ye see."

He pinned me with a belligerent stare. "That's why I thought *you* killed him, missus. Billy went off to see you the night he died. Settling his debts, he said. I reckoned he'd showed you a bit of gold, and you struck him dead for it."

26

"He was coming to see *me?*" I asked, stunned.

"I tried to tell him it weren't worth it," Mr. Smith said. "But he wouldn't listen to the likes of me." He honked into the napkin again, and the soup spoon disappeared under it. "*She can't get by without me,* he says. *She'll be chuffed I'm alive and kicking.*"

"I never saw him." I'd walked away from Bow Lane once the bailiffs had taken everything from me, vowing to never return. My existence going forward had been about Grace, whom I'd named before she'd been born. I'd known in my heart she would be a girl.

Mr. Smith laid down the napkin, the spoon beneath it, his expression sorrowful. "I never saw him after that neither. He was supposed to meet me at our pub later that evening, but he never came."

After a moment of quiet, Mr. Fielding reached over and removed the soup spoon from under the napkin, and tapped it to the table next to his plate. "Then we must find out what happened to Billy between leaving you and the time he was to meet you at the pub."

As though the tap of the spoon had been her cue, Mrs. Hodder returned with a platter of roast chicken and vegetables, which she thunked to the center of the table. Mr. Fielding took up the large knife and fork on the platter, preparing to carve and serve.

"Which pub?" Daniel asked Mr. Smith.

Mr. Smith's attention riveted to the chicken Mr. Fielding sliced, its clear juices dripping to the potatoes and carrots.

"On Cable Street," he said distractedly. "Not far from here, actually. The Speckled Hen. He left me there as the sun went down, and promised to be back."

"I know it," Mrs. Hodder said. "Near the dockyards, ain't it? Lots of sailors. I won't go near the place, meself."

"Don't blame yer, love. I haven't been since. Couldn't bear it. I remember waiting all that night, furious with the man. If I'd known he were dead, I'd have cried instead."

Mr. Smith's eyes swam with tears now, though he eagerly lifted his plate so Mr. Fielding could pile on slices of chicken and a large helping of potatoes. Mr. Fielding ought to have served Lady Cynthia first, but I knew he was trying to relax the man into revealing any secrets.

Mr. Smith said a brief word of thanks and fell to the feast without waiting for the rest of us. Mr. Fielding sent a glance of apology to Cynthia and me and filled Cynthia's plate.

I picked at the food he served me, my thoughts churning.

Joe had tried to come home to me, had he? To boast about money he'd brought with him? Or because he'd truly wanted to see me?

No, I would not let myself believe he had ever loved me. Joe had been very fond of himself, hence finding ways to do exactly as he pleased. The robbery was a good illustration of this fact; while he'd claimed to be reformed by his experience in the penal colony, he'd become a thief again as soon as presented with the opportunity.

I doubted Joe had been coming to me to share his wealth. No, he'd wanted me to be pleased and relieved he was alive and to fling myself into his arms. Little had he known that the police had already told me about Charlotte, and I'd have been more likely to smack him with a cook pot, as Mr. Smith had believed I'd done.

Who had Joe encountered between leaving Mr. Smith and reaching our old rooms? Or between those rooms and the pub he was to return to?

The answer, I felt certain, lay in Bow Lane.

I sensed Daniel watching me. I returned his gaze serenely and ate my very thoroughly cooked chicken.

The rest of the meal was uneventful. Mr. Smith, having delivered all the startling revelations he could, turned himself to consuming everything on his plate and the second and third helpings Mr. Fielding stuffed him with. Mrs. Hodder followed the main dish with a lemon tart, one of my recipes given to her via Mr. Fielding. She'd done well with it.

Mr. Fielding indicated he'd convey Mr. Smith back to his boardinghouse—Mr. Smith kept insisting he be dropped off at a pub, but Mr. Fielding ignored him. Daniel was to walk with Cynthia and me to find a hansom back to Mount Street.

As I moved from dining room to front door, I became aware of eyes watching us from above. I looked up to see two of the children Mr. Fielding was looking after, one small boy and a taller girl, hanging over the banisters two floors up.

The small boy, Michael, had regained the fire a little boy ought to have, and grinned impudently at me. The girl, about fifteen, had relaxed a bit, but she'd seen too much in her life to lose all her rigidity. Her flaxen hair had been tamed into a bun, and she wore a modest gown of dark blue. Not a penitent-like garment, but a pretty frock with lace on its hem.

I waved up at them, and Michael's grin widened. The girl, whose name was Mabel, started, then smiled uncertainly.

I would like to have spoken with them, a good, long conversation, but I hesitated to frighten them. I contented myself with giving them a nod in both greeting and farewell, before turning away.

"I am sorry you had to endure Mr. Smith," Daniel said as we walked from the house and out the gate of the churchyard to the street. "Both of you."

"No worry," Cynthia said. "We needed to know. I hope he didn't upset you too much, Mrs. H. I ought to have come on my own and broken it all to you more gently."

"Please, the pair of you, cease treating me like a delicate piece of china." I heard the waspishness in my voice, but I *had* been unnerved, which put me out of temper. "Joe was a lying blackguard and could not have had good intentions in visiting me that night. He wouldn't have reached me, in any case, even if someone hadn't done him in. I was long gone."

"The pub where he was to have met Mr. Smith is near the docks where he was killed," Cynthia mused.

"Exactly my thoughts," I said briskly. "A place to investigate."

"A place for *me* to investigate," Daniel broke in. "Please do not rush into a pub full of sailors on shore leave who haven't seen anything female in months. Lady Cynthia, your aunt and uncle, not to mention your mother and father, would thrash me soundly for allowing you to go anywhere near such a place."

Cynthia laughed. "I will leave it to you, McAdam. Though you'd faint to see the sorts of dens Bobby drags me to."

"Very dangerous," I admonished. "Please keep to places Miss Townsend recommends."

"Oh, she knows dens of iniquity too," Cynthia said. "But they are somewhat cleaner."

"Tell me no more," I said quickly. "I worry so when you are out."

Cynthia slung her arm around my shoulders and gave me a spontaneous hug. "You are too good to me, Mrs. H."

Daniel hailed a hansom, and soon it was stopping, Daniel handing in Cynthia.

He tugged me to him before I could climb in behind her. "I have things I must do," he said in a low voice. "I will call on you tomorrow night, if that is convenient."

I resisted a smile—he sounded like an overly polite suitor. "I believe I will be in to receive you."

Daniel shot me a grin, then he boosted me into the hansom.

"Afternoon, McAdam," Cynthia said. I only gazed at Daniel, who lifted his hand to us, until he stepped back, fading into the traffic that swallowed us.

The next morning, I rushed through cooking breakfast and then preparations for luncheon, wanting to steal away a few minutes early for my half day out. Tess, knowing I longed to be on my way to Grace, sent me off cheerfully.

"I won't make too many mistakes," she said with confidence. "Mr. Davis will steer me right if I do."

Her statement made me almost decide to stay a while longer, but I swallowed my qualms, changed my frock, and departed.

I splurged on a hansom, as it was quicker than the omnibus and my own feet. Instead of heading straight for the lane where the Millburns' house lay, I asked the cabbie to let me out on the corner of Cannon Street and Bow Lane.

Bow Lane was a haven of quiet after the traffic of Cannon Street. I passed the tobacconists at the corner of Watling Street and the greengrocers opposite it. Nettie was moving boxes of produce about inside the greengrocers, chatting with two women shoppers with baskets over their arms. The tobacconists was quiet at the moment, and I did not see Alice Taylor through its window.

Continuing north on Bow Lane, I came to Mr. Miller's haberdashery. Squaring my shoulders, I pushed open the door and entered the shop.

"Miss Holloway, how fine to see you." Mr. Miller turned from greeting me to his customer, a woman in an out-of-fashion but well-kept frock, cheerfully handing her the purchases he'd wrapped for her. She thanked him, nodded at me, and left the shop.

Mr. Miller set aside the paper and string with which he'd wrapped the woman's parcel and peered at me expectantly from across the counter.

"What can I do for you, Miss Holloway? I have more pretty ribbon in. Would look lovely in your daughter's hair."

I resisted the urge to ask him to show me, knowing I would purchase it. I'd come for more serious business than that.

I pressed my hands together as I approached him, deciding to come straight to the point.

"I have learned that on the night my husband died, he tried to visit me here. I'd already gone, and he would have had to ask you for the key. He never took it with him when he went to sea." I fixed Mr. Miller with a steady gaze. "*Did* he come here that night?"

Mr. Miller's smile faded in an instant, and his face grew gray as chalk. He slumped, his wizened hands bracing him on the counter's wooden surface.

"Little Kat, I am so sorry." His quiet whisper was almost lost in the gloom.

"Why?" I demanded, my fears rising. "What happened? Please tell me, Mr. Miller. Joe did come here, didn't he?"

"He did." I could barely hear his answer. "I was just closing up when he burst in, looking for you. He was excited and sneering, horrible." Mr. Miller covered his face with thin, shaking hands. "May God forgive me."

"Good gracious, Mr. Miller, what did you do?"

The door flew open, the noise and wind from the street bursting inside. With them came Nettie Sheppard, her greengrocers' apron still tethered about her waist.

"What are you doing to him?" she demanded, sallow face flushed. "You leave him be. You're not welcome in Bow Lane anymore, Katharine Holloway."

I regarded her in bewilderment. "I am doing nothing to Mr. Miller. I have been asking him whether my husband arrived here the night he died. Apparently, he did, and I see *you* must know something about it."

Mr. Miller gazed at her imploringly. "Go home, Miss Sheppard. I will be well."

I moved past Nettie—she did not try to stop me—and firmly shut the door. I locked it with the key resting in the keyhole.

"Now then," I said, turning back to them. "Both of you. This is my husband, and his death, and I need to know. What on earth happened when he came here?"

Nettie glared at Mr. Miller, but he bowed his head. "She is right, Miss Sheppard. She deserves the truth." He looked up at me, his red-rimmed eyes swimming with tears. "I killed him."

27

"Shut it, you," Nettie growled at him. "She's in thick with the police." She swung on me. "He don't know what he's saying, Kat."

"Mr. Miller?" I asked gently. "How could you have? Joe was a strong and fit man, a fighter. Even if you had crept up behind him, it would have to have been a terribly lucky blow."

Nettie continued to scowl, but Mr. Miller's misery was sad to behold.

"We both did it," he whispered. "Miss Sheppard and me."

"I said, shut it." Nettie advanced on him. "I knew she'd come here to cause trouble. Saw it in her face when she charged by."

I stepped quickly between them, bending my most flinty gaze on Nettie. "One of you had better tell me, or I *will* fetch a constable."

"It were a long time ago. What does it matter?" Nettie snapped. "He was a bad man, was your Joe."

"Did he attack you, Mr. Miller?" I asked, ignoring her. "Were you defending yourself?"

My heart was breaking—Mr. Miller was a kind man, and Joe had been horrible. I did not want my awful husband to have ruined yet another person's life.

Mr. Miller drew a breath, standing up straight as though ready to unburden himself. "Joe came here to see you, as you say. He told me he had something to show you. He was excited. Had it in a sack."

My throat tightened. Some of the money? Or a trinket he'd brought to soften me up?

"I was amazed to see him," Mr. Miller went on, "after you'd thought he was dead, and you so grief-stricken. I told him you'd gone, believing him deceased. It was mean of him to dance back in, and I said so." Mr. Miller sighed. "He didn't believe you weren't here, and he made me take him upstairs. When he found your rooms empty, he was furious. He said you'd gone to another man, and when he found you, he'd kill you. He was making all sorts of threats of what he would do—terrible things."

Mr. Miller's lined face was streaked with tears. "He tried to force me to tell him where you were. I wouldn't. I was so afraid he'd hurt you. He shook me, hit me. I fought him, but you are right. I am a feeble old man."

"Oh, Mr. Miller." I took his hand in mine. "You ought to have told him. I was safe in my boardinghouse—the landlady there would have summoned the police had he tried to enter."

Mr. Miller shook his head. "No. He was crazed, livid. Miss Sheppard came in while I fought him.

334

She'd spied him in the lane and ran here to see if it was truly him."

I turned to Nettie, who shifted from side to side, her rage at me barely contained. "You tried to help him?" I asked her.

"I *did* help him." Nettie's loathing of me was clear. "I came into the shop—Mr. Miller hadn't locked the door—and heard the scuffle upstairs. I found Joe Bristow trying to strangle Mr. Miller. I couldn't believe me eyes, but it were him. I pulled him off Mr. Miller. When Bristow stumbled, I picked up the bag he'd dropped—it was heavy. I whacked him with it, and he stayed on the floor."

"But came around," Mr. Miller said quickly. "He started to get to his hands and knees, and I knew he'd kill us both if he reached his feet. So I took the bag from Miss Sheppard and hit him again."

"Then I did it a third time," Nettie said firmly, as though trying to ensure she took the blame for the final blow. "Just to make certain. Then he stayed down, and his face turned an odd shade of red."

"I see." I could form no other words.

I believed the tale—Joe would have been very angry that I hadn't stayed in our rooms, even if the bailiffs had taken everything from me, on the off chance that he'd come back to me. That he'd immediately think I'd gone to another man was just like him as well.

The fact that he'd been infuriated by that idea while he'd been practicing bigamy with me, and had tried to hurt Mr. Miller, who was kindness itself, made the last vestiges of sympathy I'd ever felt for the man vanish.

Joe, or Billy, had been an unrepentant thief, a liar, an adulterer, and a violent brute. He could rot, for all I cared.

"You had no choice," I told them. "He might have injured you severely, Mr. Miller, or even killed you."

Also, if Joe *had* managed to reach me at the boardinghouse, he might have beaten me in his rage. Perhaps hard enough to hurt not only me but Grace. And for that, I condemned him.

"I must thank you both," I said, as Mr. Miller and Nettie watched me, the two breathing hard. "You possibly saved my life, and my daughter's."

Mr. Miller shook his head. "But it's a terrible, terrible thing."

"Joe was a terrible, terrible person." My strength returned as I squeezed Mr. Miller's hand, which I still held. "You are not to blame, nor are you, Nettie. The police don't need to know any of this."

Nettie stared, open-mouthed. "You wouldn't peach? But we killed 'im."

"Not on purpose," I said with conviction. "In defense of yourselves. He was a villain and a thief, and we are well rid of him. I have misjudged you, Nettie. You are a good woman."

Nettie continued to regard me in shock. "And you are a strange one, Kat Holloway."

"So I have been told. What I am more interested in is—" I switched my gaze to Mr. Miller. "What was in the bag. And where is it now?"

Mr. Miller swallowed. I saw him dart a quick glance at Nettie, and she gave a minute shake of her head.

"Was it some gewgaw?" I asked. "Or was it gold coins?"

Mr. Miller gaped, jerking himself from my grasp. "How did you know?"

At the same time, Nettie wailed, "No, don't tell her."

"What did you do with the money, Mr. Miller?" I asked. "Did you turn it over to the police?"

He'd certainly not spent any on repairs to the shop, that I could see. The walls were as crumbling, the wooden shelves and counter as worn as they ever had been. Nettie's greengrocers was a little less shabby, but it had obviously never been renovated.

Mr. Miller bit his lip. "I kept it. I was going to give it to you—by rights, the coins were yours. But that would lead to questions about how I came by them, questions I could not let myself answer. I was not only protecting myself, but Miss Sheppard."

"You kept it?" I asked in astonishment. I'd

been imagining the two had divided up the coins and sent them to family members to ease their lot. "For a dozen years?"

Mr. Miller's shoulders sagged. "It was blood money. I couldn't spend it, and Nettie agreed to let me look after it."

Nettie glanced heavenward. I suppose she hoped that one day Mr. Miller would wear down and give her a portion of it. The fact that she hadn't coerced the money out of him before this continued to raise her in my estimation.

"I will fetch it," Mr. Miller said breathlessly.

He turned from us and exited the room, more quickly than I thought his thin frame could move. Nettie continued to regard me in anger.

"This has been very hard for him," she said. "He has lived poorly with his guilt."

"But it has not been hard for you?" I countered.

Nettie lifted her chin. "I am made of sterner stuff. I've been fending for myself a long time. What's done is done."

Perhaps she was more ruthless than I'd imagined. We studied each other guardedly until Mr. Miller returned.

He carried a leather bag the size of his two hands, closed by a drawstring, which he plunked on the counter.

"I've not touched it since I hid it," he said.

I stepped to the counter, feeling a bit queasy. This bag had been used as a cosh to kill a man.

However, I saw no blood on the leather or any sign that the sack had been wielded as a weapon.

Willing my fingers not to tremble, I untied the drawstring and pried the bag open.

Inside, more than a dozen gold coins lay on the dark leather. My eyes widened as I took them in, the gleam of gold like a streak of sunshine in the gloom.

"Good heavens," I murmured.

"Take them," Mr. Miller said. "They have been like lead on my mind all these years."

I tore my gaze from the beautiful gold and pulled the drawstring shut. "Thank you, Mr. Miller. Nettie. For looking after it for me."

Mr. Miller's strength left him, and he crumpled. Both Nettie and I leapt to him, the two of us leading him to a chair. It was the only chair in the shop, and a rickety one at that.

"You are not a villain, Mr. Miller," I told him. "You are a good and kind man who did an honorable thing."

He was not comforted. Nettie, still angry at me, offered to make him tea.

"One thing that puzzles me," I said as I tucked the heavy bag inside my coat. "Why did you drag Joe to the London Dockyards? And how did you? Especially with no one seeing you?"

Mr. Miller raised his head, and Nettie blinked. "Dockyards?" she asked in bewilderment.

"That was where Joe was found." I took in

their blank expressions. "You did take him to the docks, did you not?"

"No," Nettie burst out. "We carried him to the church."

"Church?" I asked, my bafflement matching theirs.

Nettie pointed impatiently northward. "Bow Bells. Where'd ya think?"

"Nettie had a cart." Mr. Miller spoke as one trying to be helpful. "It was very dark by that time. We loaded him in, covered him with a tarp, and trundled him up the lane. No one paid us any mind. We decided the church was the best place for him. The vicar could look after him, inform the police, arrange for his burial."

"But he wasn't found at the church." I gazed at each of them in turn, willing them to understand. "Were you not surprised when there was no announcement of his death?"

Nettie shrugged. "Nothing to do with us, was it? We assumed the vicar would have informed you, or the police, or whomever he pleased. Or maybe no one realized who he was."

"The vicar knew him," I said. "He'd have sent word to me." My ideas, which had been untangling, had snarled again, and I once more smoothed them out. "My poor, dear Mr. Miller. Can you not guess what happened? You and Nettie very likely *didn't* kill him after all. I wager that once you left him at the church, he came to and went away to nurse himself." I smiled at them, the two regarding me in shock. "The police found Joe very dead in the London Dockyards, they having no inkling of who he was. That is why there was no hue and cry—the police assumed he was a sailor who'd either fallen and hit his head, or seen the worse end of a fight, and were done with him."

I had been right in the first place. Mr. Miller and even the steely Nettie would have been no match for Joe, hardened from his years of labor in the penal colony, plus his work as a sailor.

From what I understood, it was actually difficult to kill someone with a cosh. One had to strike very hard in just the right spot. Nettie and Mr. Miller *might* have accomplished this, but odds were they hadn't.

Joe had likely also been drunk—he'd been celebrating with Mr. Smith and then decided to come find me. Joe had always grown either very exuberant or very enraged when he was drunk.

"You did not kill him, Nettie. Nor did you, Mr. Miller." I pressed my hands to Mr. Miller's shoulders as he sat, stunned. "You are innocent of his blood. I am very glad."

I thought Mr. Miller would slump in relief, letting go of the burden he'd been carrying all these years. Instead, he burst into tears, sobbing messily into his hands.

Nettie pushed me away as I tried to comfort

341

him. "You go," she snapped. "I'll look after him."

I straightened in frustration, but I decided not to argue. The pair of them had been pressed under a load of guilt—at least Mr. Miller had—and it would take time for them to realize that load was lifted.

For me, my heart had lightened. My dear Mr. Miller was innocent, relieving me of a grief that had been forming in my heart. Joe, the savage lout, was dead and could no longer hurt them, or me, or anyone else.

I was free of him. I had been for years, but today, I felt free of my so-called husband completely. Not even the nagging puzzle of what had truly happened to him continued to fog my mind.

"Good day, Mr. Miller," I said. "And thank you. And you, Nettie."

Mr. Miller continued to weep, Nettie ignoring me as she fussed over him. I unlocked the door of the shop and let myself out into the lane.

The sun shone strongly, the September air crisp. A beautiful day.

I told a woman making for the haberdashery that Mr. Miller wasn't feeling well and his shop would be closed for the rest of the day. She raised her brows but turned and continued along the lane.

I retraced my steps toward Cannon Street, pressing my arm tightly over the bag under my coat. It felt odd to try to walk normally, aware that I carried more money than I'd ever seen in my life.

I skirted knots of people, among whom pickpockets would lurk, and emerged unscathed to Cannon Street, where I hailed a hansom cab.

"Scotland Yard, please," I told the driver crisply as I climbed in, and off we went at a rapid clip.

28

Not long later, I plunked the bag of coins onto Inspector McGregor's desk.

"From the Goldsmiths' Company robbery," I said. "Some of it, anyway."

Inspector McGregor's stupefied expression was gratifying. He came to his feet, then he gingerly worked the drawstring open and peered inside the bag.

He stared at the coins a long while, then up at me.

"How the devil did you come by this?" he demanded when he found his voice.

"They were hidden at my old flat," I said, without reprimanding him on his language. "Joe must have stashed them there when he sought me out the night of his death."

I poked my tongue into my cheek as I told the half-truth, but I did not want Mr. Miller or Nettie subjected to a Scotland Yard interrogation. They would be arrested, at best for hiding stolen goods, at worst for Joe's death. I well knew that while Joe might have walked away from Bow Bells church on his own two legs, he could have expired from his wounds later with no other interference.

"Stashed at your old flat?" McGregor's voice

dripped with skepticism. "For a dozen years? With no one being the wiser?"

"I had already moved out when Joe arrived that night, and I'd had no idea he was alive at the time, so of course, it never occurred to me that he'd left anything there. Then an old pal of his told me he'd gone to see me the night he died, so on the off chance, I went back and looked. And there it was."

I kept as close to the truth as possible, bolstering my courage with the thought that I was protecting Mr. Miller. He was too feeble to be dragged off to Newgate.

Inspector McGregor gazed into the bag. "Is this all he left?"

"It is indeed. I brought that straight to you, without dipping in to keep a few for myself. I can swear a Bible oath on it, if you'd like."

Inspector McGregor, I was pleased to see, at least believed me on this point.

"Where is the rest of it?" he asked, but I could see he did not expect me to know.

"Gone into buying a large plot of land in Antigua. Mr. McAdam has already telegraphed a firm of crooked investment bankers and land dealers in St. John's, and can tell you all about it."

Inspector McGregor leaned heavily on his desk. "Antigua."

"My erstwhile husband decided to invest the

take in land, planning to sell it after a time and settle on an estate in Kent."

"Kent." Inspector McGregor grunted. "I see. So the rest of the coins went to the Antilles, where they have been sold off or traded years ago, and are long gone."

"That is our conclusion, yes."

Inspector McGregor heaved an aggrieved sigh. "At least we can close that case. Money traced, robber Billy Glover dead long ago."

"Will you return the coins to the Mint?" I asked. "They will be happy to see them back, I think."

"They will, greedy sods," the inspector growled. "Beg pardon, Mrs. Holloway."

"I do understand your frustration. It was all so long ago, and they were likely insured for the loss."

The money could have done so much for me. I did not believe for a moment that Joe had brought it to me so I could move into nicer rooms and buy pretty frocks. He'd brought it to show off, to make me fly into his arms. I have no doubt he'd have taken it all away the next morning, perhaps leaving me only a token coin.

And yes, I could have taken this lot home to Mount Street and hidden it in my wardrobe with the rest of my carefully hoarded funds. Inspector McGregor would never have needed to know.

But it would have weighed on me, as it had

weighed on Mr. Miller. I'd have heard the coins clinking in the night, like in the best Gothic tales, where a person's guilty conscience drives them mad.

Better I handed the money to the inspector and had done with it.

"I'll leave it to you, then," I said. "My husband, I have concluded, met his killer somewhere between Bow Lane and a pub called the Speckled Hen in Cable Street near the London Docks. He either encountered someone along the way or at the pub, who went with him to the docks and finished him off there. Or else finished him off and then lugged him there. Who that person was and why they killed him, I do not know. Joe angered so many in his lifetime that it could have been any number of people."

"It was not you?"

Inspector McGregor did not joke. His glare told me that.

"No, Inspector. I admit that if I'd seen him alive after I'd thought him dead, and learned of this theft, I might have struck him good and hard. Not that it would have helped me—Joe was quite large and able to defend himself."

Inspector McGregor nodded. He believed me, but as a good policeman, he needed to be certain.

"Thank you for seeing me." I sent him a sly smile. "I hope you can find this gift from a bothersome woman useful."

Inspector McGregor's face colored satisfactorily, and he muttered something I could not make out. I left him there, hiding my glee, and exited his office.

Before I closed the door, he bellowed, "Anderson!"

The harried Sergeant Anderson passed me as I left the outer office, and I found myself once more in a rather dingy corridor.

The halls of Scotland Yard were busy, constables moving to and fro, answering orders barked from sergeants and the occasional inspector. I sidled through and started down a staircase, but when a swarm of constables flowed up it, I turned around and hastened back to the floor from which I'd come. They might be perfectly fine lads, but I did not care to be crushed among them.

I scurried along the upstairs hall, past Inspector McGregor's office, and around a corner, in search of another staircase.

A much quieter corridor led to the end of the building, and I saw the wooden end of a banister where the corridor terminated. As I sped along, the hall grew emptier until, with the exception of a lone wooden chair, I was the only thing in it.

A door stood ajar near the staircase. I scarce noticed it until a voice floated from it.

". . . Mrs. Holloway."

I paused. I knew the voice, and he was speaking

adamantly. When the icy tones of Mr. Monaghan answered Daniel, I froze, unable to make myself go any farther.

"Why?" Monaghan asked. "What is she to you?"

"A friend." Daniel's answer was firm.

"So she claimed. Trust me, McAdam, I do not care what women you tumble. I do care who you spout information to in your bed."

Daniel's growl intensified. "I'll thank you to not impugn Mrs. Holloway's character. She is innocent and respectable. Besides, do you think me that witless?"

"Innocent—that is debatable."

Daniel laughed humorlessly. "Perhaps you'll be glad to know I've been celibate as a monk since you dragooned me into doing your most repellent jobs."

"You know why I have."

I should have quickly and quietly continued my journey to the staircase, but I instead sank down on the wooden chair in the hallway. I told myself I was making certain no one else came down this corridor to hear the very interesting conversation within.

"Oh yes, I know why." Daniel's impassioned response was clear. "You have made me pay and pay and pay. When will you release me? One more, you have said—and keep saying."

"Wright was bloody good at what he did." The answer was filled with bleak fury.

"I know." Daniel's hard tones broke. "I know. But it was not all my bloody fault. I took the blame, but you have turned my contrition from penitence into crushing me to soothe your own guilt."

"You are an impertinent bastard." Monaghan's coldness returned. "A *true* bastard, aren't you?"

Daniel went silent a moment before he answered. "I honestly don't know."

"I could find out, you know."

Another pause. "You can also go to hell."

"Stay loyal to me, and all will become clear. Leave, and I will crush you as you say I have been."

"If I stay, you'll use me until there's nothing left of me. I won't do it."

"You have no choice."

Daniel's answering words were extremely vulgar, ones I'd never heard him utter. When he recovered himself, he continued, "You will leave Mrs. Holloway alone. She has done nothing to deserve your interest, and if you go near her again, I will find a way to crush *you*."

"You are in no position to threaten me, McAdam."

"No?" Daniel's tone held brittle mirth. "But I know people who are. You are of vital importance to the Home Office *now*, yes, but no one likes you, and that will be your downfall in the end."

Monaghan replied with frosty scorn. "Get

out of here, McAdam. Go do what you're told, or run and lick Mrs. Holloway's boots—it's all the same to me. But you come when I call. One more."

Another vulgar parting shot, and Daniel swung open the door so hard it banged into the wall.

I had already left the chair and was scuttling for the stairs before he emerged. In vain did I hope Daniel hadn't seen me, because his quick footfalls sounded behind me, and a strong hand soon closed around my arm, propelling me down the stairs with him.

"Damnation, Kat," he said under his breath once we'd reached the ground floor.

"I was looking for a way out," I bleated. We plunged through a side entrance to the street, a strong breeze stealing my breath. "I cannot help it if you left the door open."

Daniel's face was blotchy red. "You are a confounded nuisance."

"Am I? I thought you said I was innocent and respectable."

Daniel towed me through the lane called Great Scotland Yard, heading in the opposite direction from Whitehall, winding us through small streets leading to Charing Cross Station.

We emerged onto the Strand, its thick traffic ready to trample the unwary. From here Daniel steered me toward Trafalgar Square. Pigeons rose on clouds of wings as we hurried through, settling again behind us in their endless search for discarded food.

Daniel pulled me to sit with him on the stone steps near the National Gallery. I was out of breath, and Daniel still held my arm.

"Explain to me, Kat, why you went to Monaghan's office in the first place. I won't ask why you listened to a private conversation. I know you'd never be able to walk away from that, especially as it was about you."

"Precisely. A person does not like being discussed." I gently released myself from his grip. "First of all, I had no idea that corridor was Mr. Monaghan's domain. I truly was trying to find a way out of the building. Secondly, I did not go to Scotland Yard to see him, or you, but Inspector McGregor, to deliver him stolen goods."

"Kat—"

I could not help feeling smug at Daniel's dazed expression. "I found some of the coins. Or at least, Mr. Miller did."

Daniel regarded me, open-mouthed. "You found some of the—"

I interrupted to give him the tale, the true one, and then related what I'd told Inspector McGregor. "Please say nothing about Nettie or Mr. Miller," I finished. "The poor man has been through enough, punishing himself for the last dozen years."

"I'd feel more kindly disposed toward him if

he'd told you the truth and given you the money long ago," Daniel said grimly. "Though I can understand his fears."

"I do realize the pair of them might truly have killed Joe, injuring him enough so he died later. We must discover what exactly happened to him."

Daniel nodded. "I had planned to take myself to the Cable Street pub and find out things, but I decided first to have it out with Monaghan, as you heard." He removed his cap and scrubbed his hand through his hair. "Small good it did me, the bloo—er—blasted man."

"I heard you say worse words in that room."

Daniel's cheeks reddened. "I daresay you did. I have had my fill of him."

I took Daniel's hand, warm even through our gloves. "Will you tell me why now? You spoke of a man called Wright."

"Yes," Daniel said tightly.

"What happened to him?"

Daniel gazed across the square to the fountains playing in its center, surrounding the tall fluted column with Admiral Nelson standing grandly at its top, facing away from us. A few pigeons, tiny from this distance, decorated his hat.

I thought Daniel would not answer me, but then he said, "He died."

"Oh." My heart squeezed. "I am sorry. Mr. Monaghan was close to him?"

Daniel huffed a mirthless laugh. "Monaghan has always been a coldhearted fish, so I would not say he was close to anyone. But he respected Wright—Reginald Wright. Monaghan had been his right-hand man. I can't tell you everything about Monaghan, but when he was recruited for his position, he wasn't trusted by anyone. Rightly so, because he had done some very bad things in his past. But Wright recognized his usefulness, built him into the man he is. Monaghan took his place when he was killed." Daniel hesitated, his gaze now resting on the classic elegance of the Church of St. Martin-in-the-Fields. "Wright died because of me."

Daniel's hand tightened on mine, and a swallow moved in his throat. It had been very difficult for him to tell me this, I saw. I doubt he would have if I'd not heard his argument with Monaghan.

"I can't believe that," I said softly.

Daniel snapped to me, his eyes filled with anger and self-loathing. "Believe it. I wanted to join the police, craved it. I knew I could be a good detective, as I was already acquainted with the cruelest villains in London and knew all their secrets. I wanted to bring them all down. So I hung about Scotland Yard, in one of my masterful disguises, and followed Wright, thinking he was a high-placed inspector. At that time, he was investigating a man bent upon assassinating the prime minister, and I inserted myself into the trap to catch the man."

He gave another grim laugh. "I actually found the assassin, holed up in a deserted hotel in Whitechapel. I put myself in front of Wright and made him listen to me, then led him to the chap."

Daniel's self-deprecating amusement left him, to be replaced with a vast sadness. "But I wasn't careful. I didn't realize that the assassin not only had friends with him, but explosives. When Wright and the constables burst in, the man set off his dynamite. Wright was killed, as was the assassin and most of his colleagues, and several constables were badly injured. Monaghan was late arriving—he'd been investigating another possible hiding place. He found Wright's body, and me standing over it."

29

"Oh, Daniel." I lifted his hand between mine. "I am so sorry."

Daniel looked away again, fixing his gaze on a dancing fountain. "Monaghan blamed me, has always blamed me. He did acknowledge that I'd found the assassin when the rest of them had been searching in the wrong place. But he condemned me for dragging Wright in to die, especially when I didn't have a scratch on me."

"That was not entirely your fault," I said, my indignation rising. "The constables and Mr. Wright himself should have gone more carefully, checked as well. They were experienced policemen, were they not?"

"I thought of that," Daniel said, "though not until much later. At the time, I was too stunned and horrified. Monaghan even believed me one of the assassin's gang at first. He accused me of luring Wright to his death, but at least I was able to convince him otherwise."

"I should hope so."

Daniel's bleak humor returned. "Monaghan contrived a delicious punishment for me. He persuaded his superiors to let him take me on, in an unofficial capacity, to help him solve crimes of this sort. If I refused, he said that he would make the case I was one of the gang and deliberately led Wright in to die. I'd have been sentenced to death for it, I'm certain. I am under oath not to tell you what all I have had to investigate, and for whom, and why, but he sets me on the most dangerous tasks, half hoping one of them will kill me. That is one reason why I'm not on the rolls of Scotland Yard, or any agency: so that if I do not survive, Monaghan does not have to make amends to anyone."

I had managed to sit still while Daniel told me this tale, anger, worry, then more anger surging through me. When he at last fell silent, I climbed to my feet.

"He has no call to treat you so," I all but shouted. "It is not your fault that man was killed. As I say, he and the constables could have been more careful. They ought to have waited for Mr. Monaghan."

Daniel, instead of rising politely, rested his cap on his knee and let the wind push his hair awry. He looked defeated, and my heart ached. "Should haves won't change what happened. I've blamed myself even more than Monaghan did. I'd been cocksure, realizing I could discover what the police could not, quite proud of myself. I led good men into serious danger, stepping aside and gesturing them into their doom. When the explosion came . . ."

"Oh, Daniel." I sank beside him again as he

357

faltered, barely stopping myself from pulling him into my arms. "My poor, darling Daniel. I never knew—I didn't understand."

"Because I've never told anyone." Daniel lifted one of my hands and kissed it, breath hot through my glove. "No one knows this—not Thanos, nor James, not even Inspector McGregor or anyone else in the police. The injured constables on the case that night were either transferred or so hurt they had to resign their posts. No one knows any of my part in the incident but Monaghan. I am duty bound to Monaghan's agency within the police—I swore allegiance to it—and I have no doubt that if I tried to leave my post he would resurrect my part in Wright's death and have me stand trial for it."

His hold over Daniel was sinister. "How long ago was this?" I asked.

"Nearly ten years."

I gripped his hand. "Then I agree with what you said to him. Enough is enough. You have paid your debt, many times over."

Daniel shook his head. "Monaghan is a very angry man, with very deep grudges. He'd been a villain before he decided to turn coat and protect others from even worse villains." He let out a breath. "Sometimes I believe I'm just like him."

"You are not." I released his hand and cupped his face, not caring about the passersby who either grinned knowingly or pursed their lips in disapproval. "You have a fine, kind heart, and a forgiving one. Monaghan has let anger eat at him until he has no compassion at all. Believe me, you are *nothing* like him."

Daniel turned his head and kissed my palm before he gently lowered my hands. "You are good to me, Kat. What I fear—what I have feared since I realized how fond I was growing of you—was that Monaghan would use you against me. That he would hurt you, or worse, to make me experience the grief that he felt upon losing the only man who'd trusted him."

His words, delivered with quiet despair, filled me with new understanding. Daniel feared for me the same way he feared for James, the way I feared for Grace. To avoid this worry, he could have broken his connection with me at once, or never formed it in the first place—but he'd been brave enough to stay.

"Daniel . . ." My throat tightened, and I could not continue.

Daniel sent me his lopsided smile. "At this point in the conversation, you will declare you can look out for yourself. In most circumstances, you can. But with Monaghan—"

I touched his lips, stilling his words. "He is dangerous. I know." I returned his smile. "And you are wonderful."

Daniel's eyes filled with sudden fire, longing, hope. I lowered my hand, and we simply stared at each other, unable to do more in this open space teeming with so many Londoners.

Without words between us, I saw Daniel's love burning like the embers of the fire in my stove, having to be damped at times but never going out. I wanted to kiss him, to press his warm lips to mine, and the restraint I forced myself to have made my smile widen.

Daniel's gaze turned wicked. "Kat . . ."

I drew a breath. "Hadn't we better go investigate that pub in Cable Street?"

"We had better go somewhere," Daniel said with a growl. "Before I shock the denizens of Trafalgar Square."

He launched himself from the steps, pulling me up with him, and we joined the flowing masses of people, heading for the Strand.

I was pleased that Daniel hadn't argued about me accompanying him, but once we reached the Strand, he pulled me to a halt.

"I'll find a cab to take you to the Millburns'," he said. "As I told you, I want you nowhere near a sailors' pub by the docks."

I pried myself from his grip. We stood on the doorstep of a closed shop, out of the way of the foot traffic that streamed past without noticing us.

"I am afraid I will insist," I said. "The pub must be key. I highly suspect Joe recovered once

Nettie and Mr. Miller left him at Bow Bells and he shuffled off back to Cable Street to meet Mr. Smith. Mr. Smith says Joe never arrived, and so Joe must have met someone between Bow Lane and there, who then killed him."

Daniel made a noise of exasperation. "With the entirety of the City between the two, not to mention the many lanes of Whitechapel and Shadwell."

I shook my head. "Joe was a man of habit. He had his routes and he stuck to them. If he started from Cheapside, he'd have walked it to Poultry, then down King William Street to Eastcheap, and then to and around the Tower. When he worked odd jobs at St. Katharine Docks in between his sailing trips, he'd go that way—he told me. Cable Street is east of the Tower and north of St. Katharine Docks."

Daniel's eyes began to sparkle. "That route would take him directly past the Royal Mint. I wonder if that was how he got the idea for the robbery."

"Have you had a chance to speak to Mr. Birkett?" I asked. "The supposed inside man Mr. Smith told us about?"

"I have indeed." Daniel folded his arms and leaned against the brick doorframe. "I was going to tell you all this tonight over a warm pot of tea. Birkett retired four years ago. He is living with his sister in Hampstead, and is steeped in shame.

He did it, all right, just as Mr. Smith said. Set aside the boxes and handed them out the door to Bristow and Smith. However, Bristow vanished with the money, and Mr. Birkett got nothing. Same as Smith."

I turned away from the stiffening breeze as I pondered. "Perhaps, if we are charitable, we can believe Joe meant to pay his debts with the money he was carrying around that night. Bringing some to me and then paying out to Mr. Smith and Mr. Birkett, and anyone else he owed."

Daniel rubbed a forefinger over his chin. "Could be. Perhaps he thought that if he paid off those who'd helped him, including you, they would have no cause to seek him out once he sold his plantation and bought his estate in Kent. He'd be free to play lord of the manor."

"Neatly drawing a line between his old life and his new," I concluded. "If that is the case, he'd likely have wanted to give Charlotte money, too."

"Probably. Very well, let us say that his next stop in this journey of tying up loose ends was the pub, to pay off Smith. In that case, Smith could well be the killer, in spite of his denials. Joe left the money behind when Mr. Miller and Nettie carted him to the church. Obviously, he wasn't feeling well enough or brave enough to go back for it."

"I am pleased to imagine Joe afraid of Mr. Miller," I said. "Though Joe might simply have been dazed and not thinking straight. He let his feet take him to the pub."

"Where Smith, annoyed that he was not being paid after all, dragged him to the docks and finished him off?" Daniel shook his head. "That won't wash. Smith is a small man, and Joe might have had other stashes of the gold with which to pay him."

"I wonder if Joe had made contingency plans for having to come back from the dead?" I mused. "Not that he could have anticipated the *Devonshire* going down, but he must have thought the shipwreck a stroke of good luck—for him, that is. He'd changed his name and his profession once, and he'd know how to do it again."

"It is not easy to become someone else," Daniel said. "But I agree he developed the knack of changing his identity."

"A knack you have as well," I reminded him.

"A thing we will have to discuss later," Daniel said.

"We certainly will." I sent him a no-nonsense look.

Daniel began to laugh. "Oh, my dear, Kat. How fortunate that I had a delivery to your kitchen that day so long ago. I nearly fell flat when I saw you, your beauty so radiant."

In spite of myself, I tingled with pleasant warmth. "I am certain I was smudged with flour and cooking fat." I recalled how my knees had gone weak at his smile. Lucky we both hadn't ended up on the floor. "Let us get on for Cable Street, shall we?"

Daniel lost his smile. "For heaven's sake, Kat. I've said I do not want you there."

"And I have said I will have to insist. I have no intention of sitting and stewing while I wait for you to come and tell me what you have discovered. We'll go in a hansom, and I can stay inside it, if that will make you feel better."

Daniel's lips parted, I assumed to inform me he'd carry me bodily to the Millburns' and bid Joanna lock me in a cupboard. I watched him think it through, and then he pressed his lips together and nodded.

"Very well." He straightened and held out a hand to me. "Let us depart."

Surprised by his acquiescence, I took his hand and fell into step beside him.

Daniel first led me to Charing Cross Station, where he strode along the line of hansoms there until he found the one he sought.

"Lewis," he called to the weathered-faced cabbie. "Care to transport us to the docklands?"

For answer, Lewis carefully backed his horse from the queue and swung out toward us. Daniel handed me into the cab and sprang aboard himself as Lewis started the horse. Soon we were rolling along the Strand at a good pace, Lewis dodging through traffic with great skill.

When we reached Ludgate Hill, Daniel shouted to Lewis to stop. I sent Daniel an inquiring look.

"Errand," he said tersely. "Won't be a moment."

Daniel alighted as soon as Lewis halted, and to my surprise, he went to speak with a small boy who swept the street clean for those who wished to cross it. Daniel and the boy had a brief conversation, a coin exchanged hands, and then Daniel made his way back to the hansom.

"Having him take a message to a friend," Daniel said as he climbed inside and the cab rolled forward once more.

He wouldn't say more than that. We had a silent ride around the Tower and past the Royal Mint, then into the increasingly shabby streets that flanked the docks and warehouses.

The pub called the Speckled Hen was as insalubrious as Daniel had warned me. Though it was midafternoon, the lane outside it teemed with burly men in rough coats and hats, many of them resembling Joe, if not entirely in looks then in demeanor. The doorway was crowded, and I could see that the taproom inside was full.

A very large man dressed in similar togs and heavy boots pushed his way along the street and arrived at the hansom as soon as Lewis halted it.

"Got your message, me old china," he called to Daniel. "Came running, as you can see." He put his hands on his hips and dragged in lungfuls of the damp, sooty air. "What's the job?"

Daniel swung down from the cab and gestured to me. "This is Mrs. Holloway. Please look after her while I'm inside."

"Ah, this is she, is it?" The ruddy-faced man, with blue eyes under flat brown hair, peered into the cab. "Pleased to meet you, Mrs. Holloway. Me name's Grimes, Zachariah Grimes. Me mum had grand notions when she were a lass." He chuckled.

Mr. Grimes couldn't be much older than Daniel, but his face was lined with the weariness that came from hard labor. His countenance did not betray that weariness, however. His eyes twinkled, and the grin remained on his lips.

Daniel touched his cap to me. "I'll be as quick as I can."

Mr. Grimes and I watched Daniel slide through the crowd and into the pub.

"Where's he off to, then?" Grimes asked me. His accent put him firmly from South London. "Investigating another crime?"

"Something like that," I said cautiously.

"I see why he asked me." Grimes scanned the road. "Not a place for a lady, is it? But hard for ye not to come along, eh? Sometimes ya waits for Danny a long time."

I nodded, appreciating his understanding. "Would you like to sit inside, Mr. Grimes? The wind is brisk."

"Thank you, but no. I can better guard you from

out here, and I don't want Danny thinking I was canoodling with his lady." He laughed, a cheery sound.

I smiled with him. "I hope he did not drag you away from something important."

"He always do." Grimes shrugged large shoulders. "But Danny's summonses are important too."

"Have you known him long?" I asked, to make conversation. They must be well acquainted if Grimes referred to him by a nickname. "Mr. McAdam has told me nothing of you."

"That's our Danny. Puts things in boxes, like. I've known him for years, love. Met by fighting, like boys do. Once we sorted ourselves out, we became fast friends. I was a brawny lad, and he had a sharp and quick mind. We made a fine team."

"I can imagine." I pictured Daniel, small and fast, rattling off his schemes to the tougher Grimes, who'd nod in admiration.

It was difficult not to warm to Mr. Grimes. He had the sunny nature some do—they acknowledge life is hard but have decided not to let it bow them down. They'd get by, and as long as they can have a pint with a good friend once in a while, there wasn't much to complain about.

"He's a funny sort, inn't he?" Grimes went on, glancing into the pub. "But a good lad."

"He can be," I agreed.

Grimes burst out laughing. "He told me you were a shrewd one. And a lovely lass, to boot."

He did not say this with any sort of libidinousness, but as a friendly observation.

"You are too kind," I said.

Grimes laughed again, leaning on the wheel. The men, and very few women, who came to this part of the street gave him a wide berth. They knew hired muscle when they saw it.

Grimes, unbidden, told me more about himself—"to pass the time," he said. He was from South London, as I'd suspected, born in Southwark. He'd met Daniel, and scrapped with him, after Daniel had been taken in by Mr. Carter—Grimes, who'd roamed the metropolis looking for work, had sometimes run errands for Carter.

After Mr. Carter had been killed, Grimes hadn't seen Daniel for nearly a year, meeting him again by chance on the street.

"Danny was gutted by that man's death." Grimes lost his smile as he relayed this. "The only real father he'd had, he told me, and Carter wasn't much of one, in my opinion. Me and Danny teamed up again and . . . did some bad things, Mrs. Holloway, I won't lie to yer. But that was years ago, and we was lads. Danny turned out all right, didn't he? Smarter than most."

"Yes, Mr. McAdam is quite clever," I said without rancor.

Grimes chortled. "More than he should be sometimes, eh? But he's got a fine son, which says a lot about him, and he'd not have taken up with you if you weren't a good sort."

Grimes certainly had every confidence in Daniel. He had an ingenuousness about him that made me believe him sincere.

"I assume you also know Mr. Fielding?" I asked, curious.

"Errol?" Grimes barked a laugh. "Aye, I know him. Another clever lad, but in a different way. Slippery, wasn't he? Tell you one thing, while he was doing seven other things at the same time. And now he's a vicar." Grimes went off in hilarity. "Well, the world's a funny place, ain't it?"

I agreed that it was indeed.

"I almost put me foot in it when I met up with Danny again not long ago," Grimes said. "I hadn't seen him in donkey's years, and then there he was, crossing in front of me in the middle of the Strand. 'How are you, Daniel, old man?' I bellow. Then I notice he's in a fancy suit, all la-di-da, with his hair combed flat, but it was our Danny. What I didn't know was that he was in disguise, and a bloke just as fancy was hurrying to catch up with him. Danny looks right through me like I was a stone, and it came to me, sudden-like, that he was pretending to be someone else. I turned around and made like I was calling to another chap." He guffawed. "A close call."

I had nearly done the same thing once, so I could not be disdainful of his mistake. I'd spied Daniel in a Bond Street suit, escorting a young lady, of all things, assisting her into a carriage. I'd been heartsick before I'd understood the sorts of things Daniel did for Mr. Monaghan.

We ceased our conversation when Daniel emerged abruptly from the pub, his grim expression dimming the fine day.

"Charlotte boards near Smithfield, is that right?" he asked me.

"Yes." I moved over so Daniel could climb into the cab, my alarm rising. "Why?"

"We must go there at once. What is the address?"

I gave it to him, and Daniel shouted it up to Lewis.

"Want me along?" Grimes asked.

Daniel studied him a moment, then gave Grimes a nod. "Yes, we might need you. Lewis, quick as you can."

30

When we reached the boardinghouse where Charlotte had taken rooms, the landlady, the one who'd listened to our conversation when I'd visited Charlotte previously, said she'd gone.

"Gone where?" I asked in alarm. I had come in alone, Daniel waiting in the cab this time, as I knew the sharp-eyed woman would not allow a man to darken her doorway.

"Off with her bloke." The landlady radiated disapproval. "She's married him, hasn't she? At least, we should hope she married him. No better than she ought to be, that one."

"Thank you," I said hastily, and fled.

Daniel and Mr. Grimes waited next to the hansom. I gave them my news as Daniel handed me back in, then Daniel hoisted himself beside me, Mr. Grimes squeezing his bulk next to him.

"If she means Tuck, he has rooms in a court off Leadenhall Street," Daniel reminded me.

"Financial bloke, is he?" Grimes asked as Lewis careened the cab southward past St. Bart's Hospital toward Newgate Street. "No good can come of that."

"Possibly none at all," Daniel answered grimly.

Daniel had told me, as we'd raced from the pub to Charlotte's rooms, that the landlord of the pub remembered Joe, all right. The landlord had tried repeatedly to bar Joe from that pub, as he enjoyed stirring up trouble and getting into fights, but Joe had defied him. That night, Joe had staggered into the Speckled Hen to meet a woman, the landlord had said.

"What woman?" I'd demanded of Daniel. "And why didn't Thomas Smith see her or Joe?"

"I don't know the answer to either question," Daniel had told me. "But Joe left with a person the landlord *did* know—who has been a regular at that pub for years, before and since."

"Wasn't the landlord surprised to see Joe alive?" I had to ask. "He did not remark upon this?"

"He hadn't heard Joe went down with his ship at that time, and when he did learn the news, he assumed he'd seen Joe before that, not after. Most days are the same to him, the landlord told me. Time passes without him noticing."

Grimes snorted. "It's steady work. I'd not complain."

"He is good at noticing people though," Daniel had concluded. "Which is why we need to question Charlotte."

Lewis hauled us in a remarkably short time to the dead-end lane called Lime Court that turned off Leadenhall Street. Daniel stepped out into the quiet cul-de-sac, a great contrast to the very busy street we'd turned from.

He pushed his way past a startled porter and into the house where Mr. Tuck took rooms, but soon was out again.

"They've gone to a hotel," Daniel announced. "The one at Cannon Street Station."

"Very handy for a quick departure," Grimes said.

Daniel frowned at the passing traffic as Lewis started off again. "He left the name of the hotel and a forwarding address in Bristol with his landlord. That speaks of a planned move, not a clandestine disappearance."

"Bristol?" I settled the hansom's dust blanket over my frock. "They must be in love, after all, and starting a life together. Shouldn't we be happy for them?"

"They can be happy all they like after I ask them a few pointed questions," Daniel said sternly.

Cannon Street, as usual, was quite busy, but Lewis squeezed his hansom close to the front door of the hotel. I'd brought Grace here from time to time, for a special tea while we watched travelers from around the country stroll through the lobby or rush to catch their trains.

The three of us went inside this time, the clerk behind the counter casting a dubious glance at Daniel in his dusty working clothes, and at Grimes, who blatantly stared at the well-dressed ladies and gents around us.

"Never been in through the *front* door," he muttered.

I was in too much of a hurry to explain their presence. The clerk was courteous to me, but then I was in my best dress and hat, and I saw him decide the two men must be my servants. Daniel discerned this, and he and Grimes faded behind me, letting me speak for us.

"Mr. and Mrs. Tuck, yes," the hotel clerk responded when I pressed him. "Newlyweds, I believe. Would you like me to have a boy fetch them down?"

"I'd rather go up," I said. "A surprise, you see." I put on the smile I'd seen Miss Townsend use— sweet and gentle but with a hint of steel. "Such a dear friend, is Charlotte."

Behind me, Daniel coughed into his hand.

"Of course." The clerk gave me a room number, but hesitated. "Are you certain? They *are* newlyweds." He flushed a dark red.

"I am a widow, dear boy," I assured him. "I do understand. I will knock quite loudly." With another winsome smile, I turned from the desk.

I knew I'd never explain why I wanted to take my two ruffian servants up to a respectable gentleman's hotel room, so I flicked my fingers at Daniel and Mr. Grimes. "You, wait for me."

Daniel's face became a careful blank as he nodded, then he gestured for Mr. Grimes to follow him out to the street.

I trusted they'd find a way up through the back stairs, and my trust was rewarded when I emerged from the small lift and made my way to room number thirty-six. Daniel and Mr. Grimes popped out from a plain door at the end of the hall, both of them breathing hard from their steep climb to the third floor.

The person who answered my knock, to my surprise, was Charlotte. She stared at me in bewilderment but admitted us into the nicely furnished parlor of a suite.

"What do you want?" she demanded. "Did you find the money?"

"I'm afraid there isn't any money," I said gently as Daniel closed the door behind me. I glanced at a door opposite that must lead to the bedroom. "Is he here? Your husband?"

"You mean Mr. Tuck?" Charlotte lowered her voice. "We ain't married, not yet. But we had to say we were, didn't we? Or we wouldn't have been able to take a room."

"You are betrothed, then?" I asked.

"Just about. We're going back to Bristol. I'm missing my boy. He loves his grandmother, but . . ."

She swung away before she finished the thought. I caught, before Charlotte turned, the expression of almost despair I'd seen in her before. Unhappy about delving into the past, I'd thought previously, and having to leave her son behind to do it, but now I rearranged my thoughts.

I'd seen the bleak, haunted look in my own eyes the nights I'd longed for Joe to come home, while simultaneously fearing his return. I'd known that if he was in a fine mood, I could relax, but if he proved to be in a foul mood, I'd go to bed with bruises.

Charlotte had been married to Joe—she'd have experienced this before. But Joe was long dead, which meant she was experiencing it again.

"Where is Mr. Tuck, Charlotte?" I asked.

Behind me, I heard the door quietly open and close, but it was Mr. Grimes slipping out. He could move with great stealth for so large a man.

Charlotte swiveled to us, her face now a mask of hardness. "In the bedroom. We're packing to go."

She started for the inner door, but I stepped between her and it. Daniel had told me on our way who Joe had left the pub with the night of his death. The pieces had fallen into place in my head.

"He killed Joe," I said in a low voice.

Charlotte regarded me in both rage and fear. She must suspect I was right, but she'd choose to deny the truth to herself.

I stepped close to her, making my words almost soundless. "*Go.* Get away from him."

She glared at me. "How can I? You said there's

no money—but you're wrong. If Joe bought that plantation in Antigua, then my son inherits it, don't he? And me, as the widow. Oliver says he can get that money for me. I needs it."

I could feel sorry for her now. She had nothing, as I'd had nothing. No, not quite. Charlotte had a mum who would look after her son—she had family. I'd had no one, nothing, only my skill and my courage.

Charlotte continued to gaze at me hopefully, then at Daniel. "Are you sure the rest of the gold is gone?"

Daniel said not a word. I realized he was trying to avoid alerting Mr. Tuck in the bedroom that he was here.

"It is." I ceased trying to speak quietly. "There is no more money, Charlotte. Do you hear me, Mr. Tuck?" I spun for the door to the bedroom. "You may stop badgering her to find the gold. It no longer exists. The police know about the plantation purchased from a crooked investment firm, so she might get nothing at all."

Charlotte grabbed for me, but I flung open the bedroom door before she could stop me. Mr. Tuck was there, all right, just climbing out the window.

Daniel rushed past me, giving chase. We were on the third floor, but Mr. Tuck skillfully began to descend out of sight. To my consternation, Daniel followed him.

Charlotte and I ran to the window, jostling each other to reach it. Mr. Tuck, in his fine suit, was very out of place shimmying down the corner of the hotel. Daniel climbed like a cat after him.

Amazingly, Mr. Tuck reached the ground, jumping the last few feet without mishap. Daniel scrambled after him.

Charlotte jerked from the window, ready to rush out of the room, but I caught her and held on tight.

She clawed at me. "Let me go, you bitch."

I shook her. Out of the corner of my eye, I noted Mr. Grimes, below, emerging from the shadows of the next building to tackle Mr. Tuck.

I pulled Charlotte around so she would not see. "Why stay with him?" I demanded. "He only wants the money. It's only ever been about the money."

"So?" Charlotte jerked from me. "I need it—I need *him*. I've never been any good on me own."

So many a woman with a cruel husband told themselves. "Nonsense," I said stoutly. "You've done fine. I'm certain of it. You have a boy. Why bring in a man who might beat him? Has he beaten you?"

Charlotte nodded sullenly. "A few times. But only when I made him angry."

"There is nothing to say he will not again, or that he will not lay hands on your son," I told her. "You can get away from him. Now. Go home. Leave Mr. Tuck to the police."

Tears streaked silently down Charlotte's cheeks. "I ain't like you. I live hand to mouth, ain't got nothing. Him coming around to comfort me and give me presents is the only thing that's kept me going."

"I have no doubt," I said, not without sympathy.

Charlotte tried to run again, but I seized her. Though her tears hampered her, she fought me with strength.

"Stop," I commanded. We struggled, Charlotte trying to kick me, until I pushed her hard into a chair. I dashed for the door, turned the key in the lock, and pocketed the key. "Stay there," I said as she began to rise. "I do not advise you to try to climb out of the window yourself. You'll come to grief."

Charlotte breathed hard, her face red, but she remained on the chair. "You want to see me starve, do you?"

"I want nothing of the sort. Joe did you a bad turn. He did me a bad one too, but Mr. Tuck had no right to kill him. Mr. Tuck is no better than Joe—even worse, if you ask me."

"I didn't ask you," Charlotte snapped.

"You did, as a matter of fact," I reminded her. "When you came to find me. *He* put you up to it, didn't he? He knew full well about Joe's money, because Joe, the idiot, showed it to him and asked him to insure it. He visited you over the years, giving you these presents—even paying back the premium for the insurance Joe had given him—sweet-talking you into helping him find the cash, even convincing you to travel to London when all other efforts failed, to see what I could discover."

From Charlotte's sunken face, I'd guessed correctly. "You can't know none of this," she said sulkily.

"You asked me to find out about Joe's money and his death, and I have. Would you like to hear my conclusions?"

I thought she'd sling me out, but she nodded. "Don't matter now, do it?"

I repeated part of the story Daniel had told me in the hansom. "There is a pub on Cable Street where Joe often drank with Thomas Smith, his devoted partner in crime. Joe was supposed to meet Mr. Smith the night he was killed, except when Joe arrived, he was stumbling, hurt, and calling for a pint to ease his pain. Mr. Smith never saw him—I suspect he'd either grown tired of waiting and gone on, or fallen into a drunken stupor himself."

I paused to pull another chair over to face Charlotte, positioning it, as I sat, to block her path to the window, in case she did decide to flee that way.

"So?" Charlotte asked. "Maybe Mr. Smith offed him, and pinned it on my Oliver."

"Not quite," I said. "I believe Mr. Smith is innocent of all but robbing the Goldsmiths'

Company. The landlord of the Speckled Hen told Mr. McAdam that Joe met a woman that night, and also a well-dressed gent. I have no idea who the woman was—it could be Joe planned to use her to also ease his pain. However, the landlord knew the well-dressed gent, because he'd come to that pub for years. Mr. Oliver Tuck, a clerk in the City. Joe and Mr. Tuck went out together, and Joe wasn't seen again from that day to this, except as an anonymous body found on the docks."

"Don't mean Oliver killed him," Charlotte argued. "Why would he tell me, and you, that Joe weren't dead at sea, if he killed him? He'd keep mum about that." She eyed me in triumph.

I'd mulled that over on our swift cab ride around London. "To pique our interest," I said. "Also, to keep me—and you—from believing that the money was at the bottom of the sea. If we thought he'd gone down on the *Devonshire*, we'd conclude that the money had gone down with him too, and would not bother."

"All right." Charlotte sniffled. "But *why* should Oliver kill him? Joe never did nothing to him. Even paid him for worthless insurance and all."

"For the gold, of course," I said impatiently. "Gold does things to people—drives them a bit spare. Joe's mistake was giving Mr. Tuck a sample coin. I imagine that coin made him think about the entire two boxes of the things Joe had.

Tuck is an insurance man—he hears about or sees other people's riches and fortunes, and all he gets is his small pay packet for writing up the policies on them. He must have wondered how he could get hold of what Joe had acquired. Why should a man like Joe have that when Mr. Tuck works hard for so little?"

Charlotte had quieted to listen to me, likely putting together the pieces for herself.

I continued, "Mr. Tuck must have despaired when he heard Joe's ship had sunk. All that money—gone. Imagine his astonishment when Joe walks into the pub, alive and mostly well. Mr. Tuck saw his opportunity, welcomed Joe back, got him to talk about where he'd been and what he'd done."

Charlotte nodded. "Maybe. But even so, why should Oliver kill Joe, if he wanted the money? Oliver didn't get it, did he?"

"Mr. Tuck wasn't aware Joe didn't have the money. He'd spent it in Antigua, but Mr. Tuck wasn't such a mate that Joe would tell him all about his plantation. For some reason, they left the pub together, perhaps seeking somewhere more quiet to talk. Mr. Tuck might have asked him point blank to give him some of the gold, and Joe, being Joe, probably laughed at him for it. Or pointed out that Mr. Tuck actually owed *him* money, as he'd taken Joe's premium and then never insured the coins. Joe was a bully—I can imagine him taunting Mr. Tuck, until Mr. Tuck struck him, or they began to fight. Joe was not at his best, as he'd already been hurt that night, and Mr. Tuck managed to kill him. Whether that was intentional or not, I do not know. But now Joe is dead, and Mr. Tuck found no sign of the money."

Charlotte listened, her eyes round, any hope she'd clung to draining from her eyes.

"Mr. Tuck knew nothing of me, at this point," I went on. "He travels to Bristol to find you, Joe's widow, ready to marry you, or some such, once he works out what happened to all of Joe's cash. He's willing to wait—he's a methodical, patient man—but he'll have it in the end. One day, you must have told him about me, and he wondered. Joe had given you nothing, but he might have left the money with me. Then when I obviously knew nothing about it—why should I drudge as a cook and wear out-of-date frocks if I had any of the gold?—he stirred my curiosity to find out what became of it."

Charlotte wiped her eyes. "That could be true."

"I believe it is true. It was a job uncovering the story after all these years, but now we know." I leaned forward in my chair. "Mr. Tuck can't help you, Charlotte. He will only hurt you. It wasn't until Daniel and I explained about the plantation Joe purchased that Mr. Tuck promised to marry you, correct? But he'd have only stayed with you until he discovered whether he could profit from that land, and then he'd disappear from your life."

"Suppose," Charlotte said grudgingly.

She knew it for truth, I saw. She hadn't wanted to believe Mr. Tuck would betray her, because to believe it meant she was truly alone.

I had sympathy for her now, far more than I'd ever had. When I'd realized that Joe had been with me not because he'd loved me but because he'd wanted home comforts whenever he was in London, I'd been devastated. I had tried so hard to make a good marriage, in spite of his brutality, and I'd realized all my effort had been for naught. Charlotte must have felt the same when she'd found out about me, and I imagine she was realizing that Mr. Tuck was cut from the same cloth as Joe.

But I admired her courage. Instead of breaking down or lashing out at me, she simply sat like lead in her chair and heaved a long sigh. "Men are foul creatures, ain't they?"

"They can be," I said gently. "But not all are. I'm sure your son is a fine lad."

Charlotte's eyes warmed with sudden fondness. "He is. Nothing like his father."

That was a mercy. I'd survived because of Grace, the one person I could love without misgivings.

"I have a daughter," I told Charlotte boldly. "Her name is Grace. A beautiful lass." I paused. "She'd be your son's sister."

Charlotte started, eyes widening. "I guess she would be."

I let my smile come. Grace was my shining light. She waited for me now, not far away, and I'd go to her with joy.

"She's been asking questions about her father," I said. "Wants to know everything. May I tell her about your son? She ought to know she has a brother."

Charlotte considered, then shrugged, fresh tears filling her eyes. "Yeah, we should tell them both. I call my little boy Joe. I suppose now that was a daft idea."

"But it's a good name," I said generously. And not really Joe's at all, though I hadn't yet told Charlotte that part of the tale.

Charlotte folded her arms. "Will the peelers really keep the money from me? From the plantation, I mean."

"I honestly do not know," I said. "But it's blood money. Stolen, whitewashed. A person is not to profit from a crime, so I imagine the land will be sold, the money confiscated to pay back the Mint or whoever insured *them*."

"Too much of a mess for me to untangle," Charlotte said. "Oh well. I suppose I'm no worse off."

"Me either."

We sat in silence for a time, though it was not one I'd call companionable. We'd both been used by men who wanted only soft living and profit for themselves, but we'd never be friends, I didn't think.

The painted porcelain doorknob rattled, then someone knocked with a heavy hand. I did not recognize the knock, but it was polite, not frenzied.

I rose and unlocked the door, pulling it open to find Mr. Grimes, who crushed his cap in a beefy hand.

"Danny sent me up to fetch the pair of yer," he announced. "That insurance fellow has been arrested by some constables and marched off with Danny to Scotland Yard. Danny says, would you please join him there?"

31

When we reached Scotland Yard, Mr. Tuck was already in a bare room facing Inspector McGregor across a table. I caught one glimpse of him before Sergeant Anderson pulled the door shut. Mr. Tuck's face was wan, any superior air he'd worn gone.

Inspector McGregor would pry the truth from him, and his fate would be sealed.

I was subdued as I followed Sergeant Anderson by myself into another room, where Daniel waited, and Daniel and I told him our part of the tale. Sergeant Anderson, a quiet man, wrote it all down meticulously.

I noticed that Daniel eliminated mention of Mr. Birkett, who Joe coerced to help with the Goldsmiths' robbery. A man broken by guilt, Daniel had called him. I decided to keep silent. Let Mr. Birkett finish his life without the added misery of hard labor at Dartmoor.

Sergeant Anderson finished with us, and summoned Charlotte. She asked me to stay with her, and seeing her fear, I could not find it in my heart to leave her.

Not that she needed me. Once Sergeant Anderson made it clear that Inspector McGregor would have Mr. Tuck for murder, or manslaughter at the very least, Charlotte opened up and told Sergeant Anderson her entire tale.

She became galvanized, claiming that Mr. Tuck had hounded her for years, wanting to know about Joe and his life, and that she should find out what became of all the money he was purported to have had. Charlotte was convinced now that Mr. Tuck had coshed Joe, and he should hang, and to hell with him.

Sergeant Anderson, nonplussed, took it all down.

I did not stay to discover the final outcome. Inspector McGregor would pry a confession from Mr. Tuck in due course, but I wanted to be with Grace. Half my afternoon was already gone, and I had so little time with her as it was.

Mr. Grimes had left us before we'd set out for Scotland Yard, fading into the stream of humanity on Cannon Street. He avoided the police, for good reason, Daniel told me. But I'd been glad to meet him and learn that Daniel had such a friend.

Daniel walked me out of the building and signaled to Lewis, duly waiting for us, to take me to the Millburns'.

"I'll look after Charlotte," he promised me as he helped me in. "Best place for her is a train to Bristol. I'll make certain McGregor lets her go."

I pressed his hand. "Thank you, Daniel."

"I haven't done much." He sighed. "I couldn't find you the money."

"Blast the money," I said with feeling. "It brought anyone who touched it terrible luck. Joe died because of it. I was left destitute, and Charlotte wasn't much better off. Mr. Miller and Nettie feared for more than a decade that they'd killed a man, Mr. Smith has lived in poverty, and the two men from the Goldsmiths'—the one who actually helped, and the one who didn't—were sunk in wretchedness. I don't want a bloody penny of it."

Daniel touched my cheek. "You are a wise woman, Kat Holloway."

I sent him a wry smile. "Which is why I will always have to drudge for my living."

He brushed his glove along my cheekbone, then stepped back. "Go to Grace and give her a hug from me. May I see you tonight?"

My heart lightened. "I will put the kettle on."

Daniel grinned, a sunbeam touching his unruly hair, then he waved me off and dove back into the shadowy entrance of the police station.

Grace came flying to meet me as soon as I stepped into the Millburns' house. I gathered her to me, kissing her hair and her sweet face, blessing her and the circumstances that allowed me to keep my child safe and well.

She wanted to return to Bow Lane, and so I took her there, stopping in to greet Mr. Miller.

He appeared both relieved and subdued by the burden that had been lifted from him.

While Grace browsed the wares, I whispered to him that the true culprit was now in the hands of the police. Mr. Miller sagged at the news, but managed to remain upright as Grace made a purchase of a scrap of lace, proudly handing over her own farthing for it.

We returned to the tobacconists to say our good afternoons to Alice Taylor and purchase some lemon drops. Grace and I shared these as we strolled the lane, heading for the Church of Bow Bells and ducking inside it to admire its quiet beauty.

There, I broke the news to Grace that she had a half brother, in Bristol, by her father's first wife. I did not exactly explain that Joe had been married to both of us at the same time, though perhaps when Grace was older I could confess all that had happened.

For now, Grace looked stunned, until her excitement at the prospect began to grow.

"Can I meet him?" she asked.

"I will arrange it," I said, caution in my tone. "It might not happen for some time, and he will have to agree."

"He will," Grace said, confidence in her eyes. "A brother." She tried out the word. "How splendid."

She would not feel as alone now, is what I gathered she meant. She was part of Joanna's family of course, but not quite, and Grace understood the difference.

We walked slowly home, sucking on the remainder of the lemon drops, and all too soon, I had to say good-bye to her.

"Thursday will come quickly enough," Grace said as she embraced me.

I wondered when I'd left off comforting her at our separation and she'd begun comforting me.

Once back at Mount Street, I had to plunge myself into my duties with a vengeance. Mrs. Bywater was hosting another charity dinner—to Mr. Bywater's dismay—and we were to produce our best meal yet.

When I returned from changing my frock, Tess was screeching at passing footmen and maids to get out of her way, eyes wide with panic. I soothed her, firmly taking the knife she waved out of her hand. I tied on my apron, and resumed my daily life.

Tess had made a good start, and we were able to complete a carrot soup, whitefish with shrimp sauce, veal cutlets with mushrooms, a ham with roasted potatoes, and apricots in a honey sauce over rice. I finished with a cabinet pudding I'd begun the day before—candied lemon peel and currants laid in a pudding basin and topped with slices of sponge cake, with milk poured over and sweetened with sugar and spiced with a bit of nutmeg.

I had made up two of these puddings and left them to rest in the coolness of the larder. I retrieved them now, tied each in a pudding bag, and set them to boil. They were finished by the time the rest of the meal was ready to be served.

I unmolded one of the puddings onto a platter to go upstairs, decorating it with more lemon peel and a scattering of raisins, and sliced another for the staff's dinner. One of these slices I covered with a cloth and returned to the larder.

Only when the last of the dishes had gone up could Tess and I relax at the kitchen table, reviving ourselves with a helping of ham and potatoes and a chunk of pudding.

Cynthia came down to see us, declaring she'd begged off her aunt's supper, unable to sit through a night of ladies praising one another while they mindlessly inhaled my good food.

I served her a plate, though I knew Mrs. Bywater wouldn't approve, and the three of us ate in the kitchen while the staff helped themselves to what I'd set out in the servants' hall. I poured Cynthia, me, and Tess a small amount of the sweet white wine I'd used in the sauce for the veal.

While we ate, I told them of the end of our hunt for Joe's killer and the money he'd stolen. Both Cynthia and Tess listened in astonishment, then expressed their opinions.

"Audacious of the man," Cynthia said. "Taunting you with the fact that your husband had been murdered and then daring you to find out how so he could discover what became of the gold."

"He'd been obsessed with it a long time, I believe," I said, and then sighed. "Joe died out on the docks alone, with no one to help him. Some might say he deserved what he got, but I can almost pity him now."

"Shows you the trouble marriage can bring ya," Tess said.

"Hear! Hear!" Cynthia raised her wineglass.

"It is not necessarily always terrible," I said. I thought of Mr. Thanos and his longing glances at Cynthia. "Some men are good, and marriages prosper. Your parents are very fond of each other, Lady Cynthia."

"Huh." Cynthia shrugged. "They are feckless and soppy, but I suppose they dote on each other. Very well, here's to finding the right chaps to make us happy."

We clinked our glasses. Cynthia sent me a wink, which made my face heat.

Cynthia rose when she finished, announcing she'd run and tell Bobby and Miss Townsend the outcome of the investigation, and then relate all to Mr. Thanos when she joined him at the Polytechnic in the morning. I bade her thank each of them for their assistance, and to let them know that cake would be forthcoming for them all. I told Tess the same for Caleb.

"Caleb's happy to help," Tess said. "Says he's at your service anytime you need him."

"Indeed, no," I answered in alarm. "Inspector McGregor would never allow it."

Tess laughed, thinking me joking. Once Cynthia had gone, Tess and I cleared up and began preparations for tomorrow's meals.

It felt good to return to the routine I knew, where I could create dishes I was confident of and experiment with ones that had promise. My profession was full of hard work, but I could take satisfaction in it and watch the small amount of money I saved grow. One day . . .

But I would leave off dreaming for now, and focus on the moment.

I lingered after sending Tess and Elsie to bed, enjoying the peace of the dark kitchen and its lone candle.

By the time the knock came on the back door, I had the kettle on and the pudding warm and waiting.

Daniel rubbed his hands when he spied the slice of pudding on the table, sat down, and lifted a fork to plunge straight into it. He chewed, eyes closed, while I filled the teapot and let the tea steep.

"Marvelous," Daniel announced. "I've never tasted better."

I shrugged modestly. "It's naught but bread-and-butter pudding made fancy."

Daniel grinned as he reached for another bite. "I will inhale your fancy bread-and-butter pudding anytime you allow it."

"Silly man." I poured the tea, which had steeped to perfection. "Is Inspector McGregor satisfied?"

"He is indeed. Our culprit was happy to blurt his confession and nearly ran to the transport to Newgate to get away from him. McGregor has the touch."

"He can be terrifying," I said. "Until you grow to know him."

Daniel snorted a laugh. "I believe I will not burst his pride with that information."

"I have not quite forgiven him for his *bothersome woman* comment. But I might, in time."

"Poor Inspector McGregor." Daniel shook his head. "He ought to choose his words more carefully."

"Mr. Monaghan was very pleased to tell me about it," I said. "Wanting to create discord between me and Inspector McGregor, I'll wager."

"Mmph. About that." Daniel did not finish the sentence, waiting until he'd consumed every bite of pudding and washed it down with tea. He drained the cup, and I poured him another.

Instead of drinking it, Daniel rose and pulled me to stand before him. "I have something to tell you."

My heartbeat sped until I feared I'd grow dizzy. "Perhaps you should not."

Daniel looked puzzled, then his grin reappeared. "Let me finish, Kat. You do decide what a chap is going to say long before they do."

"Intuition."

"Rubbish. You are a clever woman who puts two and two together easier than most, but you get ahead of yourself."

"Very well, do continue," I said, trying to sound calm.

"I spoke to Monaghan again today. Forcefully." Daniel drew a breath. "I told him I'd help him with one more case, whatever it is, whenever it comes. After that, I consider my debt paid."

I could not suppress a qualm of disquiet. "And what did he say to that?"

"Not very much. But he agreed. Surprisingly."

"*Very* surprising."

"Not that I trust him. But once that case is over, I will consider myself out from under his control. Once I am . . ."

Daniel tugged me closer. I smelled the tea on his breath, which he'd sweetened with honey, and the bite of whiskey I'd put in the pudding.

"Once I am free," he went on softly, "I would like leave to court you."

I parted my lips, but no sound emerged. *To court you.* As though we were a debutante and a gentleman, a lady and a lord.

Marriages sometimes prospered, I'd told Cynthia not many hours ago. And some men were good.

This man was. I'd heard tales of him from his brother, his son, and his dear friend Mr. Thanos, as well as Mr. Grimes, who'd known him in his youth.

All those tales agreed that Daniel was a man of integrity and honor, even with the wild recklessness that his young grief had led him to.

I hadn't needed to hear these stories to realize Daniel was a fine man. I could read it when I looked into his eyes, as I had that day he'd first appeared in my kitchen, smiling at me and warming my lonely heart.

He'd become frustrated when I'd shied from his declaration that day outside the Millburns'. I'd been afraid—scared more of myself than anything else.

Now Daniel stood before me, asking if it was all right if he began the dance that might lead to us sharing a teapot for the rest of our lives.

And I knew, without thinking it through, that it would be. It would be a most excellent thing.

"Very well," I said softly.

Daniel flashed me a relieved, then stunned, smile. He began to speak, but I pulled him closer and silenced his answer with a tender and heartfelt kiss.

Jennifer Ashley is the *New York Times* best-selling author of more than one hundred novels and novellas in mystery, romance, and historical fiction. Jennifer's books have been translated into more than a dozen languages and have earned starred reviews in *Publishers Weekly* and *Booklist*. When she is not writing, Jennifer enjoys playing music (guitar, piano, flute), reading, hiking, gardening, and building doll-house miniatures.

CONNECT ONLINE

JenniferAshley.com
Facebook:
JenniferAshleyAllysonJamesAshleyGardner
Twitter: JennAllyson
Instagram: jennallyson6591
bookbub.com/authors/jennifer-ashley

Center Point Large Print
600 Brooks Road / PO Box 1
Thorndike, ME 04986-0001 USA

(207) 568-3717

US & Canada:
1 800 929-9108
www.centerpointlargeprint.com